LOVELAND PUBLIC LI
000488038
W9-DEU-500

BISON
BOOKS

Bison Frontiers of Imagination

Jules Verne

The Secret *of* Wilhelm Storitz

THE FIRST ENGLISH TRANSLATION
OF VERNE'S ORIGINAL MANUSCRIPT

Translated and edited by Peter Schulman

UNIVERSITY OF NEBRASKA PRESS LINCOLN

Publication of this book was
made possible by a grant from
The Florence Gould Foundation.

Manufactured in the
United States of America

Library of Congress
Cataloging-in-Publication Data
Verne, Jules, 1828–1905.
[Secret de Wilhelm Storitz. English]
The secret of Wilhelm Storitz :
the first English translation of
Verne's original manuscript /
Jules Verne ; translated and
edited by Peter Schulman.
p. cm.—(Bison frontiers of imagination)
Includes bibliographical references.
ISBN 978-0-8032-4675-1 (cloth : alk. paper)—
ISBN 978-0-8032-3484-0 (pbk. : alk. paper)
1. Chemists—Fiction. 2. Rejection
(Psychology)—Fiction. 3. Revenge—
Fiction. 4. Alchemy—Fiction.
I. Schulman, Peter, 1964– II. Title.
PQ2469.S413 2011
843'.8—dc22
2010031693

Set in Adobe Garamond by Bob Reitz.
Designed by R. W. Boeche.

Contents

Acknowledgments

The translator would like to thank the following for their critical and generous support throughout this project: the trustees of the North American Jules Verne Society; Arthur B. Evans; Jean-Michel Margot; Olivier Dumas and the Société Jules Verne; the editors of the University of Nebraska Press; the Old Dominion University Research Foundation; and the anonymous readers for Nebraska, whose guidance and knowledgeable readings of this manuscript were comparable to the helping hand Captain Nemo gave the castaways in *The Mysterious Island*.

Introduction

"*Storitz* is [all about] the invisible, it's pure [E. T. A.] Hoffmann, and even Hoffmann wouldn't have *dared* to go as far as I go," Jules Verne wrote to Louis-Jules Hetzel, the son of Verne's famous editor and publisher, Pierre-Jules Hetzel, with whom Verne had worked for over thirty years. Hetzel *père* had been a literary father figure of sorts for Verne, guiding him to his early triumphs and navigating his work through perilous waters when Verne's later novels became increasingly pessimistic and alarming to a young readership used to the earlier, joyous tales of travels and discoveries. "I might have to soften up a few parts for your *Magazine*," Verne conceded, "as the title of this work could very well be '*The Invisible Fiancée.*'"[1] *The Secret of Wilhelm Storitz* was in fact one of the very last novels Verne ever wrote and one he felt passionate about. He referred to it often in his correspondence and at one point, in 1904, a year before his death, declared to Hetzel *fils*, who had taken over his father's publishing house, "'The Saharan Sea' [1905, *Invasion of the Sea*] will be followed by *The Secret of Storitz*, a volume I wish to see published in my lifetime."[2]

Indeed, ever since Verne tried to publish his first novel, *Paris in the Twentieth Century*, a dystopic vision of French nineteenth-century society in 1863 (dramatically unearthed and published for the first time in the 1990s), Hetzel *père* had successfully steered him away from anything too gloomy for his target adolescent audience. Yet, as Arthur B. Evans has noted, Verne's work can be divided into three distinct periods: 1862–86, 1888–1905, and 1905–25.[3] The first, what Evans refers to as the "Hetzel period," might be considered the peak of Verne's career, during which he published most of his familiar classics, which are still immensely popular today: *Voyage au centre de la terre* (1864, *Journey to the Center of the Earth*); *De la terre à la lune* (1865, *From the Earth to the Moon*); *Le tour du monde en quatre-vingt jours* (1873, *Around the World in Eighty Days*). The second period could be called "Verne's post–P-J. Hetzel period," as now Verne worked with Hetzel's son. It was during this period that a general shift occurred in Verne's writing, as the cheery didacticism of his earlier novels gave way to a darker, deeper focus. As Evans points out, "In these later works, the Saint-Simonian, pro-Science optimism is largely absent, replaced by a growing pessimism about the true value of progress" (257). Many Verne biographers have commented on how a series of setbacks in his life might have contributed to such a sudden change in his writing. First, he had suffered unusual financial difficulties that led to the sale of his beloved yacht; second, his relationship with his son (who had been profligate, involved in a series of romantic escapades and then a nasty divorce from his wife) caused him great anxiety; third, a series of deaths of his closest friends (his mistress and Hetzel *père*) had seriously depressed him; and finally, he was shot in the leg and crippled from an assassination attempt on him by his deranged nephew Gaston.

Moreover, France's rapid defeat at the hands of the Germans during the Franco-Prussian war severely embittered him toward Germans, to the point where his most fiendish villain (and uncharacteristically his first evil scientist), the diabolical Herr Schultze in *Les 500 millions de la Begum* (1879, *The Begum's Millions*), became a caricature of a world-domination-obsessed Teutonic leader bent on destroying the world. At the beginning of the Franco-Prussian war, Verne wrote to his father, Pierre, for example, that he thought the world was collapsing: "What a great year 1870 turned out to be: the plague, the war and famine. God protect France."[4] Well after the war, when a German reader approached him to encourage him to set one of his novels in Germany (to foster better relations between the two countries), Verne replied:

I don't think I'm up to the task of reestablishing an intimacy between the two people. [. . .] If they are enemies, it is not because they do not know each other well enough; quite the contrary, and the novel which seems to haunt you would have no success. Only an act of reparation can modify French feelings toward the Germans. I can't tell you what that act might be; but anything that would be done outside that act would be in vain, illusory, unexecutable.[5]

While such beloved German figures as the absent-minded Dr. Liedenbrock in *Journey to the Center of the Earth* populate Verne's earlier work, Verne's intensely anti-German feeling culminated in the purely nefarious German Wilhelm Storitz, whose Prussian identity Verne equates with evil. Throughout the novel he is referred to as "that German," and his nationality is one of the main reasons the Roderich family rejects him as a potential suitor for their daughter. As Captain Haralan explains, "And even if he weren't the kind of person he is [. . .] he would still be a Prussian, and that would be quite enough to make us refuse such an alliance!" At another point, when Henry Vidal and Haralan are walking past Storitz's house, Storitz is described in Dracula-like terms that are equated with his being German: "Is he a foreigner?" Vidal asks. "A German," Haralan answers, as if that were sufficient to inculpate him. Similarly, when Vidal runs into him for the first time on the *dampfschiff,* his German aspects inspire immediate antipathy:

When I thought hard about this strange fellow, however, I got the distinct impression that he was German, quite probably of Prussian origin. If I had not been mistaken, he would no sooner have wanted to make contact with me than I with him once he found out I was a Frenchman. He was a Prussian, all right. I could smell it in the air, and everything about him bore a Teutonic stamp. Impossible to confuse him with those brave Hungarians, the sympathetic Magyars, the true friends of France.

Verne's venomous anti-German sentiments and darker narratives would eventually spill into what Evans understands as "the third and final phase of the Jules Verne Story, the Verne *fils* period" (259). Just as Louis-Jules Hetzel had taken over his father's publishing house, Michel Verne also inherited "the family business" in the form of several novels and plays his father left behind. In order to continue his father's legacy, he worked very closely with Hetzel *fils* to get them all published. There has been considerable discussion among Jules Verne scholars, however, as to Michel's actual involvement with these manuscripts. Did he leave them alone, or did he rewrite them? He had always been sensitive to the idea of following in his father's footsteps (he was active in trying to make films out of his father's novels, for example) and had even changed his name to Michel Jules-Verne in order to feel fully linked to his illustrious father. Although both Hetzel *fils* and Verne *fils* went to great lengths at the time to reassure the public, the public still doubted whether Verne's posthumous books were truly authentic. All in all, there were eight novels remaining in various stages of completion, published as *Le volcan d'or* (1906, *The Golden Volcano*); *L'Agence Thompson and Co.* (1907, *The Thompson Travel Agency*); *Le pilote du Danube* (1908, *The Danube Pilot*); *Les naufragés du Jonathan* (1909, *The Survivors of the Jonathan*); and finally *Le secret de Wilhelm Storitz* (1910, *The Secret of Wilhelm Storitz*). However, when Verne's original manuscripts were opened up to the public in the 1980s, the true extent of Michel's involvement was finally revealed. All of the novels had been changed to some degree. Some had been radically doctored, while others had undergone minor changes. *The Thompson Travel Agency*, for example, had been completely rewritten, while *The Golden Volcano* and *The Danube Pilot* had been only slightly modified to include happier endings or other plot devices Michel thought would be more commercial. Thanks to the painstaking efforts of France's Société Jules Verne, Verne's original manuscripts have been republished as he intended.

As for *The Secret of Wilhelm Storitz*, although Michel left the bulk of the manuscript intact, he nonetheless made several significant—if inexplicable—changes. First, he changed the era in which the story takes place from the late nineteenth century to the eighteenth. Such a century shift would have greatly annoyed his father, who wanted his novels to be contemporaneous and always used the most recent scientific research he had picked up from the latest science magazines. Moreover, because he had changed the time period, Michel had to comb through the manuscript and replace nineteenth-century references and words and make them all eighteenth-century ones. Finally, and more substantially, he changed Verne's poignant and highly original ending to a completely conventional "happy ending." As readers of this version will soon discover, Verne's original ending is particularly haunting. In fact, it is one of the many elements that contribute to *Storitz* being considered one of Verne's greatest long-lost masterpieces.

Finally, if Michel's meddling weren't enough to distort his father's final works, their previous translations into English further bowdlerized what were already bowdlerized versions. The British "Sampson Low" translations of the late nineteenth and early twentieth centuries contained many inaccuracies and abridgements, as well as gratuitous name changes and dialogue modifications that would fit into the Victorian ideologies of some British translators. Fortunately, just as the Société Jules Verne in France worked to restore accurate versions of Verne's later works, the University of Nebraska Press and Wesleyan University Press have also recently published new American translations of hitherto unauthentic versions of Verne's novels.

The only prior English version of *Storitz* was ill-served not only because it was based on Michel's modified version, but because it was also altered in translation. Its translator, I. O. Evans, had to contend with deleted passages, such as Verne's beautiful travelogue at the beginning of the novel as the *dampfschiff* goes up the Danube, and alter certain bits of dialogue and references. I. O. Evans's translation of *Storitz* first appeared in 1963 in the U.S. "Fitzroy" editions (published by Arco in Great Britain), which were meant to repopularize Verne's writings. Of course, Evans and the Fitzroy editions were pioneers of sorts and are to be commended for resurrecting Verne at the time, but because Evans and others based their translations on inauthentic versions of Verne's works, and because these versions are still distributed through libraries and secondhand bookstores, Nebraska's edition of *Storitz* represents a major step in rectifying the real Jules Verne corpus for English-speaking readers and scholars.

As he put it himself, Verne had originally thought of *Storitz* as a Hoffmanesque tale that would go well beyond Hoffmann in its use of the uncanny and the fantastic. By the same token, however, some of the gothic elements draw inevitable comparisons to Edgar Allan Poe's *Tales* (1840); Robert Louis Stevenson's *The Strange Case of Dr. Jekyll and Mr. Hyde* (1886); and of course H. G. Wells, whose *Invisible Man* was published in 1898, only a few months before Verne began his own "invisible" story. Indeed, since Verne wanted to name his book "The Invisible Fiancée," thus making the center of the story an *invisible woman* rather than an invisible man, one can also read *Storitz* as a key to a plethora of Verne dialectics involving notions of invisibility/visibility, art/life, love/illusion, and reality/imagination. *The Secret of Wilhelm Storitz* could even be read as Verne's final statement on the themes he held most dear. As Arthur B. Evans has remarked, a year after Verne's death "a pulp magazine called *Amazing Stories* first appeared on American newsstands. It published tales of a supposedly new species of literature dubbed 'scientifiction'—defined by its publisher, Hugo Gernsback, as a 'Jules Verne, H. G. Wells, and Edgar Allan Poe type of story'—and its title page featured a drawing of Verne's tomb as the magazine's logo" (261).

Could the particular poetry of *Storitz* as a mystery, as a ghost story, and as an intensely beautiful love story suggest that Verne may have indeed wanted to "speak from the grave" through his passionate account of a jilted would-be suitor terrorizing a Hungarian town through his invisibility? Is his Storitz a variant of H. G. Wells's invisible man, Griffin? If so, Storitz and Griffin would appear to be similar in the sheer panic they are able to inspire in their respective towns by their ability *not* to be seen, rather than by their flesh-and-blood incarnations. At one point in Verne's novel Vidal wonders whether Storitz is simply crazy. Yet Storitz, as opposed to Griffin, is in complete control of his actions, while Griffin progressively becomes a madman. Whereas Griffin wants to control the entire town of Port Burdock, Storitz is focused on his feelings as an unrequited lover. "The game is only the beginning," Griffin declares, for example. "There is nothing for it but to start the terror. [. . .] This day is day one of year one of the new epoch—The epoch of the invisible man!"[6] Although the villagers of Ragz are naturally superstitious and fear that an army of invisible men will come bursting into their lives, or that foreign governments will use the new invisibility technology for world conquest, Storitz himself can be seen as a romantic antihero or as a symbol of a series of inventors gone awry. From Captain Nemo (whose name literally means "no-body" in Latin), who appears and disappears in his *Nautilus*, destroying warships while simultaneously accumulating huge amounts of scientific data, to Phileas Fogg, who goes around the world so fast that he could be seen as a type of "fog," Verne's heroes often eclipse themselves through their own inventions or wild projects. Storitz, on the other hand, the son of a mad scientist, not only erases himself literally through his invisibility but uses his father's invention for purely malevolent purposes. Through his physical absence he becomes more powerful than he ever was when he was physically present.

Yet with his discussions on art and love throughout the novel, Verne seems to imply that while scientific invention can ultimately lead to vanity and destruction, art and love can withstand anything. As such, by placing a woman at the center of his piece, Verne is able to focus on the nurturing, loving earth mother who need not be seen to be powerful, while the male of the eventual title struggles to be powerful by not being seen. Storitz's work is senseless; Myra's is ethereal. While Verne devoted a vast majority of his novels to male protagonists for adolescent boy readers, his female characters are often very minor and underdeveloped. Fortunately, Verne's very last novel mystically and metaphorically gives the last word not to one of his typically male heroes, but to one of his most magical characters of all—Myra (or "See!" in Spanish), a most serene and beautiful spokesperson for a long and meaningful literary career.

The Secret *of* Wilhelm Storitz

I

". . . And get here as soon as possible, my dear Henry. I can't wait to see you. By the way, this country is magnificent and there's a lot for an engineer to see in the industrial region of Lower-Hungary. You won't regret coming.

Yours with all my heart
Marc Vidal"

I certainly don't regret my visit, but should I really be writing about it? Aren't there certain things one is better off not talking about even if they could corroborate this incredible story? . . .

It occurred to me that the Prussian from Königsberg, Wilhelm Hoffmann, author of *The Walled Door*, of *King Trabacchio*, of *The Chain of Destiny*, of *The Lost Reflection*,[1] might not have dared to publish this story, and that even Edgar Allan Poe might have thought twice before writing about it in his *Extraordinary Tales*![2]

My brother Marc, who was twenty-eight years old at the time, had been a rather successful portrait artist at the *Salons*. He won a gold medal, in fact, as well as the rosette of the Legion of Honor. He was one of the highest-ranking portrait artists of his time, and Bonnat would have been proud to count him as one of his students.[3]

We were mutually bound by the most tender and closest affection. For my part, it was a partially paternal love, as I was five years older than he was. When we were young, we had both been deprived of our mother and father, and I was the one, the big brother, who had to educate Marc. When I realized that he had a striking talent for painting, I pushed him toward a career in art, where great personal and deserved successes were awaiting him.

But here he was on the verge of a unique path, where one risks "stalling," to use an expression borrowed from modern technology. Why should anyone be surprised, after all, to read such a metaphor from the pen of an engineer working for the Compagnie du Nord?

Indeed, it had all revolved around a wedding. Marc had already been living in Ragz, an important city in meridional Hungary, for a fair amount of time.[4] A few weeks spent in the Hungarian capital, Budapest, had allowed him to make many very successful portraits (all very well remunerated) and enabled him to appreciate the particularly warm welcome that awaits artists in Hungary, especially French ones, whom the Magyars consider brothers. Once he had completed his stay, instead of taking the Pes line to Szegedin, which has a branch line linking it to Ragz, he had gone down the Danube to a major town in that district.

Once in Ragz, he was introduced to the Roderich family, which had been frequently mentioned to him as one of the town's most prestigious families and one of the most renowned names in all of Hungary. Dr. Roderich had been able to add the nice fortune he acquired from his practice to his already impressive estate. Every year he devoted a month to his travels to France, Italy, and Germany. Wealthy patients eagerly awaited his return, as did the poor, to whom he never denied his services. His charitable spirit never looked down upon the most humble and earned him the esteem of all who knew him.

The Roderich family consisted of the Doctor, his wife, his son, Captain Haralan, and his daughter, Myra. Marc was never able to visit their hospitable home without being touched by the grace, the affability, the charm of this young lady. No doubt, that's what was behind his decision to prolong his stay in Ragz. In short, if he had taken a fancy to Myra Roderich, it would not be farfetched to say that Myra Roderich fancied him as well. Allow me to add that he was truly worthy of her affections! Indeed . . . He was such a brave lad—slightly taller than average, with bright blue eyes, chestnut brown hair, a poet's brow, the happy physique of a man whom life endows with its most delightful qualities, a flexible disposition, and the temperament of an artist who fanatically believes in beauty. I didn't doubt for a second that he had been guided by that firm conviction when he chose this lovely young Hungarian girl.

I knew Myra Roderich only through Marc's passionate letters, but I was burning with a desire to meet her. As I was the head of the household, he urged me to come to Ragz and wouldn't hear of my staying for fewer than five to six weeks. His fiancée—he repeated a thousand times—wanted to meet me . . . The wedding date would be set as soon as I got there. Beforehand, Myra insisted on seeing, with her very own eyes,[5] her future brother-in-law, about whom, it would seem, she had heard so many good things in all matters—if you can imagine that! . . . Evaluating the members of the family one is about to become part of is the least one can ask . . . Assuredly, she would utter the fateful "yes" only after Henry had been introduced by Marc . . . and a myriad of other similar gestures! . . .

With great emotion, my brother told me all about this in his frequent letters to me, and I sensed how wildly in love with Myra he was.

I said that I knew her only through Marc's enthusiastic words. And yet, am I not right in saying that it would have been easy to place her, dressed in a pretty outfit, in a graceful pose, for just a few seconds in front of a camera lens? I would have been able to admire her *de visu*, so to speak, if Marc had sent me her photograph . . . But no such luck! Myra refused to . . . She would only appear to my dazzled eyes in person at first, Marc affirmed. Moreover, I can't imagine that he would have been in any rush to go to the photographer's studio! . . . No! What they both wanted was for Henry Vidal the engineer to drop everything and show his face in one of the drawing rooms of the Roderich manor, dressed in the attire worthy of such a distinguished guest.

Did I really need so many reasons in order to make up my mind? Of course not, and I would not have allowed my brother to get married without my being there at his wedding. In a rather short time, I would dutifully appear before Myra Roderich, before she would legally become my sister-in-law.

Moreover, as the letter suggested, my trip to that region of Hungary, which already attracts so many enthusiastic tourists, would be undoubtedly pleasurable if not beneficial for me. This was the Magyar land par excellence, with a past enriched by so many heroic deeds, but still a rebel in terms of any kind of blending with Germanic races, as it maintains its important position within Central European history.

As for the trip itself, here is how I planned my itinerary,—via the Danube on the way there, by rail on the way back. By all accounts, it was a magnificent river, although I could only gain access to it from Vienna. Even if I couldn't cover all of its 2,790 kilometers, I would still be able to see its most intriguing parts across Austria and Hungary, Vienna, Presburg, Gratz, Budapest, and Ragz, near the Serbian border, which would be my last stop (as I wouldn't have time to go all the way to Semlin or Belgrade). And yet the Danube seems to sprinkle so many superb cities from its mighty waters. It also separates Walachia, Moldavia, and the Bessarabia of the Bulgarian kingdom, before crossing the famous Gates of Steel, Viding, Nicopoli, Roustchouk, Silistra, Braïla, Galitzia, Izmaïl, all the way to its triple entry into the Black Sea!

I thought that six weeks' leave would be sufficient for the kind of trip I had in mind. I would spend a fortnight between Paris and Ragz; Myra Roderich would be kind enough not to get too impatient, and grant me some excursion time. After a similar fortnight at my brother's, the rest of my holiday would be spent getting back to France.

I put in my request at the Compagnie du Nord, and it was accepted. After taking care of some urgent matters, and after having procured the papers Marc had called for, I focused on my departure.

This did not require much time, as I refused to be bogged down with too much luggage—I would only bring my suitcase and a shoulder bag.

I didn't have to worry about not speaking the country's language, at least in terms of German, in which I felt fluent enough after my travels through the northern provinces. As for the Magyar language, perhaps it would not be too difficult for me to understand. As a matter of fact, French is quite prevalent in Hungary—at least among the upper classes, and on that point, my brother never encountered any problems beyond the Austrian borders.

"You're French. You have citizen's rights in Hungary," a deputy from the Diet was saying to one of our fellow citizens, and with this very cordial turn of phrase, he conveyed the warmth the Magyar people felt toward France.[6]

I replied to Marc's last letter, urging him to tell Mademoiselle Myra Roderich that my impatience matched her own, that this future brother-in-law burned with a desire to meet the future sister-in-law, etc. I was going to leave quite soon, but could not say for certain when I would arrive in Ragz, as, once aboard the *dampfschiff,* I would be at the whim of the beautiful blue Danube, as the famous waltz describes it.[7] Finally, I promised not to dawdle on the way. My brother could count on me, and if the Roderich family so desired it, they could immediately make a date for the wedding around the first days of May. I added: Please don't assail me with curses if, during the trip, each of my stages is not marked by a letter indicating my presence in this or that town. I'll write from time to time, just enough to allow Mademoiselle Myra to estimate how many kilometers still separate me from her native city . . . And in any case, I will eventually send you a telegram that will be as clear as it will be concise. If the *dampfschiff* isn't late, I'll be able to tell you on which day, at which hour, and at what exact minute I'll be in Ragz.

Since I could only embark on the Danube from Vienna, I begged the executive secretary of the Eastern Company to get me a regular ship pass with optional stopovers at various points of interest between Paris and the Austrian capital. Many companies honor such requests, and mine would surely not encounter any difficulties.

On April 4th, the eve of my departure, I went to the executive secretary to say good-bye and to pick up my pass. As soon as he gave it to me, he congratulated me, and told me he knew I was going to Hungary for the wedding of my brother, whom he knew not only as a painter but also as one of the most honorable citizens of Ragz.

"You heard about it?" I asked.

"Yes, yesterday, to be precise, at a party at the Austrian Embassy I happened to attend."

"And who told you? . . . "

"An officer attached to a garrison in Budapest who knew your brother during his stay in the Hungarian capital and praised him very highly. His success was striking, and the welcome he received in Budapest followed him all the way to Ragz, which should not surprise you, my dear Vidal . . . "

"And was this officer as generous in his praise of the Roderich family? . . . " I inquired.

"Certainly. The Doctor is a wise scholar with a reputation that is universally recognized throughout the Austro-Hungarian Empire. He received every possible distinction, and all in all, your brother will be entering into a lovely marriage, as, it would seem, Mademoiselle Myra Roderich is quite a beautiful person."

"My dear friend," I replied, "it will hardly surprise you if I tell you that Marc agrees with you and is very taken with her!"

"That's all for the best, my dear Vidal, and do pass on my best wishes and congratulations to your brother. But . . . there's something else . . . I'm not sure if I should tell you . . . "

"Tell me? . . . what? . . . "

"Hasn't your brother ever written to you about how, a few months before he came to Ragz . . . "

"Before he came to Ragz? . . . " I repeated.

"Yes . . . Mademoiselle Roderich . . . After all, my dear Vidal, it's possible that your brother knew nothing of it . . . "

"Please explain yourself, dear friend, as I am not in the know in this matter, and Marc never alluded to it in any way . . . "

"Well, it is hardly shocking—but it would seem that Mademoiselle Roderich had already been very sought after, and most persistently by a gentleman who, after all, was not the first suitor to come along. At least, that's what the officer at the Embassy told me when he was still in Budapest three weeks ago . . . "

"And what can you tell me about this rival? . . . "

"Dr. Roderich showed him the door. I don't believe there is anything to worry about on that front then . . . "

"Nothing to worry about indeed, since Marc would have surely mentioned him in his letters. But as he made no reference to him at all, I see no reason to attribute the least importance to this challenger . . . "

"No, my dear Vidal, yet the persistent claims this strange fellow has insisted on pursuing in regards to Mademoiselle Roderich's hand in marriage have caused quite a stir in Ragz, to the point where it is wisest that you be informed . . . "

"No doubt, you did the right thing in warning me, as we are not just dealing with a simple piece of gossip . . . "

"No, this information is rather serious . . . "

"But the matter isn't, that's the main thing!"

Then, as I was about to leave:

"By the way, my dear friend," I asked, "did this officer happen to mention the rival's name? . . . "

"Yes."

"What is it then? . . . "

"Wilhelm Storitz."

"Wilhelm Storitz? . . . The son of the chemist by that name?"

"Exactly."

"A scientist who was well-known for his physiological discoveries! . . . "

"And of whom Germany is justly very proud."

"Isn't he dead? . . . "

"Yes, he died several years ago, but his son is quite alive, and what's more, according to my informant, this Wilhelm Storitz is the sort of person one should be very wary of . . . "

"And we will be wary, my dear fellow, until Mademoiselle Roderich has become Madame Marc Vidal."

On that note, and without giving any further thought to this matter, the executive secretary and I exchanged a very cordial handshake before I went home to finish preparing for my departure.

II

I left Paris on April 5th, at seven forty-five in the morning, on train 173 out of the Gare de l'Est station. I would arrive in the Austrian capital in less than thirty hours.[1]

Châlons-sur-Marne and Nancy were the main stations in French territory. When it crossed the regretted Alsace-Lorraine region, the train only made a short stop in Strasbourg, but I didn't even leave my compartment. It was already too hard not being able to feel as though I were among my compatriots.[2] As soon as I was out of the city, I leaned out the door and saw Munster, the great Munster, appearing before me. It was bathed in the last rays of sunlight, which extended throughout the sky toward France at the very moment when the solar disk sank into the horizon.

The night went by as the passenger cars rattled and jiggled on the railroad tracks, a monotonous racket that lulls you to sleep even once the train has stopped. Sometimes, at irregular intervals, the names of Oos, Baden, Carlsruhe, and a few others rang in my ears, projected by the shrill voices of the conductors. Then, on the afternoon of April 6th, after a few glimpses of some vague silhouettes, I left behind those cities that had so gloriously punctuated the Napoleonic era: Stuttgart and Ulm in Wurtemberg, then Augsburg and Munich in Bavaria.[3] When we were nearing the Austrian border, a more prolonged delay stopped our train in Salzburg.

Finally, that afternoon, we made stops at several points within the territory, such as Wels, and at five thirty-five, the locomotive let out its last whinny, mixed with whistle blows, as it pulled into the Vienna station.

I stayed for only thirty-six hours, including two nights in the capital city, and left everything to chance. I planned on visiting it in more detail on my way back. One should approach the stages of a trip one step at a time, as though one were fielding questions, if one were to think like a politician.

Vienna is neither crossed nor bordered by the Danube. I had to travel around four kilometers by coach in order to reach the loading dock of the *dampfschiff* that was going down all the way to Ragz. We were no longer in 1830, when fluvial commerce was in its infancy and travel by water left little to be desired.

There was a little of everything on the deck of the *Mathias Corvin* and inside its cuddies, and by that I mean a little of everybody: Germans, Austrians, Hungarians, Russians, English. The passengers occupied the stern, since merchandise cluttered so much of the front part that there was no room for anything there. If I had looked hard among the other passengers, I would have surely run into some Poles in Hungarian dress who knew only Italian, from what Mr. Duruy writes in his account of his trip between Paris and Bucharest in 1860.[4]

The *dampfschiff* went rapidly downstream, and, with its large wheels, cleaved the yellow waters of the beautiful river, which seemed tinted with ochre rather than the ultramarine written about in so many legends. Many other ships passed by with their sails spread out to the wind as they carried products to the countryside, which was spread out as far as the eye could see on both banks of the river. We also sailed near those gigantic rafts, those types of wooden trains made out of entire forests that help build floating villages that are first erected, then destroyed upon arrival, in ways that reminded me of the prodigious Brazilian constructions along the Amazon.[5] Islands then followed islands . . . all of them, great and small, were irregularly sown, with most of them barely emerging from the water, or occasionally so low-lying that just a few inches of flooding would have entirely submerged them. It was a joy to see them so green, so fresh, with their lines of willows, poplars, and aspen, their humid foliage spruced with vividly colored flowers.

We also passed by aquatic villages built on the water's edge. It seemed as though the *dampfschiff*, going at full speed, was making them oscillate on their supporting piles. We then went beneath a rope stretched from one shore to the other that threatened to carry away our smokestack. It was the rope of a ferry that bore two poles flying the black eagle of the Austrian national flag.

Downstream from Vienna, I remembered an important historical fact, the famous date—July 6th, 1809—when I saw a circular island with a diameter that was larger than a league, flanked by woodsy embankments but made up entirely of plains in its interior, as well as furrows of dried branches that occasionally fill the river's swellings. It was Lobau Island, that cut-off camp where 150,000 Frenchmen endeavored to cross the Danube before Napoleon led them to victory at Essling and Wagram.[6]

During that day, we lost sight of Fischamout, Rigelsbrunn, and in the evening, the *Mathias Corvin* pulled into port at the mouth of the March, an eastern tributary coming down from Moravia, very close to the border of the Magyar empire. That is where she spent the night from the 8th to the 9th of April and shoved off in the morning, at daybreak, pulled along by the currents across its territories where, in the sixteenth century, the French and Turks battled each other so fiercely.[7] Finally, after letting passengers on and off at Petronell, at Altenburg, at Hainburg, and after sailing past the Hungarian Gate, where a boat bridge opened up to her, the *dampfschiff* arrived at the Presburg wharf for a transfer of merchandise.

This twenty-four-hour respite, after three hundred kilometers of travel from Vienna, enabled me to visit this city so worthy of tourists' attention. It really does look as though it were built on a promontory. No one would be the slightest bit surprised if the sea had extended itself all the way to its feet, or if its rolling edges had been bathing in the ocean rather than in the calm waters of a river. Above the rows of magnificent wharfs, one can see the sketchy silhouettes of houses built with remarkable regularity and stylistic beauty. Upstream, at the tip of the cape, where the left bank seems to end abruptly, the sharp arrow of a church stands tall in the distance, and further upstream a second arrow, and between the two an enormous hill with a castle hanging on to it as if to round out the picture.

After visiting the cathedral, which is gorgeously crowned by a golden dome, I admired the numerous townhouses (which looked more like palaces at times) that belonged to the Hungarian aristocracy. I then climbed up the hill and took a peek at the vast castle that had been constructed as a quadrangle with towers in each corner but was now almost entirely in ruins. Perhaps I would have regretted having climbed all the way up it had the view not largely extended over the superb neighboring vineyards, the infinite plains from which the Danube flows.

Presburg, where the kings of Hungary once made themselves known, is the official Magyar capital and the seat of the Diet, the Saoupchtina that was held in Budapest until the Ottoman occupation lasting over a century and a half between 1530 and 1686. But even though it counts forty-five thousand inhabitants, this city only seems populated when the Diet is in session, when deputies pour in from the four corners of the kingdom.

I have to add, however, that for a Frenchman the name "Presburg" is inexorably linked to the glorious treaty signed in 1805 after the Battle of Austerlitz.[8]

The *Mathias Corvin* continued upstream from Presburg on the morning of April 11th and crossed the gigantic plains of the Puszta. The equivalent of the Russian steppe or the American savanna, they take in all of central Hungary. A truly curious territory, with its seemingly endless grazing grounds, where one can occasionally see countless groups of horses galloping wildly at times, or herds of cattle and buffalo that the plains nourish by the thousands.

Here is where the real Danube begins its many zigzags. Already fed by the mighty tributaries of the Little Carpathians or the Styrian Alps, it now takes on the characteristics of a great river even though it was barely considered one when it went through Austria.

I could never forget that it all came from within the Grand Duchy of Baden, practically on the French border, in fact, and still sets limits on our own Alsace-Lorraine! At that time, it could be said that French rain was responsible for the very first drops of water in its course!

Once we arrived in Raab that evening, the *dampfschiff* docked at the wharf for that night as well as the following day and night. Twelve hours were all I needed to visit that town, the Gyor of the Magyars. It was more of a fortress than a town, with twenty thousand inhabitants, situated sixty kilometers from Presburg. I knew that it had been well tested during the Hungarian uprising in 1849.[9]

The next day, about ten kilometers south of Raab, I was able to take a look at the famous Cromorn citadel, where the last act of the insurrection took place. This is a fortress that Mathias Corvin created from top to bottom in the fifteenth century.

I can't think of anything more beautiful than abandoning one's self to the Danube's currents in this part of Magyar territory. Its capricious digressions, its sharp bends that add so much variety to its scenery, its low, half-drowned islands, its population of cranes and storks: the Puszta in all its glory! At times so resplendent with luxuriating prairies, and at others . . . punctuated by hills undulating toward the horizon. That's where the vineyards of the finest Hungarian vintages prosper, as Hungary is second only to France, and before Italy and Spain, in wine production. With twenty million hectoliters, the Tokay does its share for local viticulture. They say that its harvest is almost entirely consumed on the spot. I won't deny that I treated myself to a few bottles at some hotels and aboard the *dampfschiff*. I can safely say that, thanks to me, a few less bottles went down the Magyars' traps at least.

It's worth mentioning that the Puszta's crops have improved and increased considerably each year. Irrigation canals have been dug to insure an extremely fertile future. A million acacias have been planted in long and thick curtains to protect the earth against bad winds. Moreover, it won't be long before the wheat and tobacco crops double or triple their returns.

Sadly, properties are not yet properly divided in Hungary. And properties in mortmain are considerable there. There are estates of a hundred square kilometers that the owners have not even explored in their entirety, while small farmers hardly own even a third of this vast territory.

This state of affairs, which is so detrimental to the country, will change eventually, I'm convinced of it, if only as a result of that forced logic that belongs to the future. Furthermore, Hungarian peasants are not averse to progress. Rather, they are full of goodwill, courage, and intelligence. Perhaps, as has already been observed, they may even be a bit too satisfied with themselves,—yet less so than Germanic peasants. Between the two there is one common difference: one group thinks they can learn everything, while the other thinks they know everything.

It was on the right bank in Gran that I noticed a change in the general look of things. In the Puszta plains, long and whimsical hills follow each other in succession and create extreme fortifications along the Carpathian mountains or the Nordic Alps that surround the river. They force it to go through narrow channels while the depth of its bed becomes considerably deeper.

Gran is the seat of the primatial diocese of all of Hungary, and no doubt the most envied, were a Catholic prelate to have an interest in worldly possessions. Indeed, the person who now holds this seat was once cardinal, primate, legate, prince of the Empire, chancellor of the kingdom, and still benefits from a revenue that is easily worth over a million francs.

The Puszta starts up again after Gran. It was amazing to see what an artist Nature is. It's a firm believer in the law of contrasts—as with everything it comes into contact with, its approach is a grand one! Meanwhile, the short river continues to flow eastward before going back down toward the south via a type of right angle. It then goes in a general direction from which it never diverges no matter how sinuous its curves become. After intense variety between Presburg and Gran, Nature apparently wanted the landscape to be sad, morose, and monotonous.

At this point the *Mathias Corvin* had to choose which of the Saint-André Island branches it would follow. While both are practical in terms of navigation, it chose the left side, which I enjoyed because it allowed me to see the city of Waïtzen, dominated by half a dozen bell towers, as well as a church erected right on the river itself and reflected in the running waters shooting between great masses of greenery.

Beyond that point the country's landscape begins to change a bit. Fields, cultivated at the peak of their maturity, ripple through the plains as increasing numbers of boats slide down the river. Calm then yields to excitement. We are visibly approaching a capital city, and what a capital! A city made up of twins resembling certain stars. Even if some don't consider them first-rate stars, they shine significantly within the Hungarian constellation. The *dampfschiff* had to go around one last woodsy island before reaching Buda then Pest. That's where I would rest, from the 14th to the 17th of April, as I attempted to outdo myself in trying to do them justice as the conscientious tourist I had now become.

A magnificent suspended bridge crosses the Danube from Buda to Pest. It's the hyphen between the Turkish city and the Magyar one—Buda then Pest. Fleets of different crafts pass beneath its arches. The water transport consists of covered canal barges, each topped by a jackstaff and equipped with a large rudder with a bar stretching all the way over the cuddy. Both banks are transformed into wharfs bordered by architecturally interesting homes with towering spires and bells above them.

Buda is situated on the right bank, Pest on the left bank, and the Danube, still peppered with rolling green islands, is the line of this half circumference. On one side the city is able to extend itself to its heart's content in the plains. On the other side a citadel watches over the bastioned hills.

Yet as Turkish as it once was, Buda became Hungarian, and, for the very perceptive, even Austrian. It is nonetheless the official capital of Hungary, and of the 360,000 inhabitants of the two cities, it can count 100,000 for its part. More military than commercial, it lacks a certain business culture. One should not be surprised to see grass growing in its streets and surrounding the sidewalks. One might think that passersby and soldiers circulate through the city as though it were in a state of siege. It is not uncommon to see the national flag, with its green, white, and red tammy cloth, waving proudly in the wind. In short, a rather dead city, Buda, faces a considerably lively one, Pest. That's where the Danube seems to flow between the past and the future.

If Buda has a huge arsenal at its disposal, however, and if there is no shortage of barracks there, one can also visit several palaces that have preserved the grandeur of another age. I was truly impressed by the great cathedral that stood before all the old churches. It had even been converted into a mosque under the Ottoman Empire. I followed a wide street with terraced houses that, like those in the Orient, were surrounded by iron latticework. I went through the rooms of the Town Hall, with a wale of gates in blends of yellows and blacks that looked more military than civilian. I contemplated the Gull Baba tomb, which was still visited by Turkish pilgrims.[10]

Yet like most tourists, I spent more time visiting Pest. Hardly a waste of time, I can assure you. At the top of that Gellerthegy, the Blockberg, the hill south of Buda at the tip of the outlying Taban district, I was able to have a truly complete view of both cities. Between them, I admired the majestic Danube, which even at its most narrow point is at least four hundred meters wide. Several bridges cross over it, in fact, and one in particular is particularly elegant in contrast with the railway viaduct over Marguerite Island. Along the wharfs of Pest, around the squares, palaces, and townhouses, their beautiful architectural layout is splendidly showcased. Of course, the rest of the city spreads well beyond them, but of the 360,000 inhabitants of the double city, 200 of them are accounted for right there. Occasionally, I noticed domes with golden ribs, and spires fiercely drawn toward the sky. I had to admit that there were some aspects of Pest that seemed undeniably grandiose, which is no doubt why it is often considered superior to Vienna as a city.

In the neighboring countryside sprinkled with villas, I could see the vast Rakos plain, where Hungarian knights once noisily held their national parliaments.

Alas, two days would never be enough to see the Hungarian capital, that noble university town. There could *never* be enough time. How could one not carefully go through the National Museum, with its paintings and statues from the Esterhazy family, such as the superb *Ecce Homo* attributed to Rembrandt, the Natural and Prehistoric History rooms, the inscriptions, the coins, the ethnographic collections of incomparable worth! One would have to visit Marguerite Island, with its groves, prairies, thermal baths, and the public garden, the Stadtvallchen, moistened by a small river so easily accessible to light boats. Not to mention its beautiful shady trees, tents, cafés, restaurants, and games during which vibrant crowds frolic freely and easily—Ah, those remarkable men and women with their garish, colorful costumes!

On the eve of my departure I walked into one of the cafés in the city, the ones that bewilder you with the brightness of their gilding, the excessive daubing of their panels, the profusion of their shrubbery and flowers that decorate courtyards and rooms (especially the laurel roses). Pleasantly refreshed by the most popular Magyar drink, white wine mixed with a ferruginous water, I was prolonging my interminable course through the city, when my eye came across an unfolded newspaper. I picked it up without thinking. It was an issue of the *Wienner Extrablatt*. I couldn't resist reading the following article with giant gothic letters announcing, "Storitz Memorial."

That name immediately grabbed my attention. It was the one mentioned by the executive secretary of the Eastern Company, the name of the would-be suitor for the hand of Myra Roderich, as well as that of the famous German alchemist. There could be no doubt about that.

And this is what I read:

"In about twenty days, on the 5th of May, the anniversary of Otto Storitz's death will be officially observed. A big crowd will certainly be gathering at the cemetery of the town where he was born.

"As is well known, this extraordinary scholar has honored

Germany by his marvelous works, his astonishing discoveries, his inventions that have contributed so much to the progress of physical science."

Indeed, the author of that article was hardly exaggerating. Otto Storitz was justly famous in the scientific world. He was especially known for his studies of those new rays that are now too well-known to justify the X that characterized their first appellation.

But what really gave me food for thought was what followed.

"No one could be unaware that, according to those inclined to believe in the supernatural, Otto Storitz was considered a type of sorcerer when he was alive. Three or four centuries earlier, he would have surely been arrested, condemned, burned at the stake in the town square, and accused of black magic. We should add that more than ever since his death, a great number of apparently predisposed people consider him a master of incantations and wizardry and possessed with superhuman powers. Fortunately, they say, he took a good part of his secrets with him to the grave, and one would hope that his son has not inherited any of his father's extra-scientific powers. Yet one could never expect any of those poor fools to open their eyes, since for them Otto Storitz is and always will be a cabalist, a magician, and even a demoniac!"

One can say what one likes, I thought to myself; the important thing is that his son had been definitively shown the door by Dr. Roderich and that, as a rival, he was clearly out of the picture.

The reporter for the *Wienner Extrablatt* continued:

"There is therefore reason to believe that there will be an impressive crowd attending the anniversary ceremony (as usual), not including his real friends, who remain faithful to Otto Storitz's memory. It is not too bold to suggest that the extremely superstitious population of Spremberg expects some sort of extraordinary event to take place and wants to be there when it happens. From what is being said in town, the cemetery will become a theater for the most unbelievable and unlikely phenomena. One should not be surprised if, in the midst of the general horror, the tombstone rose up and the fantastical savant were resurrected in all his glory. And who knows? Perhaps some cataclysm awaits the city that witnessed his birth! . . .

"In conclusion, let us state that certain individuals are of the opinion that Otto Storitz is in fact not dead at all and that his funeral was merely a staged one. Many years will need to go by before good sense is able to demolish such ridiculous legends."

I couldn't resist a few comments of my own after an article like that. That Otto Storitz was dead and buried, there could be no doubt whatsoever. That his grave was expected to open up on the 25th of May, and Storitz arise as though he were a new Christ in the eyes of the crowd, was not even worth a moment's thought, however. But if the father's death was not in question, there was no doubt whatsoever that he had a son who was alive, very much alive in fact. That same Wilhelm Storitz who had been rejected by the Roderich family. Was there any reason to fear that he might bother Marc, or that he might create some problems at his wedding? . . .

"Fine!" I said to myself as I threw down the paper. "Now I'm the one who's being unreasonable! Wilhelm Storitz asked for Myra's hand in marriage . . . he was spurned . . . I assume he hasn't been seen again because Marc didn't mention a thing about this business. I don't see why I should attach any importance to it at all!"

I sent for pen, paper, and ink and wrote to my brother to tell him that I would be leaving Budapest the next day and that I would arrive sometime in the evening on the 22nd, as I couldn't have been more than three hundred kilometers from Ragz. I noted that until now my trip had gone by without a hitch . . . I saw no reason why it should not end just as uneventfully. I made sure to include my regards to Mr. and Mrs. Roderich, and added my warmest regards for Mademoiselle Myra.

The next day, at eight in the morning, the *Mathias Corvin* cast off her moorings along the wharf and set sail.

It goes without saying that, since we left Vienna, every stop had seen some sort of passenger change. Some had gotten off at Presburg, at Raab, at Komorn, at Gran, at Budapest; others had gotten on at the abovementioned cities. Only five or six passengers had boarded the *dampfschiff* in the Austrian capital . . . including some English tourists who were supposed to go down through Belgrade and Bucharest before hitting the Black Sea.

At Budapest, as elsewhere, the *Mathias Corvin* picked up some new passengers. One of them in particular caught my eye because of his demeanor, which seemed particularly odd to me.

He was around thirty-five years old, tall, sharply blond, with a harsh face and an imperious gaze. He was really quite off-putting. He had a rather haughty and disdainful look about him. I remember hearing his cold, dry, unpleasant voice and his abrupt tone when he asked the crew questions.

Moreover, this peculiar passenger had absolutely no desire to have anything to do with anyone. I couldn't care less at that point myself, because I too had maintained an extreme reserve in regards to my fellow traveling companions. The captain of the *Mathias Corvin* was the only person I chatted with during the trip.

When I thought hard about this strange fellow, however, I got the distinct impression that he was German, quite probably of Prussian origin. If I was not mistaken, he would no sooner have wanted to make contact with me than I with him once he found out I was a Frenchman. He was a Prussian, all right. I could smell it in the air, and everything about him bore a Teutonic stamp. Impossible to confuse him with those brave Hungarians, the sympathetic Magyars, the true friends of France.

After leaving Budapest, the *dampfschiff* chugged along with no increase in speed, which made it easy to fully appreciate the landscape. Once the double city was a few kilometers behind us, the *Mathias Corvin* followed the left branch of the river along Czepel Island.

As she made her way downstream from Pest, the Puszta began to take shape, with its curious optical illusions, its long plains, its green pastures, its tight cultures that are even richer in the neighborhoods near the big city. There will always be those low islands shaped like rosary beads, prickled with willow trees whose heads suddenly appear like large tufts of pale gray hair.

After 150 kilometers of uninterrupted navigation at night, the *dampfschiff* reached the town of Szekszard on the evening of the 19th, but the only glimpse of it I got was its misty shadow, as the sky was wet and confused.

The next day, once the weather had calmed down, we left, knowing that we would arrive in Mohacz before nightfall.

At around nine o'clock the German passenger reemerged just as I was going back down to the deck house. I was surprised by the striking look with which he greeted me. It was the first time that fate had brought us so close to each other. Not only was there a great deal of insolence in his gaze, but a tinge of hatred as well.

What could this Prussian have had against me? Had he found out I was a Frenchman? Then, all of a sudden, it occurred to me that he might have read my name from the name plate on my trunk that had been placed on one of the deck-house benches—Henry Vidal, Paris. Could that be why he looked at me so bizarrely?

In any case, if he knew my name, I couldn't be bothered to know his. He was of no interest to me at all.

The *Mathias Corvin* made a stop at Mohacz, but quite late, which for me meant that of this town of ten thousand inhabitants, I only saw two sharp steeples over a massive heap that was already engulfed in darkness. I got off nonetheless, and after about an hour's excursion, I went back on board.

The day after, the 21st, about twenty new passengers boarded before the ship went on its way at daybreak.

Later that day the individual in question ran into me several times on the bridge and affected a look I found profoundly aggressive. If that impertinent rascal had something to tell me, then he should have come right out with it! It's not with eyes that one should speak in these moments . . . if he didn't speak French, I would have been happy to answer him in his own tongue!

I hate picking a fight with anyone, but I can't stand being observed in such an offensive manner. Nonetheless, if I did manage to stop and speak to him, it would be best if I had been able to obtain some sort of information about him beforehand.

I got hold of the captain and asked him if he knew anything about the passenger.

"First time I ever saw him," he told me.

"Is he German?" I pursued.

"Without a doubt, Monsieur Vidal, and I even think that he might be German twice over, as he's got to be a Prussian . . . "

"And that's already once too many!" It was a response that the captain, who was of Hungarian descent, seemed to relish.

The *dampfschiff* worked its way to Zombor by the afternoon, but it was too far from the left bank of the river for it to be really seen. It's an important city with no fewer than twenty-four thousand citizens. Similar to Szegedin, it is situated in that vast peninsula shaped by the two waterways, the Danube and the Theiss, one of its most formidable affluents, which it would eventually absorb about fifty kilometers before reaching Belgrade.

The next day, between numerous winding bends in the river, the *Mathias Corvin* sailed toward Vukovar, a town built on the right bank. We then followed the Slovenian border, where the river modifies its southern direction and veers toward the East. That's where the military confines are located. From distance to distance, and receding further and further from the bank, numerous guard houses maintain their lines of communication from the to-and-fro of the sentinels who live in wooden cabins or sentry boxes made of branches.

It's a territory under a military administration. All the inhabitants (who are called *grendze*) are soldiers. All the provinces, districts, parishes are eclipsed by the regiments, the battalions, and the companies of this special army. There is an area of about 610,000 square meters that are also included in this denomination that stretches from the Adriatic streams to the mountains of Transylvania. Its population (over eleven thousand souls) is subjected to a strict regimen. This institution can be traced back to the reign of Mary-Theresa, who not only had her raison d'être against the Turks but created a sanitary cordon against the plague.[11] One was just as bad as the other as far as she was concerned.

I no longer saw the German on board after our stop in Vukovar. He must have gotten off there. I felt liberated from his insufferable presence,—from having to deal with him any longer.

But other thoughts soon filled my brain. In a few hours the *dampfschiff* would arrive in Ragz. I couldn't wait to see my brother, from whom I had been separated for a year. I couldn't wait to hug him, for the two of us to chat. There were so many interesting things to talk about, and I yearned to meet his new family!

At around five o'clock in the afternoon, on the left bank, between the willows lining the river's edge and a curtain of poplars, I noticed a few churches. Some of them were crowned by domes, others governed by steeples that cut up into the deep sky. A string of clouds passed by in rapid succession.

These were my first impressions of my new city: Ragz. There it was, beyond the river's last bend and emerging in all its glory. It sat regally at the foot of a picturesque landscape made up of lofty hills. An ancient feudal castle, the traditional acropolis of age-old Hungarian cities, loomed elegantly from one of the hills.

Yet with just a few spins of the wheel, as the *dampfschiff* got closer to the landing wharf, the following incident occurred . . .

While most of the passengers were rushing to go ashore, I stood near the port railing, watching the rows of wharfs. There were several groups of people standing at the far end of the landing stage. One of them had to be Marc, I thought.

Then, just as I was trying to catch sight of him, I heard the following words uttered in a distinctly German dialect and eerily close to me:

"If Marc Vidal marries Myra Roderich, woe unto her, woe unto him!"

I turned around at once . . . Although I was standing all alone, someone had just spoken to me, and I would add that the voice was similar to that of the German who was no longer on board the ship.

But there was no one, no one, I repeat! I must have been mistaken in thinking I had heard those menacing words . . . it must have been some sort of hallucination . . . nothing more . . . I disembarked with my suitcase in my hand, and my bag around my shoulder, engulfed by the deafening rockets of vapor let loose from the *dampfschiff*'s flanks.

Marc had indeed been waiting for me at the dock with his arms extended. We hugged each other tightly.

"Henry . . . Henry," he repeated, his voice filled with emotion, his eyes moist, his entire body radiating happiness.

"My dear Marc," I said, "let me give you another hug! Are you taking me to your place? . . . "

"Yes . . . to the hotel . . . the Temesvar Hotel, it's ten minutes away, on Prince Miloch Street . . . But first let me introduce you to my future brother-in-law."

I hadn't noticed that there was an officer standing slightly behind him. He was a captain, wearing the infantry uniform of the military confines. He couldn't have been more than twenty-eight years old, slightly above average height. With his chestnut mustache and beard, he had the proud aristocratic air of a Magyar but with welcoming eyes, a smile upon his lips, and a rather pleasant air about him.

"Captain Haralan Roderich," Marc explained.

I took the hand extended by the Captain.

"Monsieur Vidal," he said, "we're happy to see you, and you can't imagine what pleasure your arrival is going to give my entire family. We've been so impatient . . . "

"Mademoiselle Myra as well?" I asked.

"Indeed!" my brother proclaimed. "And it isn't her fault, my dear Henry, if the *Mathias Corvin* didn't make its ten leagues an hour since you left!"

I noticed that Captain Haralan spoke fluent French, as did his father, mother, and sister. They had all traveled throughout France. Moreover, from then on, since Marc and I both had a firm command of German and a working knowledge of Hungarian, we would converse in any one of these languages, if not all of them at once!

A carriage took my luggage. Captain Haralan and Marc got on with me, and a few minutes later, it stopped in front of the Temesvar Hotel.

Once we arranged my first "official" visit to the Roderich family, my brother and I were by ourselves. I was staying in a fairly comfortable room right next to the one Marc had occupied since he settled down in Ragz.

We continued our conversation until dinnertime.

"My dear Marc," I told him. "Here we are, together at last . . . both of us in good health, I trust? . . . And if I'm not mistaken, haven't we been separated from each other for a good year?"

"Yes, Henry, and time seemed to go by very slowly . . . although the presence of my dear Myra . . . In any case, here you are, and I haven't forgotten despite our separation . . . that you're my big brother . . . "

"Your best friend, Marc!"

"Well, Henry, you understand . . . my wedding couldn't take place without you . . . by my side . . . And by the way, don't I have to ask you for your consent?"

"My consent? . . . "

"Yes . . . I would have asked our father for it had he been here. But you won't refuse it any more than he would, especially when you get to know her! . . . "

"She's charming? . . . "

"You'll see her, you'll judge for yourself, and you'll love her! . . . The best of all possible sisters, that's what I'm giving you . . . "

"And whom I accept as such, my dear Marc, knowing full well ahead of time that you couldn't have made a more delightful choice. Why don't we call on Dr. Roderich this evening? . . . "

"No, tomorrow . . . We didn't think that the boat would arrive so early . . . We didn't expect you until this evening. Haralan and I came to the docks just in case, and it was a good thing too, since we got there right as you were getting off. Ah! If only my lovely Myra had known. She'll really regret not being here! . . . But as I said before, you weren't expected until tomorrow. Madame Roderich and her daughter have another engagement this evening . . . a service at the cathedral, and they'll offer their apologies when they see you."

"That's understood, Marc," I replied, "and we can enjoy being together for a few hours today. We can spend them chatting, discussing the past and the future, exchanging all the memories of two brothers who've been apart for a year!"

Marc then proceeded to tell me about all his travels since he left Paris, all the towns he had left his mark in, his stay in Vienna and Presburg, where the doors of the artistic world had been thrown wide open for him. None of all that told me anything new about his life, however. A portrait signed "Marc Vidal" would surely be much sought after and argued over with as much passion by rich Austrians as by rich Magyars.

"I couldn't satisfy them, my dear Henry. You should have seen the inquiries and orders from all over! What do you expect? The word had gone round from a good bourgeois of Presburg: 'Marc Vidal makes a better likeness than nature itself!' So," my brother added jokingly, "it wouldn't seem outlandish to assume that the national overseer for fine arts might whisk me away one of these days to paint the portraits of the Emperor, the Empress, and the Archduchesses of Austria! . . . "

"Take care, Marc, take care! It would be a bit awkward if you had to leave Ragz right now to accept an invitation from the Viennese Royal Court . . . "

"I would decline it in the most respectful way possible. At present, portraits are out of the question . . . or rather, I've just finished the last one . . . "

"Hers, I gather? . . . "

"Hers, and it is no doubt not the worst one I've done . . . "

"Hey! Who knows?" I cried out. "When a painter is more preoccupied by his model than he is with the portrait itself! . . . "

"Well, . . . you'll see, Henry! . . . Allow me to repeat myself . . . a better likeness than nature! . . . That's my gift, apparently . . . indeed . . . I couldn't take my eyes off of her . . . the whole time my dear Myra was posing. But to her it was no joke. It was not to the fiancé, but to the artist, to whom she had meant to devote those two short hours! . . . And my brush flew over the canvas . . . I was convinced the portrait was going to come to life, like Galatea's statue."[1]

"Easy does it, Pygmalion, easy does it, and tell me how you first got in touch with the Roderich family . . . "

"It was written."

"I don't doubt it, but still . . . "

"Several drawing rooms in Ragz honored me with a membership as soon as I arrived. Nothing could have been more pleasant, were it only a way of spending the perennially long evenings in a foreign town. I diligently went to all the homes where I was welcomed, and it was in one of them that I renewed my acquaintance with Captain Haralan . . . "

"Renewed? . . . " I asked.

"Yes, Henry, since I had already met him several times in Pest, in an official capacity. An officer of the highest merit, destined for a splendid future, but also one of the nicest men I had ever met. Fittingly, he lived up to his potential and fought heroically in 1849 . . . "

"Oh, to be born at that time!" I broke in, laughing.

"Well put," Marc continued in the same tone. "In short, we saw each other here every day, as he was on leave for a month. Our somewhat casual relationship gradually grew into a deep friendship. He wanted to introduce me to his family, and I accepted all the more willingly because I had already met Mademoiselle Myra Roderich at several functions, and if . . . "

"And," I interrupted, "the sister being no less charming than the brother, your visits to the Roderich residence multiplied . . . "

"Yes . . . Henry, as of six weeks ago, there was not a single evening that went by without my coming over! After all that, when I talk about my dear Myra, you might think that I am exaggerating . . . "

"Not at all, my friend, not at all! You're not exaggerating in the least, and I'm even quite certain that it wouldn't be possible to exaggerate when talking about her . . . "

"Oh, my dear Henry, you have no idea how much I love her!"

"It's quite apparent, and furthermore, I'm quite satisfied in thinking that you're going to be entering into the most honorable of families . . . "

"And the most honored," Marc replied. "Dr. Roderich is a physician of great repute who is also personally respected by his colleagues! . . . Moreover, he is the best of men and well worthy of being the father . . . "

"Of his daughter," I said, "as Madame Roderich is no less worthy, no doubt, of being the matriarch . . . "

"Such an excellent woman!" Marc cried out emphatically. "Loved by all, pious, charitable, immersed in good deeds . . . "

"And a mother-in-law you can't find in France anymore! Isn't that right, Marc?"

"First of all, Henry, remember we're not in France but in Hungary now, in this Magyar country where customs have kept something of their old-time severity, where the family is still patriarchal . . . "

"Come along, you future patriarch, as that's what you're going to become yourself!"

"That's a status that has its own price to pay!" said Marc.

"That's it. Go ahead and emulate Methuselah, Noah, Abraham, Isaac, Jacob! When all is said and done, I don't think your story is particularly extraordinary. Thanks to Captain Haralan, you've been introduced into his family . . . they've given you such a warm welcome, which doesn't surprise me at all, since I know you so well! . . . You couldn't look at Mademoiselle Myra without being seduced by both her physical and her moral qualities . . . "

"That's just as you say, brother!"

"The moral qualities . . . for the fiancé. The physical qualities . . . for the painter, and they shall be no more erased from the canvas than from the heart! . . . What do you think of my phrase? . . . "

"A bit overblown, but on the mark, my dear Henry!"

"As is your appreciation of it, and in conclusion, just as Marc Vidal couldn't see Mademoiselle Myra Roderich without being attracted to her grace, Mademoiselle Roderich couldn't see Marc Vidal without being attracted to . . . "

"That's not what I said, Henry!"

"But I say so, if only out of respect for the truth! . . . Monsieur and Madame Roderich, after catching wind of what was going on, were hardly offended . . . as it wasn't very long before Marc confided in Captain Haralan, who didn't take the disclosure badly at all . . . He mentioned this little business to his parents, and they, in turn, spoke about it to their daughter . . . And at once, Mademoiselle Myra, out of a sense of discretion as well as decorum, deferred to them on the matter . . . Marc Vidal then made his formal proposal, which was duly accepted. You can see why this little romance will have a happy ending, like so many others just like it . . . "

"What you call the end, my dear Henry," Marc declared, "is but the beginning, in my opinion . . . "

"You're right, Marc, and I ought to have realized the value of words! . . . And when is the wedding, exactly?"

"We were waiting for your arrival before making the date."

"Well, in that case, whenever you wish . . . in six weeks . . . in six months . . . in six years . . . "

"My dear Henry," Marc replied, "you'll be kind enough to tell the Doctor—and I'm counting on you to do so—that your holiday here is limited, and if you stay that long in Ragz, the entire transportation industry will suffer without your calculations to help it along . . . "

"So what you're saying is that I might be responsible for all the train derailments and pile-ups . . . "

"That's about right. Now you see why we can't keep on delaying the ceremony . . . "

"Then what about the day after tomorrow or even this evening? . . . Rest assured, my dear Marc, I'll say everything that's needed. In actual fact, I still have a month's worth of vacation left, and I'm counting on spending a good half of it, after the wedding, near you and your wife . . . "

"That would be perfect, Henry."

"But my dear Marc, do you intend to stay right here in Ragz? . . . Aren't you planning on going back to France . . . to Paris? . . . "

"That's what I haven't decided yet," Marc replied, "and we have ample time to study the matter! . . . All I'm thinking about is the present for the time being, and as for the future, all I care about is my wedding. There is nothing else as far as I'm concerned."

"The past is no longer," I burst out, "the future has not been . . .

there is only the present! . . . There is an Italian *concetto* all about it that every lover recites to themselves under the stars!"[2]

The conversation continued along these lines until dinnertime. Afterward, Marc and I lit our cigars and walked along the left bank of the Danube.

I wouldn't get my first real look at the city until the day after, and the days that followed. I would have ample time to fully explore it,—more likely in Captain Haralan's company than Marc's, however.

It goes without saying that our conversation had not changed its focus: Myra Roderich was all we could think about.[3]

Still, I couldn't help worrying about what the executive secretary of the Eastern Company had told me on the eve of my departure. Nothing in what my brother had told me would lead me to believe that his lovely romance had been disturbed, not even for a day. And yet, if Marc had no rival, at least there must have been one at some point. Myra Roderich had been sought out by Otto Storitz's son. Certainly there was nothing wrong in someone asking for the hand of such an accomplished young lady with such a comfortable financial situation. In any case, Wilhelm Storitz could not possibly harbor any hope of marrying her, and Marc had no reason to be preoccupied or worried about such a fellow.

Naturally, the words I thought I had heard when I was about to disembark began to haunt me. Admitting that they had indeed been uttered, that they weren't part of some illusion, I could not have attributed them to that impertinent rogue who had come aboard at Pest, since he was no longer aboard the *dampfschiff* when we got to Ragz.

Nevertheless, without describing this specific incident to my brother, I thought I might mention what I'd learned regarding Wilhelm Storitz.

Marc first replied with a characteristic gesture of disdain. He then told me:

"Haralan had indeed spoken to me about this individual. He seems to be the only son of that savant Otto Storitz, who has the reputation in Germany of being a magician of sorts—an unjust reputation, by the way, because he really did hold a high place in natural science and had made some major discoveries in chemistry and physics. But his son's advances were rejected . . . "

"Well before yours were accepted, right, Marc? . . . "

"Three or four months before, if I'm not mistaken," my brother replied.

"And did Mademoiselle Myra know that Wilhelm Storitz was all set to pop the question, as they say in operettas?"

"I don't think so."

"And he hasn't attempted anything further since then? . . . "

"Nothing at all, once he realized that he had no chance whatsoever . . . "

"And what sort of fellow is he, this Wilhelm Storitz? . . . "

"A type of eccentric, whose very existence is rather mysterious and who lives in seclusion . . . "

"In Ragz? . . . "

"Yes, in Ragz . . . in an isolated house on Teleki Boulevard that no one has ever been able to penetrate. Mind you, and this in itself would motivate repulsion, he's a German, and the Hungarians, who are quite French from this point of view, have no love lost for William II's subjects."

"And he's even a Prussian, Marc . . . "

"That's right, a Prussian from Spremberg, in the Brandenburg region."

"Have you ever met him? . . . "

"A few times, and once in the museum Captain Haralan pointed him out to me, without his appearing to notice us . . . "

"Is he in Ragz as we speak? . . . "

"I can't tell you for sure, Henry, but I don't think anyone has seen him for two or three weeks . . . "

"It would be better if he'd left town . . . "

"Well!" Marc asserted, "let's leave this man wherever he may be, and if ever there is a Madame Wilhelm Storitz, rest assured that it will never be Myra Roderich, because . . . "

"Right, "I replied, "because she will soon be Madame Marc Vidal!"

We continued our walk along the wharf until we got to the wooden bridge that connects the Hungarian bank to the Serbian one. We stopped for a few minutes and admired the great river, which, on this pure night, was bursting with stars as though they were schools of fish with brightly glowing scales.

I had to give Marc some information regarding my own matters, news about our mutual friends, and the artistic world I use to frequent regularly. We spoke primarily about Paris, where, barring some kind of unforeseen obstacle, he would soon spend a few weeks after the wedding. The traditional honeymoon that usually propels newlyweds toward Italy or Switzerland would bring this couple back to France. Myra couldn't wait to see Paris again. But to see it on the arm of a husband would be an especially delightful treat for her.

I told Marc that I had brought all the papers he had requested in his last letter to me. He could rest assured that he would lack none of the documents that he needed for his great matrimonial voyage.

And then, just as the magnetic needle turns toward the Polar Star, our conversation kept returning to our own star of such great magnitude, the sparkling Myra. We were both tireless: Marc continued to chat, and I continued to listen. He had wanted to talk to me about these things for such a long time! Yet it was up to me to be somewhat reasonable, or else our conversation would have gone on until daybreak.

We had been able to stroll without interruption, as passersby along the quay were quite scarce on that rather chilly evening. Nevertheless—was I mistaken?—it seemed as though we were being followed by someone. He was walking behind us as though he wanted to eavesdrop on our conversation. He was a man of medium height, and judging from his heavy gait, of a certain age, who eventually drifted away from us.

At half past ten Marc and I were back in our rooms at the Temesvar Hotel. Before I fell asleep, however, the words I thought I had heard aboard the *dampfschiff* returned to stalk me obsessively, . . . the very words that threatened Marc and Myra Roderich!

IV

The next day—and what a day!—I made my official visit to the Roderich family.

The Doctor's house towers over the end of the Bathiany quay, at the corner of Teleki Boulevard, which, under various names, wraps around the city. It is an old, elegant townhouse on the outside, yet modern on the inside, stylishly decorated with rich, deep rooms, and furnished with a taste that bore witness to the Roderichs' refined artistic sensibility.

It is located on Teleki Boulevard itself between two pillars crowned with vases overflowing with sprawling, leafy plants. A carriage and service entrance opens up onto a gravel courtyard. A gate separates the courtyard from a garden, where several giant trees—elms, acacias, chestnut trees, beeches—overrun the wall extending to the house next door. A verdant but irregularly shaped lawn, embellished with flowerbeds and bushes, runs toward rows of trees festooned with ivy. A variety of foliage seems to veil the back of the garden. In the right-hand corner there is a space that was once reserved for a bailey. As for the walls, they fade away behind a curtain of greenery.[1]

A series of annexes were built on the right-hand side of the house. On the ground floor: the kitchen, the scullery, the woodshed, a coach house for two carriages, a stable for two horses, a washhouse, a dog kennel. On the first floor: beams of light pierce through shuttered windows. There is also a bath room, a linen drapery, servants' quarters with a private staircase and entrance. Between the six windows that pepper the multiple branches of wild vines, one can admire the large birthworts and rising roses.

The annex is connected to the main part of the house by a stained-glass-covered corridor that, in turn, leads to the base of a round, sixty-foot-high cylindrical tower.

The tower rises from the junction between two buildings, which form a right angle with each other. Inside, a staircase with a metal ramp climbs from the first floor of the townhouse to the second, where rather svelte sculptures decorate the garret windows.

Before arriving at the residence itself, one comes across an extended gallery, supported by metal pilasters and sealed by windows that allow for a steady flow of southeastern light. From the gallery, doors draped in ancient tapestries open up onto Dr. Roderich's office, the large drawing room, and the dining room. These different rooms overlook the Bathiany quay and get their light from the six ground-floor windows, the cant-wall at the corner of the quay, and Teleki Boulevard.

This layout is duplicated on the first floor, with Monsieur and Madame Roderich's bedroom immediately above the living room and Captain Haralan's room above the dining room, for when he comes to Ragz. Mademoiselle Myra's room is on the other end of the wing, as well as her study, with three windows: one overlooks the quay, the other the boulevard, and the third the garden, at the same level as the corridor that connects the entire floor.

I have to admit that I could have easily described the Roderich home before I even saw it in person. Thanks to my conversation with Marc the night before, I knew every room. Marc had overlooked nothing about the young lady's home. I even knew precisely where Mademoiselle Myra sat at the dinner table, where she liked to sit in the drawing room, and on which bench she liked to sit in the garden (she enjoyed the shade provided by a splendid chestnut tree).

To get back to my subject, however, the tower's staircase, bright from the sun streaming through the stained-glass window of its narrow ribbed vault, leads to a circular belvedere with a circular terrace that must have an extensive view of the entire city as well as the Danube itself.

It was in the gallery, in fact, that Marc and I were received at around one o'clock in the afternoon. An elaborate copper window box, with flowers bursting with all the striking colors of Spring, stretched throughout the middle of the room. In the corners there were a few tropical shrubs, a few palm trees, a few dragon trees, a few alarias, a few other plants.[2] Marc appreciated the enormous value of the paintings from the Hungarian and Dutch masters that were hanging along the panels between the living room doors and the gallery.

I saw and admired Mademoiselle Myra's portrait, which was sitting on a little stand in a corner on the right side of the room. It was a superbly crafted piece worthy of the name of the one who had signed it, the one who is dearest to me in the whole world.

Dr. Roderich was fifty years old at that time, but he hardly looked his age. He was tall, with a straight body, a graying beard, thick hair, an inalterably healthy complexion, a vigorous constitution that was unscathed by the slightest illness. He exhibited the best of the Magyar spirit in his unique purity, his passionate gaze, his resolute step, his strong and noble attitude. His entire being exuded a type of natural pride that tempered the sunny aspect of his handsome demeanor. He had the determined look of a military doctor. Indeed, he had a distinguished record in the Hungarian army, in which he had first served before entering the professional world as a civilian. As soon as I was introduced to him, I felt by the warm grip of his hand that I was in the presence of the best of men.

Madame Roderich, who was forty-five years old at the time, had kept all of her beauty—regular features, dark blue eyes, magnificent hair that had begun to whiten ever so slightly, a delicately traced mouth with a beautifully intact set of teeth, and an elegantly maintained waistline. Even though her background was thoroughly Hungarian, she radiated a profound sense of calm and sweetness. She was a splendid woman who was endowed with every domestic virtue and who found true happiness in being a wife to her husband. She adored her son and her daughter with all the tenderness of a wise and caring mother. Moreover, she was very pious, very eager to fulfill her Catholic duties, which she nourished with an unshakeable faith as she accepted the dogma without trying to question or reason with it. That was Madame Roderich.

I was deeply touched by the warm friendship she was offering me. She would be happy to have Marc Vidal's brother in her home on condition that he would be good enough to consider it his own.

But what could I say about Myra Roderich? She approached me with a smile and an outstretched hand or rather outstretched arms! I was truly going to get a real sister in this young girl, a sister who kissed me and whom I kissed without standing on ceremony! I had reason to believe that if Marc wasn't jealous of me, there was at least a tinge of envy in his eyes!

"I haven't even gotten that far yet!" he said.

"*Mais non*, monsieur," Mademoiselle Myra replied. "You're not my brother, are you!"

Mademoiselle Roderich was indeed everything that Marc had described, and exactly as he had depicted on that canvas I had just admired. A young girl, her charming head crowned with fine blond hair, a virgin out of a Mieris painting, but also prepossessing, playful, and vivacious.[3] Her dark blue eyes sparkled with wit; her face glimmered with the warm tints of a Hungarian carnation. Her mouth was shaped with such purity; when her rosy lips opened, they disclosed dazzlingly white teeth. She was slightly above medium height, and by her graceful movements, I would have to say that she was charm itself: perfect distinction without a trace of affectation or pose.

I suddenly thought that if it was said of Marc's portraits that they were more lifelike than their models, it could equally be said that Mademoiselle Myra was more natural than nature!

If, like her mother, Myra Roderich wore modern clothes, one could still discern something very Magyar about them . . . in the cut of the material, in the assortment of colors, a blouse closed at the neck, sleeves embroidered at the wrist, a dress fastened with metal buttons, a belt knotted with gold ribbons, a skirt with folds floating down to her ankles, bronze-colored leather half-boots—an attire so pleasant that it would appeal even to the most delicate of tastes.

Captain Haralan was there, looking dashing in his uniform and bearing a striking resemblance to his sister. He too possessed a physiognomy filled with grace and strength. He extended the hand of friendship toward me and also treated me like a brother. I felt as though we were already good friends even if we had just met the day before.

So now there were no more Roderich family members to meet.

The conversation took on a life of its own, flowing randomly from one subject to another, from my travels from Paris to Vienna, my trip aboard the *dampfschiff*, my work in France . . . what little time I had left to explore this beautiful city of Ragz. It would soon be revealed to me in great detail: the great river one should follow all the way to Belgrade at least, that magnificent Danube with seemingly golden waters . . . this whole Magyar country filled with so many historical memories, the famous Puszta that should attract tourists from around the world, etc., etc. . . .

"What a joy it is to have you among us, Monsieur Vidal!" Mademoiselle Myra repeated, holding out her hands with a gracious welcoming gesture. "Your journey seemed to take a long time, and we were getting rather worried. We weren't reassured until we got the letter you sent us from Pest! . . . "

"I feel very guilty, Mademoiselle Myra," I replied, "very guilty for having been so long in coming. Had I come by train from Vienna, I should have been in Ragz a long time ago. But the Hungarians would never have forgiven me for having disdained the Danube in which they have so much pride and which deserves its great reputation . . . "

"Indeed, Monsieur Vidal," the Doctor said to me, "it's our glorious river, and it is our very own from Presburg to Belgrade! . . . "

"And we pardon you in its honor, Monsieur Vidal," Madame Roderich assured me.

"You see, my dear Henry," Marc added, "you were awaited with impatience . . . "

"And curiosity," Mademoiselle Myra declared, "a deep-felt curiosity to finally get to know Monsieur Henry Vidal . . . Your brother has spoken of you so highly, and hasn't stopped praising you . . . "

"And isn't he praising himself by the same token?" Captain Haralan observed.

"What are you saying there, my brother?" asked Mademoiselle Myra.

"Of course . . . since there is such a strong resemblance between the two of them! . . . "

"Yes, that's right . . . two Siamese twins," I replied in the same tone of voice. "And Captain, I do hope you will be so kind as to show me the same kindness you showed him, as I'm counting on you more than on Marc, who is obviously too busy to be my tour guide . . . "

"At your service, my dear Vidal," Captain Haralan replied.

And so, we spoke about many things, and I was in full admiration of this happy family. What impressed me the most was the tender affection that could be seen in Madame Roderich's demeanor as she glanced at her daughter and Marc, who were already united in her heart.

The Doctor then spoke to us about his travels abroad . . . Italy, Switzerland, Germany, France. France was particularly unforgettable for them. They covered the entire country from Provence to Brittany. And if they didn't use their French to speak about my homeland, when would they use it at all? As for myself, I was trying to use my smattering of Magyar as much as I could, and there's no question that this made them happy. As for my brother, he spoke it like a native. It was as though he had undergone a kind of "Magyarization," which, according to Élysée Reclus, is spreading very rapidly among the central populations.[4]

And what about Paris! Ah! Paris! The greatest city in the world, —after Ragz, of course, since Ragz was Ragz, after all! There was no point in trying to come up with any other reason. And to be honest, it was all Marc needed, since for him, Ragz *was* Myra Roderich! Moreover, he was rather obstinate in thinking that Mademoiselle Myra would return to Paris with him, and that they would share its myriad of wonders, its incomparable monuments, its artistic riches, its intellectual treasures, its admirable collections within its museums, which were even greater than Rome's, Florence's, Munich's, Dresden's, the Hague's, Amsterdam's! I was in constant admiration of this young Hungarian's exquisite eye for art. I was beginning to understand the irresistible attraction that so many spiritual and physical qualities (allow me to repeat them) had held for my brother's sensitive and tender soul.

Going out that afternoon was out of the question. The Doctor had to return to his usual activities. But Madame Roderich and her daughter had nothing else planned. In their company, I was able to take a tour of the house and admire all the beautiful things it contained, such as the paintings and carefully chosen curios, sideboards filled with silver dishes for the dining room, old coffers and ancient traveling boxes from the gallery, and on the first floor the little girls' library, where so many great works of ancient and modern French literature were prominently displayed.

But don't think for a minute that we sacrificed the garden for the townhouse! Not at all. We strolled under its cool shady spots; we sat on its comfortable wicker chairs protected under the trees; we picked a few flowers from the flowerbeds on the lawn, one of which, picked by Mademoiselle Myra's very own hand, landed very elegantly in my lapel.

"And what about the tower?" she asked. "Does Monsieur Vidal imagine that his first visit will be complete without his having gone up our tower?"

"Of course not, Mademoiselle Myra, of course not!" I answered. "There hasn't been a single one of Marc's letters that didn't praise the tower—almost as much as he praised you—and, to tell you the truth, I only came to Ragz so I could climb up it . . . "

"You'll have to do it without me, however," said Madame Roderich, "as it's a bit high! . . . "

"Oh, Mother! It's only ninety steps!"

"Yes . . . and at your age, that's only two steps a year," Captain Haralan interjected. "But stay here, dear Mother. I'll go up with my sister, Marc, and Monsieur Vidal, and we'll see each other in the garden a little later."

"En route for the sky!" Myra laughed.

And preceded by Myra, whose light footsteps we had trouble catching up with, we reached the belvedere and then the terrace in about two minutes.

Such an incredible panorama graced our view:

From the west one could see how the city had expanded. Its suburbs overlook Wolfgang Hill, which is topped by the old castle with its majestic donjon surrounded by waves of Hungarian tents. Toward the south, who wouldn't be impressed by the Danube's sinuous curves, which are three hundred meters wide and endlessly peppered by the traffic from the vessels that go up and down it? So many small craft chugging along by sail or steam. Beyond it the Puszta, that beautiful country with its parklike woods, its plains, its agriculture, its pastures climbing all the way up the distant mountains of the Serbian province and the Military Limits . . . To the north the whole suburb of villas, cottages, and farms so easily recognizable by their pointy columbarium.

The admirable view was such a visual treat and especially striking in its variety. Because of the clear weather, with warm rays emanating from a sharp April sun, the view extended all the way to the furthest limits of the horizon. As I leaned from the parapet, I noticed Madame Roderich, who was waving to us from a bench by the lawn.

"There," Mademoiselle Myra explained, "that's the aristocratic neighborhood, with its palaces, its mansions, its squares, its statues . . . A bit further down, Monsieur Vidal, you can see the business district with its streets crowded with people, its markets . . . And of course, the Danube, as all roads lead to our Danube . . . It's bursting with so much life right now! And that's Svendor Island over there, so green with its thickets, fields, and flowers! . . . My brother mustn't forget to take you there!"

"Rest assured," Captain Haralan replied, "I won't spare Monsieur Vidal even a corner of Ragz."

"And our churches," Mademoiselle Myra continued. "Can you see our churches and their belfries, with their carillons and their bells? You'll hear them on Sunday! And our St. Michael's Cathedral, its imposing structure, the towers of its facade, its central steeple that shoots toward heaven as if it were leading a prayer service! It's absolutely magnificent, Monsieur Vidal, as splendid on the inside as it is on the outside! . . . "

"I can't wait to see it tomorrow," I said.

"Well then, Monsieur," Mademoiselle Myra asked, turning toward Marc, "while I'm showing your brother the cathedral, what will you be looking at? . . . "

"The Town Hall, Mademoiselle Myra . . . To the right of us, with its high roof, its lovely windows, its belfry that cries out the hours, its Court of Honor between two pavilions, and especially its monumental staircase . . . "

"And why," Myra asked, "so much enthusiasm for that municipal staircase? . . . "

"Because it leads to a certain room . . . " Marc answered as he glanced at this fiancée whose charming face had begun to blush ever so slightly.

"A room? . . . " she asked.

"A room where I will hear the sweetest word from your mouth . . . the word I've waited for all my life . . . "

"Yes, my dear Marc, and that word that both of us will utter there is the one we will pronounce in the house of God!"

After a rather long time spent on the belvedere terrace, we went back down to the garden, where Madame Roderich was waiting for us.

That day, I dined at the family table. It was my first meal in Hungary that wasn't in a hotel restaurant or on a steamship. The meal was exquisite. The quality of the courses and wines led me to believe that the Doctor appreciated the finest things in life, which could be said about all doctors, I imagine, regardless of what country they happen to belong to. Most of the dishes were spiced with paprika, as they are throughout Hungary . . . the Hungarian pallet is particularly fond of that spice! It was yet another "Magyarization" my brother had adapted and that he would lead me to as well!

We spent the evening en famille. More than once Mademoiselle Myra sat down at the clavichord and accompanied herself as she sang those original Hungarian melodies, odes, elegies, epics, Petröfi ballads, that nobody can hear without being moved.[5] It was a delight that could have gone on all night had Captain Haralan not given the signal that it was time to leave.

Marc followed me into my room when we got back to the Temesvar Hotel and asked me:

"Well then, did I exaggerate in any way? Do you think there's another girl in the world like . . . "

"Another!" I replied. "But I'm beginning to wonder if there's even one . . . and whether Mademoiselle Myra really exists!"[6]

"Ah! My dear Henry, you have no idea how much I love her!"

"Well, that doesn't surprise me, my dear Marc, and if there is but one word to describe Mademoiselle Myra, one word that I'll repeat three times: she's charming . . . charming . . . charming!"[7]

V

Early next morning, I visited parts of Ragz with Captain Haralan, while Marc kept busy with various formalities he needed to carry out for his wedding. The date had just been set for May 15th . . . in twenty days. Captain Haralan was keen on giving me the grand tour of his hometown. I could never have found a more conscientious, more erudite, or more obliging guide.

Even though my memory of him recurred with a surprising obstinacy, I didn't say a word to Haralan about that awful Wilhelm Storitz, despite having already spoken about him with my brother. As for the Captain, he too kept mum on the subject. It was quite likely, in fact, that the incident would no longer be brought up at all.

We left the Temesvar Hotel at eight o'clock, and began by walking down the length of the Bathiany quay.

As with most Hungarian towns, Ragz had previously been known by several different names. According to the time period, these cities can execute a baptism record in four or five languages—Latin, German, Slavic, Magyar—that can be as complicated as those of princes, grand dukes, and archdukes. Today, however, in modern geographical terms, Ragz is Ragz.

"Our town is not as important as Budapest," the Captain

explained. "But its population, which counts over forty thousand souls, is the same as our second-tier cities, and thanks to its industry, its commerce, it is well ranked within the Hungarian kingdom.

"Is it truly Magyar? . . . " I asked.

"Assuredly, as much by its mores, its customs, as you can see, as by what its inhabitants wear. One could say with a certain amount of truth that in Hungary, the Magyar people are the ones who founded the state, and the Germans the ones who established the cities. This affirmation is no less pertinent when it comes to Ragz. No doubt, you will meet individuals of German descent among its merchant class, but they are well in the minority."

Indeed, I was aware of that . . . The Ragzians even boasted of it as well as being a pure city with no real ethnic mix.

"Moreover, the Magyars—please do not confuse them with the Huns, as people sometimes did in the past—" Captain Haralan added, "are the ones who have created the strongest political cohesion, and from that point of view, Hungary is superior to Austria in respect of the grouping of the different populations that live within its borders."

"And the Slavs? . . . " I asked.

"There are fewer Slavs than Magyars, my dear Vidal, but more than there are Germans."

"I mean, the people . . . how are they viewed in the Hungarian Empire? . . . "

"Rather poorly, I have to admit, especially among the Magyar population, because it's obvious that for folks of Teutonic origin, their capital city isn't Vienna but Berlin."

Captain Haralan didn't seem to have much affection for the Austrians either, nor even for the Russians, who had lent their support in helping to subdue the 1849 rebellion. It has always been palpable in the Hungarian psyche. As for the Germans, there has been a long racial antipathy between Hungarians and themselves.

The antipathy can be manifested in many ways that are quickly apparent to a foreigner, and it is not just the dictums, which can express this hatred in rather brutal terms:

"Eb a német Kutya nélkül!"

Which in good French can be translated as: "Wherever there's a German, there's a dog!"

While taking into consideration a certain amount of exaggeration within proverbs, that one, at least, suggests a bit of a consensus between the two races.

As for the other groups within the Hungarian population, they can be broken down in the following manner: There are half a million Serbs in the Banat, a hundred thousand Croats, twenty thousand Romanians. The Slovaks comprise a rather compact group, with only two million people. Adding a mixture of Ruthenians, Slavs, and Little Russians[1] brings us to ten million inhabitants, spread throughout the Four Circles Committees,[2] the Danube, the Theiss, and the outskirts of the Theiss.

The city of Ragz is constructed with much uniformity. With the exception of its lower part, which is concentrated on the left bank of the river, the higher neighborhoods affect a geometrical rectitude that is almost American in nature.[3]

The first square one comes across as one goes down the Bathiany quay is Magyar Square, which is flanked by magnificent townhouses. On one side, it is serviced by the bridge that crosses Svendor Island and leans on the Serbian bank; on the other, it is linked to Saint Michael Square from Prince Miloch Street (one of the loveliest streets in the city). That's where the Governor's Palace is.

Captain Haralan did not take that street but continued further along the quay and led me to Stephen II Street, where we reached the Coloman Market, which was very busy at that time of day.

In this vast hall, one can discover an abundance of diverse products, the stands teeming with them: cereals, vegetables, fruits from the fields and the gardens of the Puszta, fresh game hunted in the woods and along the riverbanks of the Danube, meat from butchers, and cold cuts sold by retailers from the great pastures around Ragz.

There were more than agricultural products to ensure local prosperity. The Hungarian countryside relies heavily on its tobacco crops and vineyards (the Tokay region itself occupies three hundred thousand hectares of its own). I would also mention all the riches found in its metalliferous mountains, where the finest metals are extracted: gold and silver, but also less aristocratic varieties such as iron, copper, lead, and zinc. The sulfur mines are still very important as well. Finally, I should mention the layers and layers of exploitable salt (estimated at 3.3 billion tons). There's so much of it in Hungary that the sublunar world will easily have enough in their kitchens for many centuries to come . . . even when all the salt from the sea has been exhausted!

Moreover, as the typical Magyar, who wouldn't even mind living at the tip of a rock, would say:

"The Banat gave us wheat, the Puszta bread and meat, the mountains salt and gold! What is there left for us to desire, nothing! Outside of Hungary, life is not life!"

At one point during our visit to the Coloman Market, I enjoyed observing a typical peasant in his traditional garb. He had preserved the very pure character of his race with his strong head, flat nose, round eyes, hanging mustache. The typical peasant usually sports a wide-rimmed hat, from which two pigtails often emerge. His jackets and vest, with buttons of bone, are made from sheepskin; his pants are made from a heavy linen that could compete with the corduroy velvet found in our own northern countryside; his multicolored belt is tightly wound around his waist. For his feet, he wears hardy boots that sometimes have spurs attached to them.

It seemed to me that the women, who are quite beautiful, had a more lively demeanor than the men . . . dressed in their short skirts with brilliant colors, corsages decorated with fine embroideries, hats with upturned rims crested with feathers over hair that, in the absence of any national hat, is covered by a kerchief around the neck over a thick ponytail.

Gypsies often came by there as well. They are so different from their counterparts in France, who are presented by impresarios in our café concerts and casinos.[4] No! These poor devils are so miserable, so worthy of our pity . . . men, women, elderly, children . . . They still preserve some of their national character beneath their pathetically tattered clothes, which feature more holes than fabric.

As we left the market, Captain Haralan led me through a labyrinth of narrow streets bracketed by stores with signs hanging outside their windows. The neighborhood then expanded as we got to Liszt Square, one of the biggest squares in the city.

There is a beautiful fountain in the middle of the square made of bronze and marble, its basin with a constant supply of water spouting from its eccentric gargoyles. A statue of Mathias Corvin seems to look down on all the activity from above. Corvin was the fifteenth-century hero who became king at fifteen and successfully thwarted attacks from the Austrians, the Bohemians, and the Poles, and saved European Christianity from Ottoman barbarism.

It was such a truly beautiful square. On one side the Town Hall, with its high garrets and weathervanes. The citizens of Ragz had wonderfully preserved the character of the old Renaissance constructions. In the main building, an iron flight of stairs leads to a gallery decorated with marble statues. The facade is pierced by stone bars on the windows that are enclosed by old stained glass. In the center, a belfry with gabled windows beneath the keeper's tiny quarters is seemingly protected by the national flag. In the back, two buildings, linked by a gate with a door opening out onto a vast courtyard, project out, with masses of greenery at each angle.

In front of the Town Hall, a train station leads to the junction between the Temesvar and the Banat. From there, Budapest is easily connected to Szegedin on the east side of the Danube and, on the other side, to the trains to the West, Mohacz, Warasdin, Narbourg and Groetz, the Styrian capital.

We stopped at Liszt Square for a moment.

"Here's the Town Hall," Captain Haralan began. "This is where Marc and Myra will have to appear before a civil servant in less than three weeks to answer that important question they will be asked . . ."

"We already know the answer!" I quipped. "Does it take a long time to get to the Cathedral from here?"

"Just a few minutes, my dear Vidal, and if you would like, we can go down Ladislas Street, which will take us right there." That street, which, like Bathiany and the other major streets of Ragz, teems with trolley cars, ends in front of St. Michael's Cathedral. It displays a mixture of Roman and gothic architecture that dates back to the thirteenth century. Although the Cathedral's style lacks architectural purity, it also has some beautiful parts that are worth the attention of connoisseurs. Its facade is flanked by two towers, with a spire that climbs over 315 feet in the air. Its central gate is known for its elaborately crafted curved arches; its large rose windows are often pierced by the rays of the setting sun, which in fact spreads its light throughout the great nave. Finally, one should admire its round apse, which lies between those multiple flying buttresses that an irreverent tourist once called an orthopedic device for cathedrals.

"We'll have enough time to look inside a bit later," Captain Haralan remarked.

"As you wish," I replied. "You'll be my guide, my dear Captain, and I'll follow you . . ."

"In that case, let's go back up to the Castle; then we'll take the boulevard line back into town. We should arrive at my mother's in time for lunch."

Although Ragz is mostly made up of Catholics, there are many other churches as well. There are Lutheran, Romanian, and Greek Orthodox places of worship, but their temples and chapels are of no architectural interest. Hungary is predominantly apostolic and Roman Catholic even though its capital, Budapest, is, after Krakow, the city with the greatest number of Jews. There, as in other places, the Grandees' fortune has fallen almost entirely into their hands.[5]

As we worked our way to the Castle, we had to cross a rather animated district where many merchants and buyers were busy doing business. Precisely at the moment when we got to a little square, we heard a din that surpassed the usual brouhaha of commerce.

A few women had abandoned their wares and surrounded a man, a peasant who was entirely spread out on the ground. He seemed to be having trouble getting up, and screamed in anger:

"I told you that someone hit me . . . pushed me so violently that it knocked me right down! . . . "

"Who hit you then?" one of the women retorted. "You were all alone at that moment . . . I had a good look at you from my stall . . . There wasn't anyone else there . . . "

"Yes, there was . . . " the man replied. "When somebody pushes you, you feel it . . . right here straight in the chest . . . that kind of thing just doesn't happen on its own!"

After he helped him up, Captain Haralan questioned the fellow and got the following explanation: the peasant had been walking along for about twenty feet from the end of the square when suddenly he felt a violent shock, as though a vigorous man had crashed directly into him, but when he looked around, there was no one anywhere near him . . .

How much truth was there to his story? Had the peasant really received such a violent if unexpected blow? There can be no push without someone doing the pushing, even if it were a gust of wind . . . but the air was perfectly calm. One thing we knew for sure: that he had fallen and that the cause of his fall was completely inexplicable . . .

Hence all the excitement when we got there.

Either the man had been the victim of a hallucination, or he had had too much to drink. A drunkard falls by himself, if only by virtue of the laws of gravity.

This was undoubtedly what most people assumed, although the peasant denied that he had had anything to drink. In spite of his protests, officers hauled him in to the police station.

As soon as the incident was officially over, we followed a few rising streets until we were going eastward. There was a network of alleys and streets, a muddled labyrinth that a foreigner would never be able to find his way out of.

Finally, we found ourselves in front of the Castle, firmly perched on one of the crests of Wolfgang Hill.

It truly was the fortress of Hungarian cities, the acropolis, or *var*, the real Magyar word for it, the citadel from feudal times, as menacing to enemies on the outside, such as the Huns or the Turks, as it was to the feudal lord's vassals. It boasted high, crenelated, machicolated walls pierced by loopholes that were flanked by giant towers. The highest one was the donjon, which overlooked the entire county.

The drawbridge, thrown over a moat bristling with a thousand wild shrubs, led us to the postern gate between two trench mortars that were no longer in use. Above it stretched the long necks of cannons belonging to the ancient artillery that is sometimes used as bollards on wharfs.

Captain Haralan's rank had opened all the doors of those old blockhouses, which are of course now classified as historical landmarks. The few old soldiers who guarded the door gave him the military salute to which he was entitled, and once we were at the drill ground, he invited me to climb up to the donjon, which occupied one of its angles.

We had to climb no fewer than 240 steps up the spiral staircase that led to the roof.

As we walked along the parapet, my eyes looked out on a horizon that was even more outstretched than the one I had observed from the tower at the Roderich house. I would have estimated no less than thirty kilometers for that part of the Danube that flowed eastward at that point toward Neusatz.

"Now, my dear Vidal," Captain Haralan began, "you're familiar with one part of our town. You can see it in its entirety at our feet . . . "

"And what I've already seen of it," I replied, "seems very interesting to me, even after Budapest and Presburg . . . "

"I'm happy to hear you say that, and once you finish your tour of Ragz, and you've grown accustomed to its mores, its customs, its idiosyncrasies, I have no doubt that you will remember it fondly when you leave. That's because we Magyars love our cities with an almost filial devotion! As a matter of fact, there is a perfect harmony here among the various classes. The entire population enjoys a most intense appreciation for independence and harbors the most ardent patriotic instincts. Moreover, the leisure class is very charitable toward the unfortunate, and in any case, individuals are rescued from misery as soon as people find out about it."

"I know that, my dear Captain, just as I know that Dr. Roderich is never frugal when it comes to the poor, and that Madame Roderich and Mademoiselle Myra are both directors of charitable organizations . . . "

"My mother and sister only do what anyone of their social status and financial situation should do. In my opinion, charity is the highest duty! . . .

"Undoubtedly," I added, "but there are many ways to fulfill it!"

"Therein lies the secret of women, my dear Vidal, and one of their callings down here on earth . . . "

"Yes . . . and assuredly the most noble of them."

"Finally," the Captain continued, "we live in a peaceful town that is unmarred or hardly troubled by political passions, yet very jealous of its rights and privileges, which protect it from any infringement by the central government. I'll admit, however, that my fellow citizens have only one flaw . . . "

"And that is? . . . "

"They can be a bit too inclined to superstition and believe too willingly in the supernatural! Legends filled with ghosts and phantoms, yarns about raising the devil, are quick to please them more than they ought! I know very well that the Ragzians are very Catholic and that the practice of Catholicism contributes to this predisposition . . . "[6]

"So," I suggested, "not Dr. Roderich—a doctor is hardly susceptible to that sort of thing—but your mother . . . your sister? . . . "

"Yes . . . and everybody else along with them. I have to admit that I haven't been able to make any headway against that weakness, for it really is one. Perhaps Marc will help me."

"Unless, of course," I joked, "Mademoiselle Myra objects!"

"And now, my dear Vidal, lean over the parapet . . . take a look toward the northeast . . . there . . . at the tip of the city, can you see the terrace from a belvedere? . . . "

"I see it," I replied. "It would seem to be the tower of the Roderich residence . . . "

"You're not mistaken, and in that mansion, there's a dining room, and in that room lunch will be served in about an hour, and since you are one of the guests . . . "

"At your orders, *mon cher Capitaine* . . . "

"In that case, let's go downstairs, let's leave this *var* to its feudal solitude we've interrupted momentarily, and let's go back up the boulevards that will allow us to cross the northern part of the city . . . "

A few minutes later, we had gone through the postern gate.

Beyond a beautiful neighborhood extending all the way to the walls of Ragz, the boulevards, with names that change at each of the big streets they intersect, delineate three-quarters of a circle that is sealed by the Danube itself. A quadruple row of trees are planted along them . . . oak, chestnut, lime trees throughout the ages, which stretch for five kilometers. On one side, a revetment wall of ancient facades that can earn you a nice glimpse of the countryside, if you look over it. On the other, a succession of luxurious homes, for the most part preceded by a courtyard bursting with flowerbeds with rear walls hiding gloriously fresh gardens that are irrigated by gushes of water.

Several well-drawn horse-and-carriages were already going down the boulevards at that time of day. Groups of horsemen and very elegantly attired horsewomen trotted down the side lanes.

We turned left at the end of the street so that we could go onto Teleki Boulevard, toward Bathiany.

From that vantage point, I noticed an isolated house standing alone in the center of its garden. Its sad appearance, as though it had been forsaken for some time, its closed and shuttered windows that seemed never to have been thrown open, its moss-encrusted wall, formed a strange contrast with the other townhouses along the boulevard.

Through an iron gate surrounded by thistles, we entered a small courtyard with two willows that had died of old age. Their trunks, split by long gashes, were entirely rotten at the core.

At the front of the building, there was a door that had been discolored by inclement weather, blasts of winter, and blizzards. One could reach it by a flight of three dilapidated steps.

Up on a roof that was heavy with purlins, on the building's first floor, there was a square belvedere with narrow windows that had been draped with thick curtains.

It didn't seem as though the house were inhabited, even supposing that it were habitable.

"To whom does it belong?" I asked.

"An eccentric," Captain Haralan replied.

"It defaces the boulevard," I remarked . . . "The city should buy it and demolish it . . . "

"The more so, my dear Vidal, as with the house torn down, its owner would no doubt leave town and go to the devil—his closest relative, if we're to believe the gossip of Ragz!"

"Is he a foreigner?"

"A German."

"A German?" I repeated.

"Yes . . . a Prussian."

"And his name is? . . . "

Just as Captain Haralan was about to reply, the door of the house opened, and two men came out. The oldest, who looked about sixty years old, waited on the steps while the other crossed the yard and reemerged through the gates.

"Well!" Captain Haralan murmured. "So he's still here? . . . I thought he had gone away . . . "

The fellow saw us as he turned around. Did he know Captain Haralan? I didn't doubt it, since they exchanged unmistakable looks of animosity.

I had also recognized him, however, and when he got a few steps away from us, I yelled:

"So it's really him!"

"You've met this strange bird before?" Captain Haralan asked, a bit surprised.

"I'm sure of it," I replied. "I traveled with him from Budapest to Vukovar on the *Mathias Corvin*, and I have to admit, I hardly expected to see him in Ragz."

"And it would be better if he weren't here!" the Captain declared.

"You don't seem to be on good terms with that German . . . " I suggested.

"And who could be!"

"Has he been living in Ragz for a long time? . . . "

"For about two years, and, I might add, he had the impudence to ask for my sister's hand in marriage! But my father and I refused it in a way that aimed to thoroughly discourage him from ever asking for it again . . . "

"What! So that's the man! . . . "

"So you knew ? . . . "

"Yes . . . my dear Captain, and I also know that his name is Wilhelm Storitz, the son of Otto Storitz, the illustrious chemist of Spremberg!"

VI

I spent the next two days exploring the city. Like a true Magyar, I spent long hours on the bridge that links the two banks of the Danube to Svendor Island. I never got tired of admiring that magnificent river.

I have to admit that, despite my better judgment, Wilhelm Storitz continued to haunt me. So he lived in Ragz, with, as I soon learned, a solitary servant known as Hermann who was no more sympathetic, nor approachable, nor communicative than his master. Moreover, there was something about Hermann's appearance and gait that reminded me of the man who seemed to have followed my brother and myself on the day I arrived, when we strolled along the Bathiany quay.

I thought it best not to say anything to Marc about the encounter Captain Haralan and I had experienced on Teleki Boulevard.[1] It might have made him uneasy to know that Wilhelm Storitz, whom he thought was no longer in Ragz, had in fact returned. I didn't want anything dimming his happiness! But I didn't like the idea that his rejected rival had still not left town. I would have liked him to be gone at least until Marc and Myra's wedding.

On the 27th, I was getting ready for my usual morning walk, and about to go downstairs, when my brother walked into my room. I was planning on exploring the areas surrounding Ragz, in the Serbian countryside.

"I have a lot to do, my friend," he told me, "and you'll forgive me if I leave you alone for a bit . . . "

"Go, my dear Marc," I replied, "and don't worry about me . . . "

"Isn't Captain Haralan supposed to come by and take you? . . . "

"No . . . He's not free today . . . I'm going to have lunch in a nearby tavern on the other side of the Danube . . . "

"Above all, Henry, make sure you're back by seven! . . . "

"The Doctor's dining room table is too delicious to forget that!"

"Gourmand . . . Ah! There is also an evening party that will be held at the Roderich house in a few days. You'll truly be able to study Ragz's high society there . . . "

"Is it an engagement party, Marc? . . . "

"Oh! It's been quite some time since my dearest Myra and I have been engaged . . . It even seems as though we've always been . . . "

"I know . . . from birth . . . "

"It could very well be!"

"Farewell, then, oh you happiest of men . . . "

"Before you say that to me, you should wait until my fiancée becomes my wife!"

After Mark shook my hand good-bye . . . I went down to the dining room and had breakfast.

I was about to leave when Captain Haralan appeared.

"You!" I said rather loudly. "Well, my dear Captain, what a pleasant surprise!"

I could have been wrong, but he had a rather worried look on his face. All he said to me was:

"My dear Vidal . . . I came . . . "

"I'm ready, as you see . . . The weather is beautiful, and if a few hours of walking doesn't scare you away . . . "

"No . . . another time, if you please . . . "

"So what brings you here then? . . . "

"My father would like a word with you, and he's waiting for you at home . . . "

"I'm all yours!" I replied.

Captain Haralan didn't utter a single word as we walked side by side along the Bathiany quay. What could have happened, and what did Dr. Roderich want to talk to me about? . . . Did it have anything to do with Marc's wedding? . . .

The servant led us into the Doctor's study as soon as we arrived.

Madame and Mademoiselle Roderich had already left the house, and Marc was probably accompanying them on their morning errands.

The Doctor was alone in his study, sitting at his table, and when he looked up, he seemed even more worried than his son.

"Something's up," I thought, "but I'm sure Marc knew nothing about it when I saw him this morning . . . Nobody told him a thing, and surely nobody wanted to tell him anything . . . "

I sank into an armchair facing the Doctor, while Captain Haralan remained standing by the fireplace, where a log was still burning.

A bit anxious myself, I waited for the Doctor to speak.

"First of all, Monsieur Vidal," he told me, "thank you for coming to visit me . . . "

"I'm always at your service, Monsieur Roderich."

"I wanted to have a word with you in Haralan's presence."

"Does it have something to do with the wedding? . . ."

"Indeed."

"Something serious? . . . "

"Yes and no," the Doctor replied. "Whichever it is, neither my wife, nor my daughter, nor your brother, knows anything about it, and I prefer for them not to know what I've got to tell you . . . You'll be able to judge for yourself whether I'm right or wrong to do so!"

Instinctively, I felt in my heart that this had something to do with our encounter in front of the house on Teleki Boulevard.

"Yesterday afternoon," the Doctor continued, "while Madame Roderich and Myra were out, and just at my hour for consultation, the servant handed me the calling card of a visitor I had not counted on ever seeing again. As I read the name that was written on that card, I felt a strong feeling of discontent . . . That name was Wilhelm Storitz."

I took the card, and I looked at it intensely for a moment.

What caught my eye was that the name, instead of being engraved or printed, had been personally autographed. It was the actual writing of this worrisome figure, his signature embellished by a complicated flourish, the beak from some sort of bird of prey.

Here is the rest of the facsimile:

Wilhelm Storitz[2]

"But perhaps you don't know about this German?" the Doctor asked . . .

"Yes . . . I am aware of the situation," I replied.

"Well then, about three months ago, before your brother's request had been made and welcomed, Wilhelm Storitz asked for my daughter's hand. After consulting my wife, my son, and Myra, who shared my dislike for such a marriage, I told Wilhelm Storitz that I could not consider his proposal. Instead of bowing to this refusal, he renewed his request in formal terms, and I reiterated my reply no less formally and in such terms so as not to leave him any room for hope."

While Dr. Roderich was talking, Captain Haralan was striding up and down the room, stopping several times at one of the windows to look toward Teleki Boulevard.

"Dr. Roderich," I said, "I knew about this request, and I knew that it was made before my brother's . . . "

"About three months before, Monsieur Vidal.

"So," I continued, "it wasn't because Marc had already been accepted that Wilhelm Storitz was refused Myra's hand, but simply because the marriage didn't appeal to you."

"We would never have consented to such a union, which would have appealed to us in no way whatsoever, and to which Myra would have given a categorical refusal."

"Was it personal . . . or was it Wilhelm Storitz's position that informed your decision? . . . "

"His position is probably good enough," Dr. Roderich replied. "We can believe that his father left him a considerable fortune, the result of his fruitful discoveries. But as to his person . . . "

"I know him, Dr. Roderich."

"You do? . . . "

I explained how I had met Wilhelm Storitz on the *dampfschiff*, without a clue as to who he really was. For forty-eight hours, that very German had been my traveling companion between Pest and Vukovar, where I thought he had gotten off, since he was no longer on board when we reached Ragz.

"And yet yesterday," I added, "during my walk with Captain Haralan, we went past his house, and I recognized him the moment he came out."

"They say that he had been out of town for several weeks," Dr. Roderich remarked.

"That's what everybody thought, and it is possible that he had gone away," Captain Haralan observed, "but what we now know for sure is that he has returned to his house, and that he was in Ragz yesterday!"

Captain Haralan's voice betrayed a sharp irritation.

The Doctor continued in these terms:

"Monsieur Vidal, I've already explained Wilhelm Storitz's position. As for his everyday life, who on earth could claim to know anything about it? . . . He's utterly mystifying! . . . It's as though the man lived on the peripheries of humanity . . . "

"Aren't you exaggerating a bit?" I pointed out.

"A little exaggeration, no doubt," he told me. "Still, he belongs to a rather suspicious family, and before him, his father, Otto Storitz, was the subject of the strangest legends . . . "

"Which have survived him, Doctor, to judge by an article in a copy of the *Wienner Extrablatt* I read in Pest. It was about the anniversary celebrated every year in Spremberg at the cemetery. If one were to believe the paper, time has not weakened the superstitious legends you spoke of! . . . The dead savant inherited from the living one! . . . He was a sorcerer . . . He possessed secrets of the Next World . . . He had supernatural powers, and each year they expect to see some extraordinary phenomenon occur around his tomb! . . . "

"In that case, Monsieur Vidal," Dr. Roderich concluded, "and based on what goes on in Spremberg, don't be shocked if our Wilhelm Storitz is perceived as a strange character in Ragz! . . . This is the kind of man who asked for my daughter's hand in marriage, and who yesterday had the audacity to repeat his request . . . "

"Yesterday? . . . " I blurted out.

"Yesterday, when he called here!"

"And even if he weren't the kind of person he is," Captain Haralan declared, "he would still be a Prussian, and that would be quite enough to make us refuse such an alliance! I think you understand this, my dear Vidal . . . "

"I do indeed, Captain!"

All the antipathy that the Magyar race, by tradition and by instinct, feels for the Germanic one burned through his words.

"This is what happened," Dr. Roderich continued. "You really should be informed. I hesitated when I picked up Wilhelm Storitz's calling card . . . Should I have had him shown in or simply replied that I could not receive him?"

"Perhaps that might have been preferable, Father," Captain Haralan remarked. "After his first attempt failed, he should have realized that under no pretext whatsoever should he ever set foot in this house again . . . "

"Indeed, you might be right," the Doctor muttered, "but I didn't want to go to such extremes for fear that it might lead to some sort of scandal . . . "

"Which I would have swiftly extinguished, Father!"

"It's precisely because I know you so well," the Doctor said, grasping the Captain's hand, "that I preferred to act so cautiously! . . . And come what may, I appeal to your affection for your mother, for me, for your sister, whose position would become very painful if her name were to be brought into it, should this Wilhelm Storitz cause any trouble . . . "

Although I had known Captain Haralan for only a few days, I regarded him as a rather short-tempered man, almost excessively concerned with any matter relating to his family. I too hated the fact that Marc's rival had returned to Ragz, and that he had had the gall to renew his request.

The Doctor continued to describe the visit in detail. It had taken place right where we were standing at the moment. Wilhelm Storitz had first spoken in a tone that revealed how unusually tenacious he was. Storitz had just returned to Ragz forty-eight hours ago, and Dr. Roderich couldn't help but be surprised that he wanted to see him once again. "If I have returned," he said, "if I have insisted on being seen, it is because I wanted to make a second attempt, but not the last . . . " "Sir," the Doctor replied, "I can understand your first request, but I cannot fathom this one, and your presence in my home . . . " "Sir," he insisted coldly, "I have not given up pursuing the honor of becoming Mademoiselle Myra's husband, and it is for this reason that I have wanted to see you again . . . " "In that case, Sir," the Doctor asserted, "your visit would be in no way justified . . . We have no reason to go back on our refusal, and I see no reason for this persistence . . . " "On the contrary," Wilhelm Storitz pursued, "there is a reason that in fact motivates my insistence. It is that another suitor has come forward, another who is happier than I am, one whom you have deemed worthy to grant . . . a Frenchman . . . a Frenchman! . . . " "Indeed," the Doctor replied. "A Frenchman, Mr. Marc Vidal, has requested my daughter's hand . . . and he has succeeded in obtaining it!" Wilhelm Storitz cried out. "Indeed, Sir," the Doctor replied once again. "And in the absence of any other motive, this in and of itself should have been enough to make you understand that you have absolutely no chance whatsoever were you to harbor any hope at all . . . " "I maintain that hope!" Wilhelm Storitz declared. "No! I will not give up on my union with Mademoiselle Myra Roderich! . . . I love her, and if she is not mine, then she will never be anyone else's either!"

"The insolence! . . . The wretch!" Captain Haralan declared. "He dared to speak like that, and I wasn't there to throw him out!"

"Indeed," I thought, "if these two men should ever come face to face, it would be difficult to prevent the clash the Doctor is so worried about!"

"With those last words," the Doctor continued, "I got up and indicated that I would listen to no more of this nonsense . . . The wedding had been decided upon and would be celebrated in a few days . . . "

"Neither in a few days, nor later," Wilhelm Storitz replied.

"'Sir,' I told him, showing him the door, 'be so good as to leave!' Anyone else would have understood that his visit couldn't possibly go on any further . . . Well, he waited, he lowered his voice and attempted to obtain with gentleness what he wasn't able to gain by violence,—at the very least a promise that the marriage would be cancelled. And so, I began to walk toward the fireplace to ring for the servant. He grabbed me by the arm, angry once again, his voice raised to such a level that it could surely have been heard outside. Fortunately, my wife and daughter had not yet come home! Wilhelm Storitz finally consented to leave, but not without uttering a slew of threats! . . . Mademoiselle Roderich would not marry that Frenchman. So many obstacles would erupt, it would be impossible for the wedding to take place . . . The Storitz family had means at its disposal that could defy all human power, and he wouldn't hesitate to use them against this impudent family that had rejected him . . . At last, he opened the study door and stormed out furiously, in the middle of a few people who were waiting outside, leaving me quite terrified by his threatening words!"

As the Doctor reminded us again, not one word of this scene had been reported to either Madame Roderich, her daughter, or my brother. It was best to spare them that kind of anxiety. Moreover, I knew Marc well enough to worry that he would bring this business to an end, as would Captain Haralan—who, however, gave way to his father's insistence.

"So be it," he said. "I won't go ahead and punish this impudent rascal. But what if he's the one who comes to me? . . . What if he's the one who attacks Marc? . . . What if he's the one who provokes us?"

Dr. Roderich had no reply to that.

On that note our conversation came to a close. In any case, we would have to wait, and no one would know a thing about this if Wilhelm Storitz decided to go from speech to action. In any case, what could he do? How could he stop the wedding from taking place? By insulting Marc in public so that he would be forced to fight a duel? . . . Or rather by some violent act against Myra

Roderich? . . . But how could he succeed in gaining entrance to a house in which he would no longer be received? . . . It was not in his power, I supposed, to break down the doors! . . . Moreover, Dr. Roderich wouldn't hesitate to warn the authorities, who would know well enough how to bring the German to reason!

Before we parted, the Doctor beseeched his son one last time not to take action against the impudent individual, and it was obvious that Captain Haralan agreed against his will. Our conversation had gone on so long that Madame Roderich, her daughter, and my brother had already come back home. I had to stay for lunch and postpone my excursion to the outer parts of Ragz until the afternoon.

Needless to say, I made up some sort of excuse for my presence in the Doctor's study that morning. Marc was not at all suspicious, as it turned out, and lunch went on very pleasantly.

And when we got up from the table, Mademoiselle Myra told me:

"Monsieur Henry, since we have had the pleasure of finding you here, I trust you will stay with us for the rest of the day . . . "

"And what about my exploring?" I replied.

"We'll explore together!"

"It's just that I had planned on going a bit far . . . "

"We'll go a bit far!"

"On foot . . . "

"On foot!"

"You can't refuse," my brother added, "since Mademoiselle Myra is the one doing the asking."

"No, you can't, or everything will be severed between us, Monsieur Henry! . . . "

"I'm at your command, Mademoiselle!"

"And by the way, Monsieur Henry, do we absolutely have to go so far? . . . I'm not sure you were able to fully admire Svendor Island in all its beauty . . . "

"I was going to see it tomorrow . . . "

"Well then, we'll go today."

And so it was in Madame and Mademoiselle Roderich's company, as well as Marc's, that I visited this island that had been transformed into a public garden, a type of park, with flowerbeds, chalets, and all sorts of attractions.

Yet my mind wasn't entirely focused on our stroll. Marc noticed that I was drifting, and I was forced to give him some sort of evasive explanation.

Was it that I feared meeting Wilhelm Storitz on our way? No, that wasn't it. I was thinking about what he had told Dr. Roderich: "So many obstacles would erupt, it would be impossible for the wedding to take place . . . The Storitz family had means at its disposal that could defy all human power." What did he mean? . . . Was he to be taken seriously? I promised myself to discuss this with the Doctor once we were alone.

Several days went by. I began to calm down. Wilhelm Storitz had not been seen again. Yet he had not left town either. The house on Teleki Boulevard was still occupied. As I passed by it, I saw his servant Hermann coming out. Once Wilhelm Storitz himself appeared at one of the belvedere windows, his gaze focused on the end of the boulevard, toward Dr. Roderich's home . . .

This is how things remained until, on the night of May 17th, the following incident occurred:

Although the Town Hall was continuously guarded by the orderlies on duty, and nobody could approach it without being seen, Marc Vidal's and Myra Roderich's wedding notice had been torn down from its place among others, found ripped to pieces only a few steps away!

VII

Who could have perpetrated such an inexplicable act—who indeed but the only one who had an interest in committing it? . . . Would it be followed by more serious attacks? . . . Was it the beginning of a series of reprisals against the Roderich family? . . .

The Doctor was informed of this incident early the next day by Captain Haralan, who got to the Temesvar Hotel as soon as he could.

One can well imagine how irritated he was.

"It's that wretch who did it," he yelled. "Yes, he's the one! . . . How he did it, I have no idea! He won't stop at that, no doubt, but I won't let him get away with it! . . . "

"Keep your cool, my dear Haralan," I said, "and don't do anything imprudent that might complicate the situation! . . . "

"My dear Vidal, if my father had warned me before the skunk left our house, or if he'd let me take action since then, we would have been rid of him by now . . . "

"I still think, my dear Haralan, that it would be better for you not to do anything right now . . . "

"And what if he continues? . . . "

"Then we'll have to ask the police to intervene! Think of your mother, your sister."

"Won't they learn what has happened to the notice? . . . "

"We won't tell them, any more than we'll tell Marc . . . After the wedding, we'll see what should be done . . . "

"After? . . . " the Captain replied. "And what if that's too late? . . . "

That day, at home, all we could think about was the engagement party. Monsieur and Madame Roderich had wanted things "to be done correctly," as the French say. The preparations were almost done. The good doctor, who only had friends in Ragz, had sent out a sea of invitations. Here, as though it were neutral territory, Magyar aristocracy would mingle with army representatives, the magistracy, public officials, and captains of industry and commerce. The Governor of Ragz, who was the Doctor's lifelong friend, had also accepted the Roderichs' invitation.

Approximately 150 people were expected in their home that evening, and its drawing rooms were spacious enough to accommodate them, likewise the veranda where supper would be served at the end of the evening.

Nobody would be surprised to learn that Myra Roderich had devoted much thought to her attire, nor that Marc was giving her the benefit of his artistic taste—which he had already provided when he began work on his fiancée's portrait. Moreover, Myra was a Magyar, and Magyars typically worry considerably about how they are dressed, regardless of their sex. It's in their blood, along with the love of dance, which verges on passion. Furthermore, as what I have just said about Mademoiselle Myra could apply to all the men and women, this soirée, during which the marriage contract was to be signed, promised to be nothing less than spectacular.

The preparations were completed that afternoon. I had spent the day waiting for the moment when I too, in true Magyar fashion, would have to start thinking about what I was going to wear.

Then, as I stared out of the window with my elbows on the

windowsill, gazing at the view of Bathiany quay, I had the extreme displeasure of noticing Wilhelm Storitz. Was it purely chance that brought him there? Most unlikely. He was slowly walking along the river with his head lowered. But when he got to the house, he straightened up, and an incredible look flashed from his eyes! His pacing back and forth a few times did not go unnoticed by Madame Roderich. In fact, she felt compelled to mention it to the Doctor, who simply reassured her without mentioning a word about Wilhelm Storitz's recent visit.

I would add that, when Marc and I were walking back to our hotel, the man met us at Magyar Square. As soon as he caught sight of my brother, he stopped suddenly and seemed to hesitate as though he meant to accost us. But he remained motionless, his face pale and his arms as stiff as those of a cataleptic . . . was he going to collapse right then and there? His eyes, his blistering eyes, fired like a shot at Marc who pretended not to pay any attention to him at all. And when we had left him a few paces behind, my brother asked:

"Did you notice that man?"

"Yes, Marc."

"That's the Wilhelm Storitz I told you about."

"I know."

"So you know him? . . . "

"Captain Haralan pointed him out to me once or twice already . . . "

"I thought he'd left Ragz . . . "

"Apparently not, or at any rate, it would appear as though he's come back . . . "

"Who cares, after all!"

"You're right. Who cares," I replied, but to my mind Wilhelm Storitz's absence would have been much more reassuring.

At around nine o'clock in the evening, the first coaches pulled up in front of Dr. Roderich's residence, and the rooms began to fill up. The Doctor, his wife, his daughter were receiving their guests at the gallery's entrance, which was glowing from the light of the chandeliers. The Governor of Ragz was announced shortly thereafter, and it was with great warmth and friendship that His Excellency presented his remarks to the Roderich family. He was particularly attentive to Mademoiselle Myra, as well as to my brother, both of whom were showered with congratulations from all directions.

All sorts of dignitaries arrived between nine and ten o'clock, all the magistrates, the officers, friends of Captain Haralan, who, in spite of the worried look on his face, continued to receive his guests with great aplomb. The ladies' dresses were resplendent amid the sea of uniforms and black suits. All these guests were milling about through the rooms and the veranda, admiring the wedding presents on display in the Doctor's study. There were all sorts of jewels and expensive objects for the guests to appreciate. It goes without saying that the gifts from my brother were of exquisite taste! The wedding bouquet, a magnificent assemblage of roses and orange blossoms, was placed on one of the tables in the great drawing room, and in accordance with Magyar custom, the nuptial crown Myra would wear when she went to the Cathedral on her wedding day had been placed next to the bouquet on a velvet cushion.

The evening would be split in two: first a concert, and then a grand ball. The dances were not to begin before midnight, and perhaps most of the guests were a bit sad that they were scheduled so late into the evening, since, as I have already mentioned, there is no entertainment that Hungarian men and women relish with more pleasure and passion!

The musical part of the evening had been entrusted to an incredible Gypsy orchestra, however. This particular orchestra, which was quite famous throughout the country, was making its first appearance in Ragz. The musicians and their leader took their seats at the appropriate time.

I was well aware that the Hungarians are great music lovers. Yet I would like to add that there is still a very distinct difference between the Hungarian and the German ways of appreciating music's charms. The Magyar is a dilettante, not an executor. He doesn't sing, or if he does, he doesn't sing much; he listens, but when it concerns the national anthem, listening is both a serious affair and an extraordinarily intense pleasure. I don't think any other group is as demonstratively impressionable, and the Gypsies, those instrumentalists from Bohemia, are the most responsive to such patriotic instincts.

The orchestra was made up of about a dozen musicians and one leader. They were about to play their most beautiful pieces, the warrior songs known as *Hongroises*, military marches that the Magyars, who are men of action, prefer to the reveries to which German music is prone.

Perhaps one might be surprised to hear that a more nuptial music, a more hymeneal sort of hymn, wasn't chosen for such an occasion. It's not part of the traditions here, and Hungary is truly a land of traditions . . . She is loyal to her popular melodies, just as Serbia is to her *pesmas* or Romania to her *doïmas*. What she needs are those spirited tunes, those rhythmic marches, that reassure her on the battlefields and celebrate the unforgettable exploits from her history books.

The Gypsies got into their original bohemian costumes. I was riveted by these curious fellows, with their weather-beaten complexions, their eyes glowing beneath hefty eyebrows, their high cheekbones, their pointy white teeth covered by their lips, their black hair with a frizziness that drifts onto their slightly furtive foreheads.

They had four types of stringed instruments. The basses and

altos were meant for the main motif. The more fantasy-oriented accompaniment came from the violins, flutes, and oboes. In two of the musicians' hands, I noticed a cymbal with metal cords. They strike these with drumsticks that endow the harmonic table with a very specific profundity that I am unable to compare to any other I have ever heard.

The orchestra's repertoire, which was superior to a similar one I heard in Paris, was quite impressive. All those in attendance listened with rapture then applauded frenetically. They particularly loved the more popular pieces, such as the "Song of Rakos" and Racoczy's "Transylvanian March," which the Gypsies tossed off with a masterfulness that was capable of awakening the entire Puszta that evening!

The time allotted to the music had already gone by. For my part, I was particularly moved by this Magyar environment. During some of the orchestra's lulls, I could even feel the distant murmur of the Danube reaching me!

I wouldn't presume that Marc was also affected by the charms of this strange music. Another, softer, more intimate air was filling his soul. As he sat near Myra Roderich, their glances would speak to each other, as they sang those romances without words that captivate the hearts of young fiancés.

After the last applause, the Gypsy orchestra leader rose, followed by his colleagues. Dr. Roderich and Captain Haralan thanked them profusely. They seemed touched as they left the room.

Between the two parts of the program, there was what I would call a type of intermission, during which the guests got up from their seats, mingled, formed new groups; some even dispersed amid the gardens, which were so brilliantly illuminated, as plates filled with refreshing beverages circulated madly.

Up until that moment, nothing had troubled the order of the festivities, and as they had begun so well, nothing would lead one to believe that they wouldn't end as seamlessly. Even if I might have feared it, or if a few apprehensions had begun to bubble within me, I had regained my initial assuredness.

Moreover, I held nothing back when it came to congratulating Madame Roderich.

"Thank you, Monsieur Vidal," she replied, "and I'm happy that our guests have spent such a pleasant evening with us here. But in the middle of such a joyous crowd, I admit that all I can see are my dear daughter and your brother! . . . They're so happy . . . "

"Madame," I answered, "this is a happiness that you deserve . . . the greatest any father and mother could wish for!"

Why would my rather banal pleasantries remind me of Wilhelm Storitz? For what strange reason? In any case, Captain Haralan no longer seemed to be thinking of him. Was that what he had in mind—was he acting naturally? . . . I couldn't say, but he buzzed from one group to another, spearheading this party with his contagious enthusiasm, and no doubt, more than one young Hungarian lass gazed upon him with admiring eyes! Admittedly, he was absolutely delighted by the goodwill the entire town showed his family!

"My dear Captain," I said to him, when he brushed by me, "if the second act of your evening is as good as the first . . . "

"You can count on it!" he cried out. "Music is fine and dandy . . . but dance, now that's so much better! . . . "

"Well then," I continued, "a Frenchman would never retreat before a Magyar . . . I reserved your sister's second waltz . . . "

"And why not . . . the first one? . . . "

"The first one? . . . But that belongs to Marc . . . by rights and by tradition! . . . Have you forgotten all about Marc, and do you want to create problems between us? . . . "

"Quite right, my dear Vidal. It's up to the two fiancés to open up the ball."

The Gypsy orchestra was followed by a dance band that had been setting up in the back of the gallery. Tables had been placed in the Doctor's study so that more serious-minded people, whose gravity might preclude any mazurkas or waltzes, would be able to surrender to their love of gambling.

Yet as the new orchestra waited for Captain Haralan to give them the signal to begin playing, a voice could be heard from the side of the gallery whose door opened on to the garden. The voice was still rather distant, but it was strikingly loud and coarse, and it was singing a strange song, with a bizarre rhythm and a complete lack of tonality. No melodic line tied its phrases together.

The couples who were ready for the first waltz had stopped . . . They were listening . . . Was this some sort of surprise that had been added to the evening? . . .

Captain Haralan ran up to me.

"What's going on? . . . " I asked.

"I haven't the foggiest idea," he replied in a tone that revealed a certain anxiety.

"Where's the song coming from? The street?"

"No . . . I don't think so."

Indeed, the voice must have been coming from the garden and making its way toward the gallery . . . Perhaps even on the verge of coming in? . . .

Captain Haralan grabbed my arm and led me to the door that opened onto the garden.

There were only about ten people in the gallery at that time, without counting the orchestra in the back, behind the music stands . . . The other guests had gathered in the living room and in the main hall. Those who had gone into the garden had just come back indoors.

I followed Captain Haralan and went out on the steps, where we had a view of the entire garden, which had been illuminated at each end . . .

No one.

Dr. and Mrs. Roderich joined us, and the Doctor said a few words to his son:

"Well . . . do we know? . . . "

Captain Haralan replied only by a shake of his head.

Yet the voice was still making itself heard, louder and more imperiously, and approaching steadily . . .

With Mademoiselle Myra on his arm, Marc came to join us in the gallery while Madame Roderich went back among the other ladies, who asked her many questions to which she had no reply.

"I'll find out!" Captain Haralan shouted as he went down the steps.

Dr. Roderich followed him, along with a few servants and myself.

Suddenly, when the singer seemed but a few steps from the gallery, the voice fell silent.

The garden was scrutinized carefully, and searched meticulously . . . The lights left no corner in shadow . . . and yet . . . there was no one there.

Could the voice have come from Teleki Boulevard . . . from a belated wayfarer?

That seemed quite unlikely, and we could see that the boulevard was completely deserted at that hour.

One solitary light was burning five hundred yards away to the left, a light that was scarcely visible. It came from one of the windows in the belvedere of Wilhelm Storitz's home.

As soon as we went back to the veranda, the only answer we could give to the questions the guests were firing at us was to make a gesture for the waltz to begin.

Captain Haralan did exactly that, and the couples began to form up again.

"Well," Myra asked me with a laugh, "haven't you chosen your partner? . . . "

"My partner? That would be you, Mademoiselle, but only for the second waltz."

"Then, my dear Henry," Marc added, "we won't keep you waiting!"

The orchestra had just finished the prelude to a Strauss waltz when the voice broke out once again, but this time from the middle of the drawing room . . .

The guests' palpable alarm was mixed with a genuine feeling of indignation.

With all its lungs, the voice was bawling out that German hymn, Georg Herwegh's "Song of Hatred."[1] It was a direct and deliberate insult to Magyar patriotism!

And yet, as for the one whose voice was raging from the middle of the drawing room . . . nobody could see him . . . He was certainly there, but no one could even catch a glimpse of him! . . .

The dancers had scattered about the drawing room and flowed into the gallery and the main hall. A kind of panic was spreading among them, especially among the ladies.

Captain Haralan strode across the drawing room, his eyes on fire, his hands held out as if to seize this person who was able to escape our field of vision . . .

At that moment, with the last strains of "Song of Hatred," the voice again fell silent.

That's when I saw . . . actually, a hundred people could see what I was seeing, but we all refused to believe it.

Here was the bouquet lying on the table—the engagement bouquet, suddenly ripped to shreds; its flowers were apparently being stomped upon and strewn all over the floor . . .

This time it was a sensation of terror that fell upon us! Everyone wanted to flee the scene of such strange goings-on! . . . I was even asking myself if I were completely sane amid such irrational occurrences.

Captain Haralan had just joined me, and pale with anger, he announced:

"It's Wilhelm Storitz!"

Wilhelm Storitz? . . . Had he gone mad? . . .

At that very moment, the bridal wreath rose from the cushion upon which it had been placed, traveled across the drawing room, then, without our being able to see the hand that was holding it, flew through the gallery and vanished into the garden.

VIII

Even before day had a chance to break, rumors of the incidents that had taken place at the Roderich residence spread uncontrollably throughout town. The morning papers dutifully recounted the events that had transpired the night before without the slightest exaggeration, were it possible, for that matter, to exaggerate . . . First of all, as I might have expected, the general public refused to admit that the phenomena that had occurred could have been anything less than supernatural in nature. And yet, they couldn't have been more natural. As to giving them an acceptable explanation, that was quite another matter altogether.

I need hardly add that the evening's festivities had come to a halt after the scene I just described. Marc and Myra seemed deeply affected. The trampled bouquet, the bridal wreath that had been stolen beneath their very eyes! . . . Such a bad omen on the eve of their marriage.

Crowds had been standing in front of the Roderichs' house all morning. Groups of women, mostly, were congregating along the Bathiany quay, beneath a row of not yet opened windows.

People chatted very animatedly among the groups. Some yielded to the most extravagant ideas; others were content to cast somewhat uneasy glances at the house.

Neither Madame Roderich nor her daughter had gone to mass that morning as they usually did. Myra had stayed with her mother, who had been dangerously affected by the episode and needed complete rest.

At eight o'clock, Marc opened the door to my room, joined by the Doctor and Captain Haralan. We had to discuss, perhaps even to agree upon, some urgent steps, but we knew our discussions had to take place anywhere but at the Roderichs'. My brother and I had stayed together all night. As soon as the sun rose, he had gone over to seek news of Madame Roderich and his fiancée. Then, at his suggestion, the Doctor and Captain Haralan had taken him back to the hotel.

We began our conversation at once.

"Henry," Marc began, "I've given orders not to let anybody in. Nobody can hear us here, and we're all alone . . . quite alone . . . in this room!"

But what a state my brother was in! His face, radiant with joy the night before, looked suddenly defeated, frightfully pale. In short, he seemed more beaten down than the circumstances might have warranted.

Dr. Roderich endeavored to maintain his self-control. How different he was from his son, who, with lips pressed tightly together and his eyes troubled, clearly revealed the obsession that was preying on him.

I made up my mind to keep cool during this situation.

My first care was to inquire about Madame Roderich and her daughter.

"They're both very distressed by last night's events," the Doctor replied, "and they'll need a few days to recuperate. But Myra, who was greatly upset at first, has summoned up all her energy and is striving to reassure her mother, who is even more overcome than she is. I hope that the memory of that evening will soon be wiped away from her mind, unless, of course, these deplorable scenes are renewed . . . "

"Renewed?" I asked. "We needn't be afraid of that, Doctor. The circumstances in which these phenomena appeared—can I call them anything else?—will not occur again . . . "

"Who knows?" the Doctor replied, "Who knows? I'm also very eager for the wedding to take place, as it would truly appear as though . . . "

He didn't finish the sentence, which was all too clear. As for Marc, he remained silent, as he still knew nothing about Wilhelm Storitz's latest steps.

Captain Haralan had come to his own conclusion. But he remained tight-lipped, no doubt waiting for me to weigh in on what had transpired the night before.

"Monsieur Vidal," the Doctor continued, "what do you think of all this?"

I thought it would be best if I played the role of a skeptic who had no intention of taking the strange events he had witnessed too seriously. It would be better to pretend not to see anything extraordinary in them, if only because of their very inexplicability, if that's the right word. Yet in truth, the Doctor's question made me feel rather uncomfortable, and I wondered what kind of evasive answer I could come up with . . .

"Dr. Roderich," I said, "I must tell you that 'all this,' to use your own expression, doesn't seem to deserve a lot of our time. What are we to think, other than that we were victims of some practical joke? A trickster wriggled his way among your guests and allowed himself to add a pathetic display of ventriloquism to the evening's entertainment . . . You know how wonderfully these magic tricks are done nowadays . . . "

Captain Haralan had turned to face me and was staring into my eyes as if to read my thoughts. His look clearly meant: "We didn't come here to indulge in such feeble explanations!"

"You'll allow me, Mr. Vidal," the Doctor replied, "not to buy into the idea of some sort of conjuring fob . . . "

"Doctor," I replied, "I wouldn't imagine anything else . . . except for an intervention that I for one reject completely . . . a supernatural intervention."

"Natural," Captain Haralan interrupted, "due to methods we don't know the secret of yet."

"All the same," I insisted, "regarding the voice we heard yesterday, it was certainly a human one . . . why couldn't it have been a result of some sort of ventriloquism?"

Doctor Roderich shook his head, as he was a man for whom such an explanation was utterly unacceptable.

"Allow me to repeat," I maintained. "It is not at all impossible for some intruder to have made his way into the drawing room, with the intention of outraging Magyar nationalism by insulting us with that German-made 'Song of Hatred'! . . . "

After all, this hypothesis was the only plausible one, assuming we were going to stay within the limits of what was purely human. But even if he admitted it, Dr. Roderich had a very simple answer, which he put in the following terms:

"If I were to agree with you, Mr. Vidal, that a trickster, or rather an insulting wretch, had been able to introduce himself into the building and deceive us with some ventriloquist act,—which I absolutely refuse to believe—what do you have to say about the bouquet that was ripped up, and the wreath that was carried away by an invisible hand? . . . "

Indeed, to attribute these two incidents to a conjuror, no matter how skillful, was beyond all reason. It was time for Captain Haralan to add his two cents:

"Speak, my dear Vidal. Was it your ventriloquist who destroyed that bouquet flower by flower, who picked up that wreath, who strolled with it through the drawing room . . . and carried it off . . . like a thief?"

I had no answer.

"Are you by any chance insinuating," he continued more excitedly, "that we were all victims of a giant illusion?"

"No, certainly not! Over a hundred people witnessed it!" After a few seconds of silence I had no intention of breaking, the Doctor concluded:

"Let's take things as they are, and let's try not to deceive ourselves . . . We are in the presence of facts that seem beyond any kind of natural explanation, and yet that cannot be denied. Still, if we stick to reality, let's see if someone . . . not a practical joker but . . . an enemy . . . wanted . . . to take vengeance upon us . . . by disturbing the engagement party!"[1]

This was to place the question on solid ground.

"An enemy? . . . " Marc cried out. "An enemy of your family or mine, Monsieur Roderich? . . . I don't know of any myself! . . . Do you? . . . "

"Yes," Captain Haralan confirmed.

"Then who is it? . . . "

"The one who asked for my sister's hand before you, Marc."

"Wilhelm Storitz?"

"Wilhelm Storitz!"

That was the name I had been waiting for . . . the name of that mysterious and suspicious character!

We then told Marc about all the events he had been hitherto unaware of. The Doctor described Wilhelm Storitz's recent visit just several days before. He had come to renew his request, even though it had been firmly rejected, even though Myra's hand had been given to another, even though he should have harbored no hope whatsoever! My brother learned of the Doctor's categorical refusal, and of the threats that his rival had made against the Roderich family. The threats were of such a nature as to justify to a certain extent the suspicion that this fellow had some sort of hand in the scenes of the night before.

"And you never told me a thing about all this!" Marc burst out. "Now only, when Myra has actually been threatened, that's when you've finally warned me! . . . Well, rest assured, I'm going to track down this Wilhelm Storitz, and I'll know . . . "

"Leave that to us, Marc," Captain Haralan told him. "It was my father's house that he soiled with his presence."

"It's my fiancée he insulted!" Marc raged, barely containing himself any longer.

Clearly, anger had made them both go astray. That Wilhelm Storitz should want to get revenge on the Roderich family and put his threats into motion, so be it! That he had intervened in the antics of the previous evening, that he had personally played a role . . . well, that was impossible to establish for sure. We couldn't rely on mere presumptions to accuse him and declare: "You were there yesterday evening among our guests. You're the one who insulted us with that 'Song of Hatred' . . . You're the one who ripped the engagement bouquet . . . You're the one who stole the bridal wreath!" Nobody had seen him, nobody! . . . Indeed, these phenomena had occurred seemingly without an apparent cause!

I repeated all of that. I insisted, in fact, so that Marc and Captain Haralan would pay attention to my comments, which were appreciated for being logical by Dr. Roderich at least. But they were too carried away to listen to me, and they immediately wanted to storm that house on Teleki Boulevard.

At last, after long deliberations, we came to the only reasonable thing to do. I suggested it along these lines:

"My dear friends, let's go to the Town Hall . . . Let's bring the Chief of Police up to date with this business, if he hasn't been caught up already . . . We'll let him know about the situation between that German and the Roderich family, what kind of threats he has made against Marc and his fiancée . . . Inform him of all the evidence against him. We can even let him know that he claims to make use of methods that can defy all human power! . . . Pure boasting on his part, of course! It will then be up to the Chief of Police to see if he cannot take any steps against this foreigner!"

Was it not the best thing to do, and indeed all that could have been done under these circumstances? The police could intervene more effectively than private individuals. If Captain Haralan and Marc had gone to Wilhelm Storitz's house, the door would surely not be opened for them, as it opened for no one. Would they try to force their way in? By what right? . . . Only the police would have that right. So it was up to them: they alone were the ones we could turn to.

That being said, it was decided that Marc should return to Dr. Roderich's, while the Doctor, Captain Haralan, and I went to the Town Hall.

It was half past ten. All of Ragz knew what had happened the night before. When people saw the Doctor and his son on their way to the Town Hall, they could easily guess why.

When we arrived, the Doctor sent his card in to the Chief of Police, who issued orders to show us into his office at once.

Mr. Henrich Stepark was a rather short man, with an energetic physique, an inquisitive gaze, a finesse and intelligence that were quite remarkable, a very practical mindset, a certain confident panache; he had what we now call "superior tact." On many an occasion, he had demonstrated great zeal matched only by great skill. We could rest assured that he would do whatever was humanly possible to throw light on the obscure events that had transpired at Dr. Roderich's home. But was it within his power to intervene usefully in such special circumstances, which seemed to overcome the limits of the unbelievable? . . .

The Chief of Police had already been alerted to the details of this affair, except for what was known only to the Doctor, Captain Haralan, and myself.

Moreover, his first care was to tell us:

"I was expecting your visit, Monsieur Roderich, and if you hadn't come to my office, I would have been the one to come see you. I knew that very night that strange goings-on were occurring in your home, and that your guests had been seized by a rather natural terror. I would like to add that this terror has spread throughout the town, and Ragz doesn't seem at all close to calming itself down."

We understood by his initial demeanor that the easiest route to take would be to wait for Stepark to interrogate us about the Roderich family.

"I would first like to ask you, Dr. Roderich, if you have inspired anyone's hatred, if you believe that, as a result of this hatred, vengeance had been aimed at your family specifically because of the proposed marriage of Mademoiselle Myra Roderich to Monsieur Marc Vidal?"

"I believe so," the Doctor replied.

"And who might this person be? . . . "

"The Prussian, Wilhelm Storitz."

It was Captain Haralan who uttered his name, although the Chief of Police didn't seem the least surprised.

He then let his father speak. Stepark knew that Wilhelm Storitz had sought Myra Roderich's hand in marriage. But what he didn't know was that he had renewed his request, and that, after a further refusal, he had threatened to thwart the marriage by methods that defied all human capabilities! . . .

"At that point," Stepark added, "he began by lacerating the wedding announcement without anyone noticing him!"

We were all in agreement, but our unanimity couldn't help us explain the phenomena any better, unless they had been perpetrated by a hand of shadows . . . as Victor Hugo would say![2] In the mind of a poet, perhaps! But not in the realm of reality, which, unfortunately, is the realm in which the police operate. It is on the necks of flesh-and-blood people that they lay their brutal hands. They are not in the habit of arresting ghosts or phantoms! . . . The person who ripped the announcement, the bouquet destroyer, the wreath thief, was a human being whom one was perfectly capable of catching—and he had to be caught.

Indeed, Stepark recognized that our suspicions and presumptions against Wilhelm Storitz were hardly far-fetched.

"I've always had my doubts about the man," he continued, "although I've never received any complaints against him. He lives in secret, but nobody knows how he lives or what he lives on . . . Why did he leave Spremberg, his birthplace? . . . Why should he, a Prussian from South Prussia, come to settle down in a Magyar country that remains so unsympathetic to his fellow countrymen? . . . Why has he locked himself up in the house on Teleki Boulevard with that old servant, in that house that no one ever enters? . . . I repeat, all this is suspicious, highly suspicious . . . "

"And what do you intend to do about it, Mr. Stepark?" Captain Haralan asked.

"What is plainly indicated," replied the Chief of Police, "is to effect a descent upon that house, where we may find some documents . . . some indication . . . "

"But in regards to that descent," Doctor Roderich remarked, "wouldn't you need a warrant from the Governor? . . . "

"We are dealing with a foreigner here, and a foreigner who has threatened your family. His Excellency will issue the warrant. There's no doubt about it."

"The Governor was at the engagement party yesterday," I volunteered.

"I know that, Monsieur Vidal, and he has already discussed the events he witnessed."

"Could he explain them?" the Doctor asked.

"No! . . . Sadly, he couldn't come up with a single explanation."

"But," I suggested, "when he finds out that Wilhelm Storitz is involved in this business . . . "

"That'll make him even more eager to throw light upon it," Stepark replied. "Be so good as to wait for me, gentlemen. I'll go straight to the Palace, and within half an hour I'll have the warrant to ransack that house on Teleki Boulevard."

"We'll go with you," offered Captain Haralan.

"If it pleases you to do so, Captain, and you too, Monsieur Vidal," the Chief of Police added.

"As for myself," said Dr. Roderich, "I'll leave you to go off with Mr. Stepark and his men. I'm eager to get back home, where you should come after the search has been carried out . . . "

"And after the arrests have been made, if there are any," Stepark declared, implying that he was determined to carry out his mission in a military manner as he set off toward the Governor's residence.

The Doctor went out with him, then went back home to await our return.

Captain Haralan and I stayed in the Chief of Police's chambers. Few words were exchanged. So we were actually going to cross the threshold of that suspicious house! . . . Would we find its owner at home at that moment? . . . And I also wondered whether Captain Haralan would be able to restrain himself in the man's presence.

After about a half hour's absence, Stepark reappeared. He brought with him the search warrant that gave him permission to take any measures he needed in regards to a foreigner.

"Now, gentlemen," he proposed, "please go ahead of me. I'll go on one side, my men on the other, and within twenty minutes we'll be at the house. Are we in agreement?"

"Agreed," replied Captain Haralan. I left the Town Hall with him, and made for Bathiany quay.

The direction pursued by Stepark led him toward the northern part of town, while his men, working in pairs, went through the central neighborhoods. Once we got to the end of Stephen II Street, Captain Haralan and I followed the quay along the banks of the Danube.

The weather was overcast. Puffy gray clouds chased each other in rapid succession from the east across the river valley. Under the fresh breeze, the boats were furrowing the yellowish waters of the river. Pairs of storks and cranes uttered piercing cries as they headed into the wind. It wasn't raining yet, but the lofty clouds threatened to burst into a torrential downpour.

With the exception of the commercial district, which was filled at that hour with crowds of townspeople and peasants, passersby were rare. Yet if the Chief of Police and his men had come with us, it would have surely attracted attention; it was better for us to separate as soon as we left the Town Hall.

Captain Haralan continued his silence. I was still afraid that he was not master of himself, and that if he were to meet Wilhelm Storitz he would unleash some sort of act of violence. That's why I almost regretted that Stepark had let us go with him.

A quarter of an hour later, we reached the end of the Bathiany quay, on the corner where the Doctor's house stood.

None of the ground-floor windows were open yet, nor were those of the room occupied by Madame Roderich and her daughter. What a contrast with the liveliness of the previous evening!

Captain Haralan stopped, and his gaze became momentarily glued to the tightly closed shutters.

He let out a sigh followed by a threatening gesture, but he never said a word.

Having gone round the corner, we went up Teleki Boulevard via the sidewalk on the right-hand side and stopped a hundred steps before Wilhelm Storitz's home.

A man paced nonchalantly back and forth in front of the gate, his hands in his pockets. It was the Chief of Police. Captain Haralan and I joined him as we had arranged.

A few steps away, six plainclothes policemen appeared, who, on Stepark's sign, lined themselves up in front of the railings.

They had brought a locksmith along as well, just in case the gate wouldn't open.

The windows were shut as usual. The curtains of the belvedere were drawn, rendering them opaque.

"I'm sure that nobody's there," I commented to Stepark.

"We'll soon find out," he answered. "But I would be surprised if the house were empty. Look at that smoke coming from the chimney, that one on the left."

And indeed, a wisp of sooty smoke was rising above the roof.

"If the master isn't at home," Stepark added, "the servant is likely to be, and for letting us in, it doesn't matter if it's the one or the other."

For my part, considering that Captain Haralan was present, I preferred not to run into Wilhelm Storitz, and ideally for him to have left Ragz altogether.

The Chief of Police pulled at the bell attached to an iron plate on the railings.

We waited for someone to appear, or for the gate to be opened from the inside.

A minute elapsed. Nobody. Another try at the bell . . . Nobody.

"They have deaf ears in this house!" Stepark grumbled. Then turning toward the locksmith:

"Get it done," he said.

From his set of keys, the locksmith selected a special passkey that was thrust into the keyhole, and the gate opened without difficulty.

The Chief of Police, along with Captain Haralan and myself, entered the courtyard. Four of the policemen joined us; the other two remained outside.

In the background, a flight of three steps led to the front door of the house, which was closed, just like the gate of the courtyard.

Stepark knocked twice with his cane.

His knocks went unanswered. Not a sound could be heard from within the house.

The locksmith went up the steps and inserted one of his keys into the lock. This might possibly have been doubly or triply locked, or the door might have been bolted on the inside, if Wilhelm Storitz, after seeing the policemen, had tried to prevent them from entering.

But nothing of the sort. The lock gave way, and the door opened easily.

Moreover, the policemen's sweep had gone practically unnoticed. At most, two or three passersby had stopped to see what was going on. Few were on the streets that foggy morning on Teleki Boulevard.

"Let's go in!" Stepark announced.

The corridor was lit by the grill of the fanlight above the door, and at its far end by the glass window, from a second door that gave access to the garden.

The Chief of Police took a few steps down the corridor and cried out distinctly:

"Hey! . . . Anybody here!"

No response, not even when his words were hurled a second time. Not a sound inside that house,—unless one counted some sort of sliding noise in one of the side rooms . . . But we were no doubt letting our imaginations get the better of us.

Stepark went right down the corridor. I walked behind him, and Captain Haralan followed me.

One of the policemen had stayed on guard on the steps.

With the door open, we had a view of the entire garden. It was walled in, and in the center of it, there was a lawn that had not been cut for a long time, and whose long grass was lying half-withered on the ground. Along the very high walls, there were five or six trees whose heads seemed to dominate the epaulements of the ancient fortifications.

Everything suggested complete negligence or abandonment.

The garden was thoroughly examined, but the policemen found no one in it, though there were recently made footprints on the paths.

On that side, the windows were closed by outside shutters, with the exception of the last one on the first floor, which lit the stairs.

"It couldn't have been long since these people came in," the Chief of Police remarked, "since the door's only locked and hasn't been bolted . . . Unless of course, they were alerted to . . . "

"You think they could have known? . . . " I asked. "No, I expect them to come back any minute now."

Stepark shook his head skeptically.

"Mind you," I added, "that smoke escaping from one of the chimneys proves that . . . "

"Proves that there's a fire someplace . . . Let's find that fire," the Chief of Police asserted.

After making sure that the garden was indeed as deserted as the courtyard, and that nobody was hidden in it, Stepark urged us to go back into the house, and the door to the corridor was shut behind us.

The corridor served four rooms. In one of them, next to the garden, one of the rooms was being used as a kitchen; the other, for all practical purposes, was just a stairway that rose to the first floor and then to the attic.

We began our search in the kitchen. One of the policemen opened the window and threw back the shutters; these were pierced by a small diamond-shaped opening, which let in very little light.

Nothing could have been simpler or more rudimentary than the furniture in that kitchen,—an iron stove, whose chimney vanished under the hood of a giant hearth; an armoire on each side; in the middle a table covered by an oilcloth, two cane chairs, and two wooden stools; miscellaneous utensils hanging from the walls; in a corner a grandfather clock that ticked regularly. Its weights revealed that it had been wound up the night before.

Some fragments of coal were still burning in the stove. That's what had produced the smoke we saw outside.

"Here's the kitchen," I remarked, "but where's the cook?"

"And his master?" added Captain Haralan.

"Let's keep on looking," Stepark decided.

The other two rooms on the ground floor, which were lit from the courtyard, were visited in order. One, the drawing room, was decorated with furniture of ancient work, with old tapestries of German origin that were badly worn in places. On the mantelpiece, above the great andirons, there was an ornamental clock of rather questionable taste; its motionless hands and the dust on its face showed that it had not been used for quite some time. On one of the walls hung a portrait in an oval frame with the name on a scroll in red letters: Otto Storitz.

We looked at that portrait, bold in design and crude in coloring, and signed by an unknown artist. It was a real work of art.

Captain Haralan could not tear his eyes away from that canvas.

As far as I was concerned, Otto Storitz's face made a deep impression on me. Was this due to my state of mind? . . . Or rather was I giving in, unconsciously, to the influence of my surroundings? But here, in this abandoned living room, the savant appeared before me like a fantastic creature, a character out of Hoffmann; Daniel from "The Walled-in Door"; Denner from "King Trabacchio," the Sandman from "Coppelius"![1] With that powerful face, that white disheveled hair, that lofty forehead, those eyes glowing like embers, that mouth with lips that seemed to quiver, I felt as though the portrait were alive, as if it were going to leap out of its frame and cry out like a voice from beyond:

"What are you doing here, intruders! . . . Get out!"

The living-room window, which had been closed by Venetian blinds, let in a little daylight. There had been no need to open the blinds, and in that comparative darkness, perhaps the portrait may have seemed even stranger and had even more of an effect on us?

What the Chief of Police seemed particularly struck by was the resemblance between Otto and Wilhelm Storitz.

"But for the difference in age," he told me, "that portrait might have been of the son instead of the father. They've got the same eyes, the same forehead, the same head set upon those great shoulders, and that diabolical demeanor! . . . One would be tempted to have them both exorcized . . . "

"Yes," I replied, "there's a shocking resemblance! . . . "

Captain Haralan seemed nailed to the floor in front of the canvas, as though the original were in front of him.

"Are you coming, Captain?" I asked.

He turned around and followed us.

We went along the corridor to the room next door. It was his workshop—in complete disarray. White wooden shelves, cluttered with volumes, most of which were unbound, the majority of them works of mathematics, chemistry, and physics. In a corner, several instruments, apparatus, machines, jars, a portable furnace, a pile of batteries, a Ruhmkorff coil,[2] one of those electrical fire-pots based on the Moissan system[3] that can produce temperatures of up to 4–5,000 degrees, a few retorts and alembics, several specimens of those metals and metalloids that are classified under the category of "rare earths," a small acetylene gasometer to fuel the lamps that were hanging here and there. In the middle of the room, there was a table overflowing with papers and other writing materials, and three or four volumes of Otto Storitz's complete works, opened to the chapter on Roentgen rays.[4]

The search that was undertaken in this room yielded no new information that could be of any help to us. We were about to leave it, in fact, when Stepark noticed a blue-tinted, bizarrely shaped vial on the mantle. There was a tag stuck on its side, and the cap that sealed it had been pierced with a tube plugged with a cotton pad.

Whether it was to satisfy a feeling of curiosity or his detective instincts, Stepark stretched out his hand to grasp the vial, so as to examine it more closely. But he must have been clumsy—it was certainly possible—as the vial, which had been placed on the edge of the mantelpiece, fell just as he was about to pick it up and smashed on the floor.

A thin, yellowish liquid escaped from it at once. It was so volatile that it evaporated into a vapor with such a unique smell that I can't compare it to anything else, although it was so weak that we could hardly detect it at all.

"My goodness," Stepark let out, "that vial . . . it fell at just the right time . . . "

"No doubt," I commented, "it contained some sort of preparation invented by Otto Storitz . . . "

"His son must have the formula, and he'll be able to make more of it!" Stepark replied.

Then, turning toward the door:

"On to the first floor," he said.

Before leaving, he urged his two men to remain in the corridor.

In the back, on the other side of the kitchen, the door led to a staircase with a wooden handrail; its steps creaked under our feet.

On the landing two rooms opened side by side. Their doors were not locked, and all it took was to turn the copper door handle to get into them.

The first one, which was above the living room, must have been Wilhelm Storitz's bedroom. All it contained was an iron bedstead, a night table, an oak linen armoire, a toiletry table on copper legs, a couch, an armchair in thick Utrecht velvet, and two chairs. No curtains on the bed, no curtain on the windows, furniture reduced to the bare minimum. No documents, neither on the mantelpiece nor on a small round table in one of the corners. The bed was still unmade at that early-morning hour, but we could reasonably assume that it had been occupied during the night.

Nonetheless, as he approached the toiletry table, Stepark noticed that the basin contained some water, with soap bubbles floating on its surface.[5]

"Supposing that twenty-four hours had elapsed since somebody used that water, those bubbles would have already been dissolved," he remarked. "From which I infer that our man washed here this morning before going out."

"So it's possible he'll come back?" I repeated. ". . . Unless of course he sees your men."

"If he sees my men, my men will see him, and they are under orders to bring him in. But I'm not banking on his allowing himself to be caught! . . . "

At that moment, we heard a sound like the creaking of a badly adjusted floorboard that had just been trodden on. This noise seemed to come from the room next door, above the workshop.

There was a communicating door that connected the bedroom to this room, which obviated our going back to the landing to get into it.

Ahead of the Chief of Police, Captain Haralan reached that door in one bound and flung it open . . .

No one! No one!

It was after all possible that the noise had come from the room above, from the attic that led to the belvedere.

This second room was even more rudimentarily furnished than the first one,—a frame supporting a length of strong canvas, a mattress much flattened by use, some thick rugged blankets, a woolen bed cover, two unmatched chairs, a jug of water and a sandstone basin on the mantelpiece of a hearth that refused to disclose even the smallest trace of cinders, some articles of clothing made from a thick material that were hanging from the pegs of a coatrack, a round-topped chest, or rather an oak coffer that served as both a closet and a chest of drawers, in which Stepark found a fair quantity of household linen.

This was obviously the old servant Hermann's room. The Chief of Police knew, from the reports coming from his men, that if the window of the first bedroom was sometimes opened to let in some air, the one in the second room, which likewise opened onto the courtyard, remained invariably shut. Moreover, one would have discovered this in any case just by examining the window fastening, which was very stiff, and the ironwork of the shutters, which had been eaten by rust.

In any case, this was an empty room, and if this were also true of the attic, the belvedere, and the cellar beneath the kitchen, the only thing one could state with accuracy was that master and servant had left the house with perhaps no intentions of ever coming back.

"You wouldn't suppose," I asked Stepark, "that Wilhelm Storitz could have been tipped off about this investigation?"

"No, Monsieur Vidal . . . unless he'd hidden himself in my office or in His Excellency's when we were discussing this business!"

"He might have spotted us when we got to Teleki Boulevard . . . "

"Granted—but how would they have gotten out? . . . "

"By getting into the open courtyard . . . from the back . . . "

"The garden walls are too high, and what's more, on the other side there's a moat surrounding the fortifications that nobody could possibly cross."

The Chief of Police was of the opinion that Wilhelm Storitz and Hermann were already outside the house before we entered it.

We walked out of the room through the door leading to the landing and in a minute reached the second floor, at the corner of the last step.

This consisted only of the attic, which stretched from one gable end to the other. It was lit by narrow skylights let into the roof, and one glance was all it took to show us that no one had taken refuge there.

In the center, a rather steep ladder led to the belvedere, which dominated the roof. Its interior was reached by a trapdoor swinging on a counterweight.

"The trapdoor is open," I commented to Stepark, who had already put one foot on the ladder.

"Yes, Monsieur Vidal, and there's quite a draft coming down through it . . . That's what must have made the noise we heard. There's a strong wind today, and the weathercock is creaking on the top of the roof! . . . "

"And yet," I interjected, "it seemed as though we heard footsteps . . . "

"Then who could have been doing the walking since nobody's here?"

"Unless he's up there . . . Mr. Stepark? . . . "

"In that aerial nest? . . . No, not more than in any other room in the house!"

Captain Haralan had been listening to our exchange. He curtly pointed to the belvedere and commanded: "Let's go up!"

Stepark was the first one to mount the rungs, with the help of a thick cord hanging down from the floor.

We climbed up after him, first Captain Haralan then myself. It seemed quite likely that three people would be enough to fill that narrow skylight.

It was, in fact, nothing but a sort of cage, measuring eight by eight feet, and about ten feet high.

It was fairly dark, even though a sheet of glass was set between the uprights that supported the beams of the ridge.

This darkness was due to the drawn thick woolen curtains that we had already noticed from outside. But as soon as they were thrown back, the light flooded in through the glass.

We had a panoramic view of all of Ragz from the four sides of the belvedere. Nothing obstructed the vista, which was more extensive than the one from the Roderichs' house, but not as impressive as the one from Saint Michael's tower or the Castle's donjon.

From there, I could once again admire the Danube at the tip of the boulevard, the developing township toward the south, dominated by the Town Hall belfry and the Cathedral's spire, the donjon on Wolfgang Hill, and all around the green prairies of the Puszta, surrounded by her distant mountains.

I hasten to add that the belvedere was just like the rest of the house—not a soul! Although Stepark had done his part, the police sweep had been fruitless, and we still knew nothing about any of the mysteries hidden within the Storitz house.

I had thought that the belvedere might be used for astronomical observations, and that it might contain apparatus for studying the sky. I was mistaken. There was just a table and a wooden armchair.

There were some documents on the table, among others a copy of that *Wienner Extrablatt* in which I had read the article about Otto Storitz's birthday.

No doubt, this is where the son came to rest for a few hours on coming out of his workshop, or rather his laboratory. In any case, he too had read the article, which had been marked with a red-ink cross he had undoubtedly drawn himself.

Suddenly we heard a violent cry. A cry of surprise and fury.

Captain Haralan had just opened a cardboard box he noticed sitting on a shelf fixed to one of the uprights . . .

And what did he take out of the box? . . .

The bridal wreath that had been carried off from Dr. Roderich's home the night of the engagement!

So there was no longer any doubt that Wilhelm Storitz was involved! We were in possession of material evidence and were no longer reduced to mere presumptions. At the very least, whether he or another was the actual culprit, it was certainly for his benefit that this bizarre robbery had been carried out, even though the method and the explanation still eluded us! . . .

"Are you still a doubter, my dear Vidal?" Captain Haralan yelled, his voice trembling with rage.

Stepark kept quiet, as he knew that in this strange affair, there was still a great deal that remained unknown. Indeed, even though Wilhelm Storitz's guilt screamed out at us, we were unable to figure out how he had pulled the deed off, and even if we continued our investigation, would we ever find out? . . .

As for myself, even though Captain Haralan had addressed me more directly, I still couldn't tell him anything. What could I have told him anyway? . . .

"And wasn't it that miserable wretch," he continued, "who came to insult us by flinging that 'Song of Hatred' in our faces as an affront to Magyar patriotism? . . . You never saw him, but you heard him! . . . He was there, I tell you, even if he managed to escape without being seen! . . . He was in the middle of the drawing room! . . . And that crown, sullied by his very hand, I don't even want a single leaf of it to remain intact! . . . "

Stepark stopped him right before he was about to rip it apart.

"Don't forget that it's a piece of evidence that could convict him," he said, "and that could be useful if, as I predict, this matter must continue!"

Captain Haralan handed the crown back to him, and we returned to the staircase, after having gone through each of the rooms in the house one last futile time.

The doors to the steps and the gate were locked shut, and the house remained in the same state of neglect in which we had found it. Yet under Stepark's orders, two of his men remained in the area to monitor the situation.

After having said good-bye to Stepark, who asked us to keep the police sweep between ourselves, Captain Haralan and I took to the boulevard as we returned to the Roderich residence.

This time, however, my companion could no longer restrain himself, and his anger spilled over into extremely violent words and gestures. My attempts to calm him down were all in vain. I was hoping, in fact, that Wilhelm Storitz had left or would leave town as soon as he realized that his house had been searched, and that the crown that he had stolen—or had ordered stolen (I still had my doubts about that)—was now in the hands of the police.

I stubbornly persisted in saying:

"My dear Haralan, I understand your anger . . . I can understand that you don't want to allow these insults to go unanswered! . . . But you mustn't forget that Stepark asked us to keep the wreath we discovered in the Storitz house a secret . . . "

"And what about my father . . . and your brother . . . won't they be informed about the results of our search? . . . "

"Of course, and we'll tell them that we were unable to find Wilhelm Storitz . . . that he must no longer be in Ragz . . . which seems quite probable at the moment!"

"You mean you won't tell him that we found the wreath in his house? . . . "

"Yes . . . they need to know, but there's no point in mentioning it to either Madame Roderich or her daughter . . . What good would it do to worsen their fears by uttering that name, 'Wilhelm Storitz,' in front of them? . . . And even in regards to the wreath, if I were you, I would say that it had been found in the garden of your own home, and I would give it back to your sister! . . . "

"What! . . . " Captain Haralan cried out, "After what that man did! . . . "

"Yes . . . I'm sure that Mademoiselle Myra will be very happy to have it back! . . . "

Despite his initial repugnance, Captain Haralan understood my reasoning, and we agreed that I would get the crown back from Stepark, who would surely not refuse to part with it.

Nonetheless, I couldn't wait to see my brother, to bring him up to date, and more importantly to see him get married.

As soon as we arrived at the residence, the servant ushered us into the study, where the Doctor was waiting with Marc. Their impatience had reached a boiling point, and we were interrogated even before we walked through the door.

As one could imagine, they reacted with intense surprise and indignation when we told them what had happened in the strange house on Teleki Boulevard! My brother could barely get himself under control! Just like Captain Haralan, he wanted to punish Wilhelm Storitz before justice could intervene.

"If he's not in Ragz, he's got to be in Spremberg!" he yelled.

I had trouble calming him down, and it took the Doctor's help to subdue him.

I kept stressing the idea that Wilhelm Storitz must have already left town, or was rushing to leave it, the minute he found out we had searched his house . . . there could be no doubt about that. By the same token, nothing pointed to the notion that he might be hiding in Spremberg, and we would probably not find him there or anywhere else for that matter.

"My dear Marc," the Doctor suggested, "listen to your brother's advice, and let this story—which has been so painful for your family—die down. Let's keep quiet about all of this, and soon it will all be forgotten . . . "

It was so painful to see my brother in this state: his head in his hands, his heart heavy. I could feel his suffering! And what would I have given to be older by just a few days, so that Myra Roderich would at last be Myra Vidal!

The Doctor then added that he planned on seeing the Governor of Ragz. Wilhelm Storitz was a foreigner, and His Excellency would not hesitate to issue a warrant for his expulsion. The most urgent thing was to prevent any recurrence of the events we had recently witnessed, even if we had to give up all hope of finding a reasonable explanation for them. As for the idea that Wilhelm Storitz had a type of superhuman power at his disposal, as he had boasted . . . that was something none of us could accept.

As for Madame Roderich and her daughter, I stressed the reasons why we had to maintain an airtight silence with them. They couldn't be allowed to learn of the police's intervention or that there could no longer be any doubt whatsoever about Wilhelm Storitz's involvement.

My suggestion regarding the wreath was accepted. We would stick to the story that Marc had found it in the Roderichs' garden. This would show that the whole thing was the work of a malevolent practical joker whom we would eventually unmask and give the punishment he so richly deserved.

That very day, I went back to the Town Hall, where I informed Stepark of our decision regarding the wreath. He wasted no time returning it to me, and I brought it back to the house.

That evening, we were in the drawing room with Madame Roderich and her daughter when all of a sudden Marc, having gone outside for a moment, returned, saying: "Myra . . . my dear Myra . . . look what I've brought you!"

"My wreath! . . . My wreath! . . . " Myra cried out, jumping into my brother's arms.

"That wreath . . . Marc?" Madame Roderich asked, her voice trembling with emotion.

"Yes . . . " Marc continued, ". . . there . . . in the garden . . . I found it behind some of the shrubbery, where it had fallen."

"But . . . how . . . how? . . . " Madame Roderich repeated.

"How? . . . " the Doctor answered. ". . . An intruder managed to infiltrate our guests . . . Well . . . in any case . . . here it is . . . "

"Thank you . . . thank you, my dear Marc," Myra said, as tears streamed down her face.

The following days produced no new incident. The town resumed its normal calm. Nothing leaked out about the search that had been made of the house on Teleki Boulevard, and nobody mentioned Wilhelm Storitz's name. All we had to do was to wait patiently—or rather, impatiently—for the day Marc and Myra Roderich's wedding could be officially celebrated.

I spent most of my time without my brother walking through the neighboring areas around Ragz. Occasionally, Captain Haralan would accompany me. We rarely left town without taking Teleki Boulevard. We were clearly attracted to that suspicious-looking house. In any case, it allowed us to see if it was indeed still deserted . . . Indeed! . . . And if it was still guarded by Stepark's men . . . day and night, by two policemen, and if Wilhelm Storitz had made an appearance, the police would have been immediately alerted of his return and would have arrested him on the spot.

Moreover, we received proof of his absence and the assurance that for the time being, at any rate, we would not be running into him on the streets of Ragz.

As a matter of fact, in the May 9th issue, the *Pester Loyd* devoted a page to Otto Storitz's commemoration ceremony, which had taken place just a few days before. I couldn't wait to tell Marc and Captain Haralan about it.

The ceremony had attracted a significant number of spectators, not only from Spremberg, but also thousands of curious people from the neighboring towns and even from Berlin. The crowd was so large that the cemetery was unable to contain it, and the overflow spread throughout the surrounding area. There had been many accidents; some people had been suffocated and had, the next day, found that spot in the cemetery they were unable to find on the day itself.

It had not been forgotten that Otto Storitz lived and died surrounded by legends. All those superstitious people were expecting some sort of prodigious posthumous act . . . Nothing less than fantastic phenomena had to occur on that anniversary. At the very least, the Prussian scientist would surely rise from his grave, and it would not be surprising in the least if, at that moment, the order of the universe were singularly perturbed . . . The Earth would reverse its rotation and turn from east to west, and this would bring about a complete upheaval of the solar system! . . .

This is what the reporter had to say, but as it turned out, nothing really extraordinary took place . . . the gravestone didn't budge at all . . . the cadaver didn't get up from his sepulchral dwelling place . . . and the Earth went on moving according to the immutable rules laid down from the world's birth! . . .[1]

Yet what was of particular interest to us was the fact that according to the newspaper account, Otto Storitz's son had attended the ceremony in person, and we thus had extra proof that he had fled Ragz . . . As for myself, I was hoping that it was with the formal intent of never coming back, but I had reason to fear that Marc and Captain Haralan wanted to seek him out in Spremberg! . . .

Perhaps I could succeed in making my brother listen to reason! He wouldn't leave for such an insane excursion on the eve of his wedding . . . But Captain Haralan . . . that was another story. I promised myself that I would watch over him and, if need be, call on paternal authority.

Although the uproar caused by this affair subsided significantly, the Governor of Ragz was still a bit uneasy. The fact that these prodigious phenomena, for which no one could provide the slightest plausible explanation, could have been caused by a type of sleight of hand executed with extraordinary skill had not really disturbed the town very seriously. But it was essential to make sure that they were not repeated.

It shouldn't be surprising then that His Excellency was extremely impressed when the Chief of Police informed him of Wilhelm Storitz's situation in regards to the Roderich family and about the threats he had uttered!

Furthermore, when the Governor learned of the results of that investigation, he decided to take serious measures against the foreigner. There had been a theft—that was clear—a theft he had carried out himself, or with an accomplice . . . If he had not left Ragz, he would have been arrested, and once firmly surrounded by the four walls of a prison cell, it's unlikely that he would have been able to escape without being seen, as he had managed to do when he had entered the Roderichs' drawing room!

And on that day, His Excellency and Stepark exchanged the following words:

"Nothing new to report?"

"Not a thing, Your Governorship."

"Is there any reason to believe that Wilhelm Storitz may have returned to Ragz?"

"None."

"His home is still kept under surveillance?"

"Day and night."

"I thought it my duty to write to Budapest," the Governor continued, "to tell them what has been going on here. The incident has aroused more excitement than it deserves, and I've been authorized to take steps to put an end to it once and for all."

"So long as Wilhelm Storitz hasn't reappeared in Ragz," replied the Chief of Police, "we've nothing to fear from him, and we know for sure that, as of a few days ago, he was still in Spremberg . . . "

"Indeed, Mr. Stepark, at that anniversary ceremony! . . . But he might be tempted to return here, and that's what we have to prevent."

"Nothing could be easier, Your Governorship. Since this concerns a foreigner, all we'll need is an order for his expulsion."

"An order," the Governor continued, "that will banish him not only from the city of Ragz but from the entire Austro-Hungarian territory."

"As soon as I have that order, Your Governorship," the Chief of Police confirmed, "I'll have it disseminated to all the border guards."

In sum, once the order had been signed, the entire kingdom was heretofore off-limits to that German, Wilhelm Storitz. The authorities then proceeded to close off his house, the keys of which were deposited at the Chief of Police's headquarters.

These measures were meant to reassure the Doctor, his family, his friends. But we were far from uncovering the secret of the affair, and who knew if we'd ever be able to unravel it at all!

The wedding date soon approached. Only two more days to go, and the sun would rise over Ragz's horizon announcing the arrival of May 15th.

I realized, not without a certain true sense of satisfaction, that Myra, impressionable as she was, didn't seem to remember those inexplicable incidents. I would like to stress the fact that Wilhelm Storitz's name had never been pronounced in front of either her or her mother.

I was her confidant. She spoke to me of her plans for the future, without really being too sure that they would be carried out. Would she and Marc go off and live in France? Perhaps, but not immediately . . . To be separated from her father, her mother, would be too painful . . .

"Yet," she added, "for the time being, it's only a question of spending a few weeks in Paris, where you'll join us, won't you?"

"Unless of course you'd rather not have me around!"

"It's just that . . . two newlyweds make for rather dreary travel companions . . . "

"I'll try to put up with it!" I answered with resignation.

The Doctor also approved of this resolution. Leaving Ragz for a month or two would be better all around. No doubt, Madame

Roderich would be quite distressed at the absence of her daughter, but she would make the best of it.

For his part, during the hours he spent by Myra's side, Marc forgot—or rather he wanted to forget—everything. It was true that when he was with me, he was again seized by those fears that I sought, in vain, to dissipate. Invariably he would ask me:

"Hear anything new, Henry? . . . "

"Nothing, my dear Marc," I always replied no less invariably, and absolutely truthfully.

One day, he felt the need to add:

"If you knew something . . . either from town . . . or via Stepark . . . if you heard people mentioning . . . "

"I would let you know, Marc."

"I would be very cross if you hid anything from me . . . "

"I wouldn't hide anything from you . . . but . . . I can assure you that nobody's talking about this affair anymore! . . . The city has never been calmer! . . . Some people are going about their business as usual, others are pursuing their own pleasures, and the market-rates are rising full force!"

"You're joking, Henry . . . "

"Just to prove to you that I no longer have any fears at all!"

"And yet," Marc's face darkened, "if that man . . . "

"No! . . . He knows that he would be arrested if he returned to Ragz, and in Germany there is no end to the amount of carnivals where he could practice his many talents as a magician!"

"So . . . those are the powers . . . he speaks of . . . "

"That would be fine for the simpleminded, it would!"

"You don't believe in them?"

"No more than you believe in them yourself. So, my dear Marc, focus on counting the days, on counting the hours, on counting the minutes that separate you from the big day! . . . You don't have anything better to do, so you might as well start counting them all over again."

"Oh, my dear friend!" Marc cried out, his heart thumping to exhaustion.

"You're not being reasonable, Marc. Myra's more reasonable than you are."

"That's because she doesn't know what I know."

"What you know? . . . Allow me to remind you! You know that the fellow in question is no longer in Ragz, and that he can no longer come back here . . . that we will never see him again, make no bones about it . . . and that should be enough to calm you down . . . "

"What do you expect, Henry? I've got a premonition . . . it seems."

"That's senseless, my poor Marc! . . . Come on now . . . trust me . . . go back to the Roderich residence and be near Myra . . . "

"You're right . . . And I should never leave her . . . no . . . not for a moment!"

My poor brother! He was so painful to watch, painful to listen to! His anxieties increased as the wedding date grew nearer. As for myself, to be perfectly frank, I was also awaiting that day with great impatience!

And yet, for all intents and purposes, although I could count on Myra, on her influence, to calm my brother down, I was at wits' end about what to do with Captain Haralan.

It was hard to forget how, upon learning from the article in the *Pester Loyd* that Wilhelm Storitz was in Spremberg, I had so much trouble preventing him from going. There are only eight hundred kilometers between Spremberg and Ragz . . . He could be there in twenty-four hours . . . In the end, we were able to hold him back, but despite the arguments that his father and I pressed upon him, in spite of the plain desirability of letting the affair drop into oblivion, he kept reverting to his plan, and I was afraid that he would elude us.

That morning, he came and found me, and right from the offset of our conversation, I knew he had decided to go.

"You can't do that, my dear Haralan," I told him. "You can't! . . . An encounter between that Prussian and you! . . . No . . . now . . . it's impossible! . . . I'm begging you not to leave Ragz."

"My dear Vidal . . . That miserable wretch must be punished . . . "

"And he will be, sooner or later," I cried out. "Yes, he will! . . . The only hand that ought to touch him, so that he can be dragged before a judge, is a policeman's! . . . You want to leave, think about your sister! . . . I implore you . . . listen to me . . . as a friend . . . In two days: the wedding . . . and you think you'll be able to be back in Ragz by that time? . . . "

Captain Haralan sensed that I was right, but he didn't want to give in.

"My dear Vidal," he replied in a tone that led me to believe that there might still be some hope, "we don't . . . we can't see things the same way . . . My family, which will soon be your brother's, has been outraged, and shouldn't it be my right to avenge these outrageous acts? . . . "

"No! . . . That's the law's job!"

"How do you expect that to happen if the man doesn't . . . can't come back! I have to find him on his own turf then . . . where he ought to be in any case . . . in Spremberg!"

"Agreed," I suggested as a last argument, "but be patient for just two or three days, and I'll accompany you to Spremberg myself! . . . "

In the end, I pressed this view with such warmth that our conversation ended with a formal promise that he would wait, on the understanding that once the wedding had been celebrated, I would no longer oppose his plan, and that I would go with him.

The two days that separated us from May 15th seemed absolutely endless! And although I considered it my duty to reassure everyone else, I felt rather uneasy myself at times.

Making matters worse, I would walk up and down Teleki Boulevard from time to time as though I were pushed by some sort of premonition.

The Storitz house remained just as the police had left it after their sweep: doors closed, windows shut, deserted courtyard and garden. On the boulevard, a handful of policemen whose surveillance extended to the parapet of the old fortification and the surrounding countryside. No attempt to get back into the house had been made, by either master or servant. And yet,—as a testament to the power obsession can have over someone—despite everything I was telling Marc and Captain Haralan, and despite what I was telling myself, if I had seen a wisp of smoke rising from the laboratory chimney, or a face appearing behind the windows of the belvedere, I would not have been at all surprised.

The truth of the matter was that, while the people of Ragz were recovering from their initial fright and no longer mentioned those strange happenings, it was really Dr. Roderich, it was really my brother, it was really Captain Haralan, it was really myself—we were the ones haunted by Wilhelm Storitz's ghost.

On that day, the 13th of May, I decided to take my mind off of the situation in the afternoon by taking a walk toward the Svendor Island Bridge so that I could stroll along the right bank of the Danube.

Before getting to the bridge, I passed by the landing stage where the *dampfschiff* was arriving from Budapest . . . the *Mathias Corvin*, in fact.

The incidents of my own journey flashed back in rapid succession . . . my encounter with the German, his insulting attitude, the feeling of antipathy he had inspired in me at first sight; then, when I thought he had gotten off at Vukovar, the words he had uttered!

He was the one indeed, it could only be him, that same voice that we had heard in the Roderich drawing room . . . the same articulation, the same roughness, the same Teutonic harshness!

And in the grip of these thoughts, I looked at each of the passengers who were getting off at Ragz, one by one . . . I was looking for that pale face, those strange eyes, the Hoffmanesque demeanor of this strange character! . . . But as they say, I got nothing for my trouble.

At six o'clock, as usual, I went to take my place at the family table. Madame Roderich seemed much better, and fairly in control of her emotions. My brother forgot everything when he was beside Myra, on the eve of his making her his wife. Even Captain Haralan seemed calmer, albeit a bit gloomy.

Besides which, I had made up my mind to do whatever possible to enliven that little world and to banish the last clouds of those memories. I was ably seconded by Myra. She was the charm and delight of the evening, which lasted until quite late. Without any prodding from us, she sat down at the piano, and we sang the old Magyar songs, as though to erase that dreadful "Song of Hatred" that had resounded through the room!

Just as we were about to retire, she said with a smile:

"That will be for tomorrow! . . . Monsieur Henry . . . You won't forget . . . "

"Forget, Mademoiselle? . . . " I answered with a similar lighthearted tone.

"Yes . . . forget that the wedding is taking place at the Town Hall . . . "

"Ah! It's tomorrow! . . . "

"And you are one of the witnesses for your brother . . . "

"You're quite right to remind me, Mademoiselle Myra . . . Witness for my brother! . . . I had already forgotten that! . . . "

"That doesn't surprise me. I've noticed that you've seemed occasionally distracted . . . "

"I plead guilty, but I won't be tomorrow, I promise . . . and so long as Marc doesn't forget either . . . "

"I'll answer for him! . . . "

"See to it! . . . "

"So at four o'clock sharp . . . "

"Four o'clock, Mademoiselle Myra? . . . And there I was thinking that it was at half-past five! . . . So don't worry about a thing . . . I'll be there at ten minutes to four . . . "

"Goodnight . . . goodnight . . . to Marc's brother, who will soon be my own! . . . "

"Goodnight, Mademoiselle Myra . . . goodnight!"

Marc had several errands to do in the morning the next day. Since he seemed to have regained his calm, I let him go alone.

As for myself, by an excess of prudence, and to feel certain, if possible, that Wilhelm Storitz had not been seen in Ragz, I went to the Town Hall.

Stepark received me immediately, and asked me the reason for my visit.

I urged him to tell me if he had any news.

"None, Monsieur Vidal," he answered. "You can rest assured that our man has not reappeared in Ragz . . . "

"Is he still in Spremberg? . . . "

"All I can say is that he was still there yesterday."

"Did you receive a dispatch to that effect?"

"From the German police, who've confirmed it."

"That's reassuring!"

"Yes, but it bothers me, Monsieur Vidal."

"And why is that? . . . "

"Because that devil of a man—and devil is the right word—doesn't seem much inclined to ever cross the border . . . "

"And that's just as well, Mr. Stepark!"

"It's just as well for you, but a pity for me! . . . "

"I hardly understand your regrets! . . . "

". . . As a policeman, I would have preferred to get my hand on his collar, and lock up that sorcerer within four walls! Well, later perhaps . . . "

"Oh! Later, after the wedding as much as you like, Mr. Stepark!"

And after expressing my thanks, I left.

At four in the afternoon, we all gathered in the Roderichs' drawing room. Two coaches were waiting on Teleki Boulevard—one for Myra, her father, her mother, and a friend of the family, Judge Neuman; the other for Marc, Captain Haralan, one of his comrades, Lieutenant Armgard, and myself. Judge Neuman and Captain Haralan were the bride's witnesses, Lieutenant Armgard and I were Marc's.

At that time, after long discussions in the Hungarian Diet, civil weddings existed just as in Austria, and were usually carried out with the utmost simplicity,—en famille. Moreover, all the pomp was reserved for the religious ceremony held the next day.

The young fiancée was very tastefully dressed in a pink crêpe de Chine gown, with chiffon trim void of any embroidery. Madame Roderich's dress was also very simple. The Doctor and the Judge, like my brother and myself, wore frock coats, and the two officers were in full uniform.

A few people were waiting for the vehicles to emerge on the boulevard, mostly women and girls from town, for whom a wedding is always an exciting and fascinating event. But it was most likely that the next day would see a large crowd at the Cathedral, an homage rightfully due to the Roderich family.

The two coaches left the main door of the mansion, turned the corner onto the boulevard, followed the Bathiany quay, Prince Miloch Street, and Ladislas Street, and stopped in front of the gates of the Town Hall.

The sightseers were most numerous in Liszt Square and in the Palace courtyard. Perhaps, after all, a recollection of the previous incidents had attracted them? . . . Perhaps they were wondering if some new phenomena were about to take place in the wedding hall? . . .

The vehicles entered the courtyard of honor and drew up before the steps.

Immediately afterward, Mademoiselle Myra on her father's arm, Madame Roderich on Mr. Neuman's, then Marc, Captain Haralan, Lieutenant Armgard, and myself, took our places in the hall, lit by tall stained-glass windows and lined with extremely valuable sculptures. In the center, a large table bore two magnificent baskets of flowers on each side.

In their capacity as father and mother, Dr. and Madame Roderich sat down on each side of the armchair reserved for the civil officer. Behind them the four witnesses took their places, Mr. Neuman and Captain Haralan on the right, Lieutenant Armgard and I on the left.

A doorkeeper announced the Mayor of Ragz, who wanted to officiate at the ceremony himself. Everyone rose as he entered.

The Mayor, standing in front of the table, asked the parents if they consented to the marriage of their daughter to Marc Vidal. Then, after an affirmative reply, there was no need to ask that same question of our side of the family, as Marc and I were its only members.

It was then to the young people themselves that the Mayor spoke.

"Mr. Marc Vidal, do you promise to take Mademoiselle Myra Roderich as your wife?"

"I do."

"Mademoiselle Myra Roderich, do you promise to take Marc Vidal as your husband?"

"I do."

And the Mayor, in the name of the law, from which he had read all the pertaining articles, declared them both united in matrimony.

In this way, everything had gone off as simply as usual. No supernatural activity had disturbed the event and,—although the idea had crossed my mind for a second,—the document on which we had placed our signatures after the reading by the civil officer had not been torn to pieces, nor the pens wrenched from the hand of the engaged couple or the witnesses.

Obviously, Wilhelm Storitz was not in Ragz, and if he's still in Spremberg, I thought, let him stay there for his compatriots to enjoy!

Marc Vidal and Myra Roderich were now united before Man and tomorrow would be united before God.

XII

May 15th had arrived. The date that had been so impatiently awaited seemed as though it would never come!

May 15th at last. In a few more hours, the religious ceremony would be consecrated in the Ragz Cathedral.

Any apprehension that might have been left over in our minds, any trace of those inexplicable events that had taken place a fortnight ago, had been entirely eradicated after the civil wedding celebration. The Town Hall was completely unperturbed by any of the phenomena that had taken place in the drawing rooms of the Roderich residence.

I got up early, but Marc was ahead of me. I still hadn't finished getting dressed when he came in.

He was already in his bridegroom attire, or should I say—his marriage uniform; he was dressed entirely in black, as though headed for a funeral, in that worldly uniform by which the severity of men's clothing contrasts with the brilliant outfits of women.

Marc was beaming with happiness. No shadow could obscure his radiance.

He kissed me effusively, and I hugged him tightly.

"My dear Myra," he began, "urged me to remind you . . . "

"That it's today!" I laughed. "Well then, tell her that since I didn't miss the hour at the Town Hall, I'm certainly not going to miss the one at the Cathedral! Yesterday . . . I set my watch to the belfry! But you, my dear Marc, make sure you don't keep them waiting! . . . You know, your presence is indispensable! . . . We can't start without you! . . . "

He left, and I hurriedly finished dressing. Mind you, it was not even nine thirty yet.

We agreed to meet at the Roderich home. That's where the "nuptial" carriages were supposed to leave from (I enjoyed calling them by that fanciful name). Moreover, as a testament to my punctuality, I arrived earlier than I needed to—which earned me a lovely smile from the bride as I took my place in the drawing room.

One after another, the people—or rather the personages, given the solemnity of the occasion—who had been present at the ceremony at the Town Hall appeared, only this time in full regalia: the black suit, the black vest, the black pants, nothing Magyar obviously, as they couldn't have looked more Parisian. A few medals, however, were shining from some lapels: Marc with his Legion of Honor rosette; the Doctor and the Magistrate with their Austrian and Hungarian decorations; the two officers, in their splendid uniforms from the Military Territories regiment, with their crosses and medallions; and me with my simple red ribbon.

Myra Roderich,—but why wouldn't I just say Myra Vidal, since the engaged couple were already bound together by civil law,—Myra, all in white, with a long train of watered silk and orange blossom, was ravishingly dressed. At her waist, the bride's bouquet was in full bloom, and on her magnificent blond hair rested the bridal wreath, from beneath which flowed the layers of her white tulle veil. She wore the wreath that my brother had brought back: she would not have any other.

As she entered the drawing room with her mother, who was also beautifully dressed, she came toward me and held out her hand, which I shook affectionately, even fraternally. Then, with her eyes bursting with joy, she said to me:

"Ah! How happy I am, my brother!"

And so there remained not even the slightest trace of all those nasty days in the past, of those sad trials that this worthy family had undergone. This wasn't necessarily the case for Captain Haralan, who clearly had not completely forgotten the events. As he shook my hand, he said:

"No . . . let's not think about it anymore!"

The program for the day had been approved by everyone: At a quarter to ten, we would leave for the Cathedral, where the Governor of Ragz, with the authorities and notables of the town, would be waiting for the young couple to arrive. Introductions and compliments, followed by the nuptial mass and the signing of the records in the sacristy of St. Michael's. A return for lunch, when about fifty guests would be present. In the evening, a ball to which nearly two hundred invitations had been sent out.

The coaches were occupied in the same order as the day before; in the first was the bride, the Doctor, Madame Roderich, and Judge Neuman; in the second Marc and the three other witnesses. On returning from the Cathedral, Marc and Myra Vidal would take their place in the same coach. Other vehicles were sent to fetch the people who were to participate in the religious ceremony.

It goes without saying that Stepark had taken measures to maintain order, since without a doubt, there would be a considerable crowd both at the Cathedral and in St. Michael Square.

At a quarter to ten, the coaches left the Roderich residence and went down the Bathiany quay. After having reached Magyar Square, they crossed and went up the most beautiful quarter in Ragz, via Prince Miloch Street.

The weather was splendid, the sky brightened by the May sun. Under the street corridors, passersby in great numbers made their way to the Cathedral. All eyes were focused on the leading coach, with glances of sympathy and admiration for the young bride, though I had to admit that my dear Marc had his share of them as well. The windows allowed people to catch a glimpse of the smiling faces, and from all sides came greetings too numerous to be acknowledged.

"My goodness," I thought out loud, "I'll bring back some pleasant memories of this town!"

"The Hungarians are honoring in your person the France they're so in love with, Monsieur Vidal," Lieutenant Armgard replied, "and they're delighted with a wedding that will bring a Frenchman into the Roderich family."

As we approached the square, we had to harness our horses to a walking pace, as it was so difficult to move.

From the towers of the Cathedral, one could hear the joyful sounds of the bells, borne by the eastern breeze, and just before ten, the carillon in the belfry mingled its sharp notes with the sonorous voices of St. Michael's.

When we got to the square, I noticed the procession of vehicles that had brought the guests as they lined up to the right and left with their doors fully opened.

It was exactly five past ten when our two coaches drew up at the foot of the steps, the central door having been thrown wide open.

Dr. Roderich got out first; then came his daughter, who took his arm. Mr. Newman offered his to Madame Roderich. We were soon on the ground, following Marc between the rows of spectators who were stretched out along the forecourt.

At that moment, the great organs resounded inside the Cathedral, playing the Hungarian composer Konzach's wedding march.

In Hungary at that time, because of a liturgical ordinance that has not been adopted by any other Catholic country, the benediction can only be given to the married couple at the end of the wedding mass. And it would seem that it might be better if, in fact, the fiancés rather than the married couple attended the service. Mass first, sacrament afterward.

Marc and Myra advanced toward the two chairs that were placed for them before the High Altar; then the parents and witnesses took the seats that were assigned to them.

All the chairs and the choir-stalls were already occupied by a numerous assembly, the Governor of Ragz, the magistrates, the officers of the garrison, the principal civil servants of the administration, the friends of the family, captains of industry and commerce. Special places had been reserved along the stalls for the ladies in their brilliant outfits. Not a single one had been left empty.

A huge crowd of oglers had gathered behind the gates of the chancel, a masterpiece of thirteen-century craftsmanship, and by the entrance of the doors leading toward them. As for the people who weren't able to get so close, they found a spot in the middle of the great nave. Every seat had been taken.

In the counter-nave's transept, along the aisles, the populace had accumulated and overflowed all the way to the steps outside. One could enjoy a sampling of Magyar dress among the masses, made up mostly of women.

And now, if a few of those brave townspeople or peasants remembered those phenomena that had disturbed the city, could they possibly have imagined that they might be reproduced in the Cathedral? . . . Plainly not, and for as much as they had been attributed to a demoniacal intervention, it was certainly not in a church that such an intervention could take place. Doesn't the devil's power stop at the doorstep of God's sanctuary? . . .

A movement began to the right of the choir, and the crowd had to part to make way for the Arch-Priest, the Deacon, the Sub-Deacon, the beadles, the children of the choir.

The Arch-Priest stopped before the steps of the altar and said the first phrases of the *Introit*, while the singers burst into the verses of the *Confiteor*.

Myra was kneeling on the hassock of her prie-dieu, her head bowed in a position of devotion. Marc was standing beside her, and his eyes never left her.

The Mass was said with all the pomp in which the Catholic Church wishes to engulf its most solemn ceremonies. The organ alternated with the plain-song of the *Kyrie* and the stanzas of the *Gloria in Excelsis*, which reverberated under the high vaults.

There was an occasional vague rumble from the crowd's movements, the clatter of displaced chairs, the comings and goings of the officers of the church, who were ensuring that the passage remained free down the full length of the nave.

The interior of the Cathedral was normally plunged in a twilight that enabled the soul to yield itself more freely to religious impressions. Only an uncertain light was able to pierce through the ancient stained-glass windows, where biblical figures were outlined in sumptuous colors, through the narrow first-century ogival windows, and through the lateral sun lounges. On those rare occasions when the weather was overcast, the great nave, the aisles, the apse were all dark, and this mystical obscurity was broken only by the points of light that shone on the ends of the long altar candles.

Today it was different. Under that magnificent sunlight, the windows facing east and the rose window of the transept were effulgent. A ray of sunlight, crossing one of the bay windows in the apse, fell directly onto the pulpit supported by one of the pillars of the nave, and seemed to bring life to the tormented face of the Michelangelo-like figure that bore it upon his enormous shoulders.

When the bell was heard, the congregation rose, and after their noisy movements, a sudden silence emerged as the Deacon chanted the Gospel according to St. Matthew.

Then the Arch-Priest turned around and addressed a few words to Marc and Myra. He spoke in a slightly feeble voice, the voice of an old man crowned with white hair. He said very simple things that must have gone straight to Myra's heart; he praised the virtues of the Roderich family, its devotion to the less fortunate and its inexhaustible charity. He blessed this marriage that would unite a Frenchman and a Hungarian, and he invoked the blessing of Heaven upon their union.

As soon as he had finished his address, the old priest turned toward the altar for the offertory prayers, while the Deacon and the Sub-Deacon took their places at his side.

I've been giving a step-by-step account of every detail of that nuptial mass because it has remained profoundly engraved upon my spirit; its memory must never be washed from my mind.

A brilliant voice then rose from the altar loft, accompanied by a quartet of stringed instruments. Gottlieb, a famous tenor throughout the Magyar world, sang the offertory hymn.

Marc and Myra left their chairs and took their places before the altar steps. And there, after the Sub-Deacon had received their generous alms, they pressed their lips, as though in a kiss, to the paten that was offered to them. Then they went back to their places side by side. Never—no! Never had Myra seemed more radiant with beauty, more haloed with happiness!

Then those who were taking up the collection for the sick and the poor came by to receive their alms. Preceded by the beadle, they wove into the rows of the chancel and the nave amid the sound of moving chairs, the rustle of dresses, the shuffle of the crowd, as coins fell into the purses held out by young girls.

The *Sanctus* was sung in four parts by the choir, dominated by all the children with their high-pitched sopranos. The moment of the consecration was approaching, and as soon as the first ring of the bell chimed out, the men got up, and the women began to kneel on their prie-dieus.

Marc and Myra were kneeling too, in anticipation of that miracle that has been renewed for eighteen centuries from the hand of a priest, the supreme mystery of transubstantiation.

During this gravely serious moment, who could not be impressed by the deeply religious attitude among the faithful, by that mystical silence, just as all the heads are bowed and as all the thoughts are climbing toward God!

The old priest leaned toward the chalice in front of the altar that his word was about to consecrate. His two assistants, on their knees on the highest step, held the bottom of the chasuble, so that he wouldn't be hindered during his liturgical genuflection. The choirboy was getting ready to shake his handbell.

In short intervals, two protracted rings echoed through the collective meditation, while the officiating priest methodically articulated the sacramental words . . .

It was at that moment that a cry rang out—a gut-wrenching cry, a cry of terror and horror.

The handbell, dropped by the choirboy, rolled down the altar steps.

The Deacon and the Sub-Deacon had moved apart from each other.

The Arch-Priest, partially knocked over, held himself up by the tips of his contorted fingers, his mouth still quivering from that cry he had let out, his face unraveled, his eyes wild, his knees bent and about to collapse . . .

And this is what he saw—what a thousand others saw, what I saw . . .

The consecrated wafer had been ripped from the old priest's fingers . . . the symbol of the Word incarnated had just been grabbed by a sacrilegious hand! And then it was torn to shreds, its pieces thrown across the choir . . .

Faced with this profanation, the congregation succumbed to total panic.

And at that moment, this is what I heard—indeed what a thousand other people heard, those words pronounced in a horrific voice, the voice that we knew all too well, the voice of Wilhelm Storitz, standing right there on the steps, but as invisible as he was in the Roderichs' drawing room:

"Woe to the married couple! . . . Woe! . . . "

Myra let out a cry and, as though her heart had been shattered, fainted into Marc's arms!

XIII

These strange acts, the ones in the Cathedral of Ragz, and the ones in the Roderich home, tended toward the same end and must have had the same origin. It was Wilhelm Storitz, and he alone, who could have masterminded them. A magic trick? Not a chance . . . not the snatching of the sacramental wafer nor the theft of the bridal wreath! I began to consider that this German had inherited some kind of scientific secret from his father, the secret of some unknown discovery that gave him the power to make himself invisible . . . just as certain rays of light are able to pass right through opaque objects, as though those objects were translucent[1] . . . but my thoughts were leading me astray, no doubt, and I made sure to keep them to myself.

We had taken Myra home without her regaining consciousness. She had been carried into her room, placed upon her bed, but the care bestowed on her wasn't able to revive her. She was still inert, numb! The Doctor felt impotent in the wake of her inertia, her limpness. And yet she was still breathing, she was still alive. Indeed, how had she managed to survive so many trials? It was a miracle that she hadn't been killed by this last one!

Several of Dr. Roderich's colleagues had rushed over. They surrounded Myra's bed, where she lay motionless, her eyelids lowered, her face pale as wax, her chest lifted only by the irregular beating of her heart, her breathing reduced to a gasp, a gasp that could pass away from one moment to the next! . . .

Marc was holding her hands; he called out her name; he begged, he cried.

"Myra . . . my dear Myra! . . . "

She no longer heard him . . . her eyes were not opening . . .

And in a voice choked with sobs, Madame Roderich repeated:

"Myra . . . my child . . . my daughter . . . I'm here . . . near you . . . your mother . . . "

She didn't respond.

But the physicians tried the most vigorous remedies, and it seemed for a moment that she was about to regain consciousness . . .

Yes, her lips babbled vague words that were impossible to decipher . . . her fingers quivered in Marc's hands . . . her eyes opened halfway . . . but what an uncertain look beneath those half-raised eyelids . . . A vacant stare devoid of understanding! . . .

And Marc realized this all too well as he fell back and let out a cry . . .

"Mad . . . mad! . . . "

I had to race toward him and hold him up with the help of Captain Haralan, asking myself if he too were about to lose his reason! . . .

He had to be taken into another room, where the doctors tried everything to solve this crisis with a potentially fatal outcome.

How would this drama end? Could there be any hope that, in time, Myra would regain her intelligence, that care would triumph over the loss of her mind, that this was only a fleeting form of madness? . . .

When Captain Haralan was alone with me, he affirmed:

"We've got to put a stop to this!"

Put a stop to this? . . . What did he mean by that? . . . What did he have in mind? . . . That Wilhelm Storitz had returned to Ragz, and that he was responsible for this profanation, there was no doubt whatsoever! . . . But where could we find him, and how could we hold on to this unattainable creature? . . .

Now what impression would the town abandon itself to? Would it accept a natural explanation of these events? This was not France, where no doubt these wonders would have been made into jokes by the press and ridiculed in song in all the taverns of Montmartre![2] Things were different in this country. As I have already pointed out, the Magyars have a natural tendency toward the marvelous, and superstition, among the uneducated classes, is ineradicable.[3] For the most sophisticated, these strange goings-on could only be the result of some discovery in Physics or Chemistry. But when it comes to unenlightened minds, everything is explained by the intervention of the devil, and Wilhelm Storitz would pass for the devil incarnate.

Indeed, there was no way we could think about hiding the conditions in which this foreigner, against whom the Governor of Ragz himself had signed an expulsion order, was involved in this affair. What we had kept secret so far could no longer remain in the shadows after the scandal at St. Michael's.

First of all, the local newspapers resumed the campaign that they had dropped weeks ago. They swiftly linked the events that had transpired at the Roderich residence with the ones in the Cathedral. The calm that the public had embraced gave way to fresh apprehension. The populace could finally understand the connection between the various incidents. In every house, among every family, the name of Wilhelm Storitz could no longer be uttered without arousing the memory, or rather, the ghost, of this strange character whose existence was spent between the silent walls and behind the closed windows of the house on Teleki Boulevard.

It was not surprising, then, that as soon as the news had been circulated through the newspapers, the mob rushed toward that boulevard, swept along by some irresistible force of which they might not have been fully aware.

This was how the crowds had thronged into the Spremberg cemetery around ten days before. There, however, the savant's compatriots had come to witness some sort of wonder and hadn't been motivated by any feelings of animosity. Here, on the contrary, there was a spasm of hatred, a need for vengeance, that had been justified by the intervention of a malevolent being.

Moreover, let us not forget the horror that must have seized such a religious town, the scandal that had just been played out in the Cathedral! The most abominable of sacrileges had been committed there. During the mass, we had seen, at the very moment of elevation, the consecrated wafer seized from the hands of the Arch-Priest, carried across the naves, then shredded and thrown from atop the throne! . . .

And the doors of the church, until reconciliation rites could purify it, were to remain closed to the prayers of its faithful!

This overexcitement could do nothing but grow and take on worrisome proportions. The majority would never accept the only thing that was plausible: the discovery of invisibility.

The Governor of Ragz was forced to address this public opinion and instructed the Chief of Police to take all the steps that the situation demanded. He had to be ready to defend himself from the excesses of the general panic, which could have grave consequences if it spiraled out of control. Furthermore, as soon as Wilhelm Storitz's name had been revealed, it had become necessary to protect the house on Teleki Boulevard—in front of which hundreds of workers, peasants, had assembled—against invasion or plundering.

Yet if a man had the power to make himself invisible,—which no longer seemed debatable as far as I was concerned—if the fable of the ring of Gyges at the court of King Candaule should come true—then public order would be completely compromised![4] No more personal security. As such, Wilhelm Storitz had come back to Ragz, and no one was able to see him there. Whether he was still there, no one could know for sure! And then, had he kept the secret of this discovery, a secret that his father had in all likelihood bequeathed to him, all to himself? . . .

Could his servant Hermann also make use of it? . . . Could others use it for his benefit or their own? . . . And who would stop them from breaking into houses whenever and however they pleased, from taking part in the daily lives of others? . . . Wouldn't the intimacy of family life be destroyed? . . . Even in one's own home, could anyone be certain of being alone, certain of not being overheard, or not being spied upon, unless one kept oneself in total darkness? And then outside in the streets, this perpetual fear of being followed without knowing it by an invisible being who would never let you out of his sight, who could mistreat you if he wanted to! . . . And was there any way of avoiding attacks of all sorts, now made so easy? . . . Would this not lead to a permanent problem resulting in the complete annihilation of social life as we knew it? . . .

The papers also reminded their readers of what had happened in the Coloman Square marketplace, what Captain Haralan and I had both witnessed. A man had been violently thrown to the ground by an individual he was unable to see, he claimed . . . Well then, who now could say that the man had been wrong? He had surely knocked into Wilhelm Storitz or Hermann or someone else of that ilk . . . With every step we took, weren't we all vulnerable to such encounters? . . .

Other things came back to me then . . . the notice torn down from the frame in the Cathedral, and, during our search of the house on Teleki Boulevard, the noise of footsteps we had heard in the rooms, the vial that had so inopportunely fallen and broken! . . .

Well, he had been there himself, and no doubt Hermann too. They had never left town after the engagement party, as we had suspected, and that explained the soapy water in the bedroom, the fire in the kitchen stove. Yes! They had both been present during our search of the courtyard, the garden, the house . . . and if we had found the nuptial crown in the belvedere, it was because Wilhelm Storitz, taken by surprise, had not had time to take it away! . . .

And so, as far as I was concerned, the incidents that had punctuated my journey on the *dampfschiff*, when we went down the Danube from Pest to Ragz, could now be explained. That passenger whom I supposed had gotten off at Vukovar had still been on board and no one could see him! . . .

And so, I told myself repeatedly, this invisibility must be something he can produce instantaneously . . . he can appear or disappear at will . . . like those characters in fairy tales with their magic wands. But we were dealing neither with magic, nor cabalistic secret words, nor incantations, nor phantasmagoria, nor sorcery! If he could make his body invisible, as well as the clothes that covered him, we couldn't say the same for objects that he held in his hand, since we had been able to see the ripped-up bouquet, the stolen wreath, the wafer broken and hurled to the foot of the altar. Wilhelm Storitz clearly had the formula of some concoction that could simply be drunk or absorbed . . . Which one? . . . The formula, no doubt, that had been in that vial and that had evaporated almost instantaneously when it had been broken! But what was the formula for that potion? That's what we didn't know, and that's what we absolutely needed to know, but might *never* know! . . .

As for that Wilhelm Storitz, now that he was invisible, was he impossible to seize? If he eluded the sense of sight, he did not, I imagined, escape the touch. His material frame did not lose any of the three dimensions common to all bodies: length, breadth, depth . . . He was still there, in flesh and blood, as they say. Invisible, granted, but intangible, no! That was for ghosts, and we were definitely not dealing with a ghost!

Nonetheless, I told myself, if chance were to allow us to grab him by the arms, by the legs, by the head, then even if we didn't see him, we should at least still hang on to him . . . And no matter how amazing the power that he had at his disposal, it would not enable him to go through the walls of a prison! . . .

This was nothing but a train of thought, on the whole acceptable, quite common no doubt, but the situation was still rather worrisome, and public safety had been completely compromised. We were living as though we were in a trance. We felt safe in neither houses nor streets, neither at night nor in the day. The slightest sound in a room, the creaking of the floor, a blind shaken by the wind, a squeak from the weathervane on the roof, the buzzing of an insect in our ears, the whistling of the wind through a badly closed door or window, everything seemed suspicious. During the comings and goings of domestic life, at table during meals, in the evenings during get-togethers, at night during sleep—supposing that sleep were possible—we never knew whether some intruder were violating, by his presence, the inviolability of hearth and home! Whether this Wilhelm Storitz, or someone else for that matter, might not be there, spying on our actions, listening to our words, at last penetrating the most intimate of family secrets.

It was possible, no doubt, that the German had left Ragz and gone back to Spremberg. And who knows whether, his discovery in hand, he might have been tempted to yield his formula to his country, to place this awful might into German hands for all to see, for all to hear. And so, in all the embassies, in all the chancelleries, in all the government cabinets, secrets would no longer be possible; international security would be a thing of the past!

But when we thought it all over—in the minds of the Doctor and Captain Haralan, as well as of the Governor and the Chief of

Police—could we reasonably suppose that Wilhelm Storitz had finished with all his deplorable acts? . . . If the civil wedding had been able to take place, it must have been because he was unable to prevent it, perhaps because he wasn't in Ragz on that day. But in regards to the religious wedding, he had successfully interrupted its celebration; and in case Myra should ever recover her senses, would he not try to prevent it again? Had the hatred he had vowed against the Roderich family been extinguished? . . . Had his vengeance been quenched? Could we ever forget the threats that had reverberated throughout the cathedral . . . "Woe to the married couple . . . Woe! . . . "

No! The last word on this matter had not been spoken, and how horrific the means this man had at his disposal for carrying out his schemes for vengeance!

Indeed, even though Dr. Roderich's house was under surveillance day and night, might he not succeed in getting into it? And once inside, could he not do whatever he liked? Was he not free to hide in some corner somewhere, and then to gain entrance to either Myra's or my brother's bedroom . . . and would he at all balk at committing some sort of crime? . . .

After all this, one can gauge the level of obsession among the people, the ones who remained within the realm of facts as well as those who abandoned themselves to the exaggeration of a superstitious imagination!

And yet, was there a remedy to this situation? . . . I couldn't see any, and even Marc and Myra's departure couldn't change anything. Wouldn't Wilhelm Storitz still be able to follow them freely, and for that matter, taking into account Myra's mental state, would it even be possible for them to leave Ragz at all ? . . .

Moreover, there could no longer be any doubt that this character was lurking somewhere among a people whom he could terrorize with impunity.

That very night, in the Town Hall district,—and it was even visible on Liszt Square and in the Coloman Square marketplace,—a powerful flash of light appeared from the highest window in the belfry. A flaming torch rose, fell, and moved from side to side, as though an arsonist wanted to engulf the Town Hall in flames.

Racing from their headquarters, the Chief of Police and his men quickly mounted the belfry.

The light had disappeared, and—as Stepark had expected—there was nobody to be found. The extinguished torch, lying on the floor, emitted a fuliginous odor; resinous sparks were still sliding down the roofing; but there was no longer any danger of a fire.

And thus: nobody! . . . Or the individual,—let's say Wilhelm Storitz,—had had enough time to escape, or else he was hiding in a corner of the belfry, invisible and intangible.

The mob that had assembled in front of the Town Hall got no return for their cries of vengeance: "Death! . . . Death to Wilhelm Storitz!" aroused the culprit's laughter, no doubt.

The next day, this time in the morning, more bravado was hurled at the entire half-crazed city.

Ten-thirty had just sounded when a sinister volley of bells, a funeral knell, a sort of tocsin of fear, proliferated throughout town.

This time, it was not one solitary man who could have brought the Cathedral's campanological apparatus into action. Wilhelm Storitz must have been aided by several accomplices, or at least by his servant Hermann.

The townspeople crowded into St Michael Square, even hurrying from the distant parts of the city, into which the clang of the tocsin had hurled total terror . . .

Once again, Stepark and his men rushed toward the staircase leading to the northern tower; they swiftly climbed up the steps;

they reached the bell chamber, which was flooded by the daylight streaming in through the louvers . . .

But they examined that floor of the tower and the gallery above in vain . . . Nobody! Nobody! . . . When the policemen entered the chamber where the muted bells had just stopped swinging, the invisible bell ringers had already disappeared.

XIV

This was the state Ragz was now in. Once so tranquil, so happy, to the point where it was the envy of all other Magyar cities. The best way to describe it would be to compare it to a town in a country that had just been invaded, that constant fear of bombardment as everyone wonders where the next bomb will drop, and whether one's own house will be the first one destroyed! . . .[1]

Indeed, was there anything that we *couldn't* fear Wilhelm Storitz might do? . . . Not only had he not left town, but he made a point of letting everyone know that he was still there.

At the Roderich home, the situation had become even more serious. Two days had gone by, and poor Myra had still not come to her senses. When her lips did open, it was only to utter incoherent words; her haggard eyes could focus on no one. She didn't hear us; she could recognize neither her mother nor Marc at her bedside, in her girlish room, so filled with joy at one time, so sad at present. Was this just a passing delirium, a crisis in which care would vanquish what was ailing her . . . Was it an incurable madness? . . . Who could say? . . .

She was extremely weak, as though the springs of life had been crushed within her. She was stretched out on her bed and practically motionless. As soon as she barely lifted her hand, it would drop back down immediately. We then wondered if she might have been trying to lift the veil that was hanging over her consciousness and enveloping her completely . . . perhaps her will was struggling to manifest itself one last time . . . Marc leaned over her, he spoke to her, he tried to speak to her, he tried to catch some response from her lips, any sign from her eyes . . . and nothing . . . nothing! . . .[2]

As for Madame Roderich: at home, the mother had gotten the better of the woman. She held herself together by an extraordinary moral strength. At best, she got a few hours of sleep, and only because her husband forced her to, and what kind of slumber? One troubled by nightmares, interrupted by the slightest noise! . . . She thought she heard someone walking in her bedroom; she said to herself that he was there, him, the one who had barged into their home . . . and that he was prowling around her daughter! . . . During those moments, she would get up, and allow herself a bit of reassurance only after having seen either the Doctor or Marc, who was watching over Myra's bedside . . . And what if this lasted for weeks, months, would she be able to hold out? . . .

Each day, several of Dr. Roderich's colleagues came over in consultation. One of them, a renowned psychiatrist, had been summoned from Budapest. After having examined her at length and scrupulously, he was incapable of coming up with anything that might cure the case of intellectual inertia that lay before him. No reaction, no crises. No! . . . An indifference to everything that surrounded her, a complete obliviousness, a deathly tranquility, before which art remained powerless.

My brother now occupied one of the rooms in the annex; perhaps it might be more accurate to say that he was in Myra's room, from which he was unable to tear himself away. With the exception of my visits to the Town Hall, I hardly left the Roderich residence. Stepark kept me abreast of everything that was being said in Ragz. Through him, I knew that the population was gripped by the wildest of apprehensions. It was not only Wilhelm Storitz they were afraid of, but a whole gang of invisible men under his tutelage who had invaded a city that was now made up of the defenseless victims of their infernal machinations! . . . Ah! If they could have gotten their hands on one of them, they would have torn him to pieces!

I met much more infrequently with Captain Haralan since the events in the Cathedral. I only saw him at the Roderichs'. I knew he was in the throes of an obsession and endlessly patrolled the city. He no longer asked me to accompany him. Had he come up with some sort of plan he feared I would try to dissuade him from? . . . Was he counting on the most unrealistic of chance encounters to bump into Wilhelm Storitz? . . . Was he waiting for that criminal to show up in Spremberg or some other place before attempting to meet up with him? . . . I wouldn't have tried to stop him, however . . . No! I would have gone with him . . . I would have helped us all get rid of this savage beast!

Would this contingency have any chance of occurring? . . . No, assuredly not. Neither in Ragz nor anywhere else for that matter!

I had a long conversation with my brother on the evening of the 18th. He seemed more overwhelmed than ever, and I worried that he was going to become seriously ill. One would have had to drag him far from the city, or take him back to France, but how would he ever have agreed to separate himself from Myra? . . . And yet, ultimately, was it at all possible for the Roderich family to get away from Ragz for some time? . . . Wasn't this an idea worth looking into? . . . I gave it some thought, and I promised myself that I would discuss it with the Doctor at some point.

Finally, on that day, as we were finishing our conversation, I said to Marc:

"My poor brother, I see that you're about to lose all hope, but you're wrong to . . . Myra's life is not in danger . . . All the doctors are in agreement about that . . . If her reason seems to have abandoned her, it's only temporarily, you've got to believe me . . . She'll regain control over her intelligence . . . she'll come back to her senses . . . to you . . . to her loved ones . . .

"You're asking me not to despair," Marc replied, his voice muffled with tears. "Myra . . . my poor Myra . . . regain her reason! . . . Listen to him, God! . . . But wouldn't she still be at the mercy of that monster? . . . Do you think for a minute that his hatred is at all appeased by what he's done up to now? . . . And what if he wants to go further in his vengeance . . . and what if he wants to? . . . Come on, Henry . . . try to understand me . . . How can I tell you! . . . He can do anything he feels like, and we're helpless against him . . . I can do nothing . . . nothing! . . .

"No . . . no!" I cried out—and, I have to admit, despite thinking the contrary, I replied, " . . . No, Marc, protecting ourselves is not impossible . . . it's not impossible to avoid his threats."

"But how . . . How? . . . " Marc continued as he became increasingly more agitated. "No, Henry, you're not telling me what you're really thinking . . . You're going against all reason! . . . No! We're defenseless against that wretch! . . . He's in Ragz . . . He can, at any moment, burst into the house without being seen! . . . "

Marc's carrying on made it impossible for me to discuss anything with him. He could only listen to himself at this point.

"No, Henry," he repeated. "You're trying to put blinders on this situation . . . You refuse to see what's really going on! . . . "

And then, as he grabbed my hands:

"And who's to say that he isn't in the house at this very moment? . . . I can't go from one room to the other, in the gallery . . . in the garden . . . without thinking he might be there! . . . It's as though someone were walking with me! . . . Someone who avoids me . . . who retreats when I advance . . . and when I want to seize him . . . there's nothing there . . . nothing!"

He stormed off and threw himself in total pursuit of an invisible man. I could no longer come up with ways of calming him down! . . . The best thing would have been to pull him away from the Roderich house . . . to take him far away . . . very far away . . .

"And," he persisted, "who knows whether he listened to every word we just said when we thought we were alone? . . . Say . . . I can hear his footsteps behind this door . . . He's here . . . You and I, come on! . . . We'll take him . . . and I'll punch him! I'll kill him . . . But . . . the monster . . . could it be possible . . . that death has no hold over him? . . . "

That's how bad things had gotten with my brother. Was I not right to worry that his rational side would succumb to one of his attacks? . . .

Ah! Why did this awful discovery of invisibility have to be made . . . just so this fiend could have such a weapon at his disposal, as though he hadn't already been overly armed on the side of evil!

In the end, I always came back to my initial plan: to convince the Roderich family to leave . . . to take Myra, who had lost her senses, as far away as possible from this cursed town, as well as Marc, who was on the verge of losing his!

And yet, even though no other incident had taken place since Wilhelm Storitz had, for all intents and purposes, screamed from the top of the belfry, "Here I am . . . still here!" the horror had taken over the entire city. There was not one single house that hadn't thought it was haunted by the invisible one! And he wasn't alone! . . . He had his gang at his command! . . . The churches couldn't even be used as safe havens anymore after what had happened in the Cathedral! . . . The papers tried very hard to intervene, but without success, and what could they do against the terror in any case? . . .

And here's an example of how high the level of madness had gotten.

On the morning of the 19th, I had left the Temesvar Hotel to meet with the police chief.

Once I got to Prince Miloch Street, two hundred steps before St. Michael Square, I noticed Captain Haralan and proceeded to join him:

"I'm going to see Stepark," I told him. "Would you care to join me, Captain? . . . "

He followed me mechanically without answering me. As we were approaching Liszt Square, however, we heard cries of terror.

A charabanc, led by two horses, was galloping down the street with excessive speed. Passersby saved themselves by jumping to the right and to the left to avoid being crushed. No doubt, the charabanc's driver had been thrown to the ground, and the horses, left to themselves, had gotten carried away.

Well, not surprisingly, several of the passersby, no less carried away than the horses, came up with the idea that an invisible man was the one driving the vehicle . . . that Wilhelm Storitz himself was the one in the driver's seat. The scream that carried all the way over to where we stood confirmed this: "Him! . . . Him! . . . It's him! . . . "

I had hardly had enough time to turn toward Captain Haralan when I saw that he was no longer next to me, but was dashing toward the charabanc in order to stop it right when it was about to thunder past him.

The street was bustling at that time of day, and that name—"Wilhelm Storitz! . . . Wilhelm Storitz!"—reverberated in every direction! The level of overexcitement was so high that rocks were hurled against the vehicle, along with a few gunshots fired from a store on the corner of Prince Miloch Street.

One of the horses fell from a bullet that had hit him in the leg, and the charabanc, having collided with the animal's body, tumbled over.

As soon as that happened, it was the crowd's turn to thrust themselves onto the vehicle, grab onto its wheels, onto its chassis, onto its shafts . . . as twenty arms reached out to apprehend Wilhelm Storitz . . . Nobody! . . .

Had he been able to jump out of the charabanc before it toppled over? It certainly wouldn't have been farfetched to assume that he would have wanted to terrify the city by trotting through it at the head of this fantastical team of horses! . . .

There was nothing to it this time, we had to admit. A few moments later, however, a peasant from the Puszta ran toward the scene of the accident. His horses, which had been parked at the Coloman Square marketplace, had gone wild, and one can imagine how angry he was when he saw one of them stretched out on the ground! . . . Nobody wanted to listen to anything he had to say, and I thought that the crowd was going to mistreat this poor man, whom we had some trouble bringing to safety.

I took Captain Haralan by the arm, and without uttering a word, he accompanied me to the Town Hall.

Stepark had already been informed about the events on Prince Miloch Street.

"The town is in a state of panic," he told me, "and who can possibly predict how far this collective madness will go! . . . "

And so I asked my familiar questions:

"Anything new to report? . . . "

"Yes," Stepark replied, handing me an issue of *Wienner Extrablatt.*

"And what does the paper have to say? . . . "

"It reports that Wilhelm Storitz is in Spremberg . . . "

"In Spremberg? . . . " shouted Captain Haralan, who had quickly read the article and now, turning toward me, said:

"Let's go! . . . You promised me . . . By nightfall we'll be in Spremberg . . . "

I didn't know what to tell him, convinced as I was that such a trip would be useless.

"Wait, Captain," Stepark suggested. "I've asked Spremberg to confirm this information. I could get a telegram any minute now."

Not three minutes had gone by when the orderly handed a dispatch to the Chief of Police.

The news had been unfounded. Not only had Wilhelm Storitz's presence not been reported in Spremberg, but the authorities believed that he had never left Ragz.

"My dear Haralan," I declared, "I gave my word to you, and I'll keep my word. But right now, your family needs us to stay by its side."

Captain Haralan took leave of Stepark, and I went back to the Temesvar Hotel by myself.

It goes without saying that when it came to the charabanc incident, the newspapers of Ragz rushed to explain what had really happened, but I'm not at all sure they were able to convince everybody!

Two days went by, but there was still no improvement in Myra's condition. My brother seemed a bit calmer, however. As for myself, I was waiting for the chance to discuss a departure plan with the Doctor, whom I was hoping to rally to my idea.

The 21st of May went by less peacefully than the two previous days, and this time the authorities understood just how impotent they were in holding down a crowd that had reached such an intense level of hotheadedness.

At around eleven o'clock, as I was taking a walk along the Bathiany quay, the following remarks caught my attention:

"He's back . . . he's back!"

Who was this "he"? Well, it wasn't hard to guess from the two or three passersby I spoke to:

"We've just seen some smoke coming out of his chimney!" one of them told me.

"We saw his face peeking through the belvedere curtains!" affirmed the other.

Whether I was wise to give credence to these prates or not, I nonetheless headed toward Teleki Boulevard.

And yet, no matter how impudent it was for Wilhelm Storitz to make an appearance . . . there was no way he could have been oblivious to what was in store for him if anyone ever got their hands on him! . . . But would he have run that risk? There was certainly nothing out there to encourage him. Would he have allowed himself to be seen from one of the windows of his residence? . . .

True or false, the news had its effect. When I got there, several hundred people had already encircled the house via the boulevard and the ramparts. Soon police detachments charged forward under Stepark's orders; they were unable to contain the crowd and unable to evacuate the boulevard. From all sides, feverishly overexcited masses of men and women arrived, demanding death to Storitz.

What could the authorities do, faced with such an irrational but ineradicable conviction that he was there, "him"? Possibly with his servant Hermann by his side . . . perhaps even with his accomplices . . . The mob surrounded the cursed house so closely that neither of them could possibly flee . . . or pass by without being captured in the process! . . . Moreover, if Wilhelm Storitz had indeed been seen by the belvedere windows, it was in his physical form, before he had time to make himself invisible. He'd be caught, and this time he wouldn't escape the masses' lust for vengeance! . . .

In sum, despite the opposition of the policemen, despite the efforts of the Chief of Police, the gates were stormed, the house invaded, the doors knocked down, the windows broken in, the furniture hurled into the garden and the courtyard, the laboratory instruments torn to pieces; then flames devoured the top floor, whirled above the roofing, and shortly afterward the belvedere collapsed into the inferno.[3]

As for Wilhelm Storitz, they searched for him in vain . . . in the residence, in the courtyard, in the garden . . . He wasn't there, or at least no one was able to come up with him, nor anybody else for that matter . . .

At this point, the house was in the process of being annihilated in the inferno that had been ignited from six different spots, and an hour later, four walls were all that remained.

Perhaps it was better off destroyed . . . Perhaps some sort of relaxation of tensions might follow . . . Perhaps the Ragzian people might even come to believe that Wilhelm Storitz, as invisible as he was, had nevertheless perished in all the flames? . . .

Fortunately, Stepark succeeded in saving a fair amount of the papers that were in the study. They were taken to the Town Hall. By studying them, it was hoped, he might be able to crack the secret . . . or Otto Storitz's secrets, which his son had so fiendishly exploited! . . .

Once the Storitz house had been completely destroyed, it seemed as though the state of exponential edginess that had consumed Ragz dissipated slightly. The townspeople felt more reassured. Without actually seizing the fellow, they had at least burned his house to the ground, even though they regretted not having burned him along with it. Furthermore,—a few brave citizens endowed with strong imaginations continued to stubbornly ask themselves: Why couldn't he have been in the house at the time it was invaded by the mob? And why, even in an invisible state, couldn't he have perished amid the flames? . . .

The truth was that in sifting through the ruins, in shaking the ashes, nothing was found that could corroborate their theory. If Wilhelm Storitz had been there during the blaze, it could only have been in a spot the fire couldn't reach.

Nevertheless, new letters, new dispatches from Spremberg, received by the Chief of Police agreed on one point: Wilhelm Storitz had not reappeared in his native town, his servant Hermann had not been seen there, and nobody had any idea where the two of them could have sought refuge. It was very possible then that they had never left Ragz at all.

Sadly, if a relative calm prevailed in town, it was not so at the

Roderich home. The mental condition of our poor Myra hadn't improved a bit. Unaware of her actions, indifferent to the care that was increasingly administered to her, she still couldn't recognize anyone. Nor did the doctors dare hold out the slightest hope. There were no visible attacks, no outbursts that they could battle in order to provoke a possible curative reaction! . . .

Yet Myra's life did not seem in any danger, despite her extreme fatigue. She lay almost motionless on her bed and pale as a corpse. If anyone tried to lift her, sobs swelled from her breast, horror burst from her eyes, her arms were tossed about, incoherent phrases escaped from her lips. Was her memory coming back to her? Was she reliving, in the midst of her troubled mind, the scenes from the engagement party, the scenes in the Cathedral? . . . Was she still listening to the threats directed against her and against Marc? . . . Perhaps it was better that way, that her mind should preserve the memory of the past! There was nothing we could wait for besides Time, and would Time do what all our care had not succeeded in doing up to now? . . .

One can imagine what life had become for that ill-fated family! My brother never left the house. He stayed by Myra's side, with the Doctor and Madame Roderich. He would make her take a bit of food from his hand, and look to see if any glimmer of reason reappeared in her eyes . . .

I wanted Marc to go out, if only for an hour or two, but I knew he would refuse. I only saw him, or Captain Haralan for that matter, during my visits to the Roderich home.

On the afternoon of the 22nd, I wandered the streets by myself, haphazardly, feeling as though only some random occurrence could lead to any kind of change in the situation . . .

For some reason, I suddenly felt like crossing to the right bank of the Danube. This was an excursion I had planned on for a while, though circumstances had not allowed me to carry it out, and I was hardly likely to enjoy it in my present state of mind. Nonetheless, I made my way toward the bridge, crossed Svendor Island, and set foot on the Serbian bank.

I delighted in the magnificent countryside that was spread before my eyes, so much agriculture and pastures in full greenery at that time of the year. It's worth noting the resemblances between rural Serbians and Hungarians. The same handsome faces, the same attitude, men with somewhat hard faces and a military demeanor, women with an imposing bearing. But it's a country where political passions run a bit higher than in the Magyar kingdom, among the peasants as well as the city folk. Serbia is considered the vestibule of the Orient, while Belgrade, the administrative city, is the doorway. If it is nominally dependent on Turkey, to which it must pay an annual tribute of three hundred thousand francs, it still remains the most important Christian population within the Ottoman Empire. As a French writer rightly said in reference to the Serbian race, so blessed with military talents: If there is one country where one could make battalions appear by stomping one's foot on the ground, it would surely be this patriotic warrior province. The Serb is born a soldier, lives the life of a soldier, dies a soldier. Isn't it to Belgrade, its capital, that all the aspirations of the Slavic race turn? And if, one day, this race rises against the Germanic one, if revolution erupts, the flag of freedom will surely be carried by a Serbian hand![1]

These were the kinds of thoughts that went through my mind as I followed the winding banks of the river, leaving to my left those vast plains that regrettable clearing had substituted for the forests in spite of the national proverb: "He who kills a tree kills a Serb!"

My memory of Wilhelm Storitz was also pursuing me, however. I was wondering if he had taken refuge in one of those villas that could be seen across the fields, or if he might have regained his visible self. But no such luck! His story was as famous on this side of the Danube as it was on the other, and if anyone had seen him or his servant Hermann, the Serbian police would not have hesitated to arrest him and hand him over to the Hungarian authorities.

At around six o'clock, I returned to the first part of the bridge I had crossed and went down the great central walkway on Svendor Island.

I had scarcely walked ten steps when I caught sight of Stepark. He was by himself. He came over to me, and our conversation immediately turned to the subject that preoccupied us both.

He had nothing new to report, and we both agreed that the town was beginning to recover from the hysteria it had experienced over the last couple of days.

We chatted during our walk, which lasted about forty-five minutes before we reached the northern point of the island. Night was falling. The shadows were spreading under the trees and in the deserted walkways. The chalets were closing for the night. We met no one on our path.

It was time to go back to Ragz. We were about to head toward the bridge when a few words reached us.

I stopped suddenly, and I stopped Stepark by grabbing his arm; then, leaning across so that only he could hear me, I said:

"Listen . . . Somebody's talking . . . and that voice . . . it's Wilhelm Storitz's."

"Wilhelm Storitz?" the Police Chief asked in the same tone.

"Yes, Mr. Stepark."

"If it's him, he hasn't seen us, and he mustn't see us! . . . "

"He's not alone . . . "

"No . . . his servant's with him, no doubt!"

Stepark led me under the cover of trees, crouching to the ground.

The darkness protected us, and we could speak freely without being spotted.

Soon we were hidden under a stretch of foliage, about ten steps from where Wilhelm Storitz must have been; if we saw no one there, it was of course because he and his companion were utterly invisible.

So he was in Ragz with Hermann. This was soon to be confirmed.

There had never been as good a chance of surprising him, or even of learning what he was planning next, or perhaps finding out where he was hiding out after his house had been burned down. Best of all, this was a shot at getting rid of him once and for all.

I was confident that he had no clue we were there, listening with all our ears. Crouched down among the branches, hardly daring to breathe, we listened with an indescribable emotion to the words they were exchanging. These were more or less distinct, as the master and his servant got further away and then came nearer, walking up and down between the trees.

This was the first sentence that we heard clearly, uttered by Wilhelm Storitz himself:

"We can get in there as early as tomorrow? . . . "

"Tomorrow," Hermann replied, "and no one will know that we're there."

It goes without saying that they were both speaking in German, a language we both knew well, Stepark and I.

"And when did you get back to Ragz? . . . "

"This morning. We agreed that you would be here on Svendor Island, but this time once everyone was gone . . . "

"Did you bring the liquid? . . . "

"Yes, two vials that I put under lock and key in the house . . . "

"And that house, is it rented? . . . "

"In my name!"

"You're certain, Hermann, that we can live in it quite openly, and that we're not known at . . . "

To our great disappointment, we couldn't make out the name of the town that Wilhelm Storitz was on the verge of identifying because the voices were just out of earshot. When they got nearer, Hermann repeated:

"No, there's nothing to worry about . . . The Ragz police can't find us under the names I gave . . . "

The Ragz police? . . . So they were going to live in another Hungarian town? . . .

Then the noise of their steps died away as they went farther off. This enabled Stepark to ask:

"What town? . . . What names? . . . That's what we've got to find out . . . "

"And why did they both come back to Ragz?" I asked out of concern for the Roderich family.

Just as I was thinking this, they got closer again:

"No, I won't leave Ragz," Wilhelm Storitz insisted, in a voice through which we could feel all his rage, so much insatiable hatred for this family, " . . . so long as Myra and that Frenchman . . . "

He didn't finish his sentence, or rather, it was as though a roar had been let out of his chest! At that moment, he was close to us, and maybe all it would take was to reach out and grab him! But the following words from Hermann got our attention.

"In Ragz, they now know that you have the power to make yourself invisible, even if no one knows how you do it . . . "

"And that . . . they'll never know . . . never!" Wilhelm Storitz shouted. "Ragz hasn't seen the end of me! . . . First the family, then the city! . . . Ah, because they burned down my house, they think they burned my secrets too! . . . The fools! No! . . . Ragz will not escape my vengeance, and I won't leave one of its stones upon the other! . . . "

This sentence threatening the town had hardly been spoken when the trees of the coppice started to shake violently. Stepark had just thrust himself in the direction of the voices, which were no more than three steps away from us. As I got out of his way, he yelled:

"I've got one of them, Vidal. You get the other!"

Without a doubt, his hands had fallen on a tangible if not a visible body . . . But he was hurled back so violently that he would have fallen had I not clutched his arm.

For a moment, I thought that we were going to be attacked under very disadvantageous conditions, as we couldn't even see our aggressors. But nothing of the sort. An ironic laughter rang out somewhere on our left, with the sound of footsteps dying off in the distance.

"Missed him!" Stepark shouted. "But at least now we know that even when we can't see them, we can hold on to their bodies! . . . "

Unfortunately, they had escaped our grasp, and we didn't know where their hideaway was. What we did know was that the Roderich family, along with the town of Ragz, was still at the mercy of this evildoer!

So Stepark and I walked back down Svendor Island. After crossing the bridge, we went our separate ways when we got to Bathiany quay.

That very evening, just before nine, I was back at the Roderich house, alone with the Doctor, while Madame Roderich and Marc watched over Myra. It was crucial that the Doctor be updated immediately about what had transpired on Svendor Island and that he be alerted to Wilhelm Storitz's presence in Ragz.

I told him everything, and he understood that, faced with that man's threats, faced with his intense will in pursuing his plan of vengeance against the Roderich family, it became increasingly apparent that they ought to leave Ragz. They had to leave . . . to leave clandestinely . . . and better today than tomorrow!

"My only question is," I added, "is Mademoiselle Myra in a state to bear the strains of travel? . . . "

The Doctor lowered his head, and after a long silence, gave me the following answer:

"Her health isn't any different . . . she isn't suffering . . . Only her reason is affected, but I hope with time . . . "

" . . . with calm, especially," I affirmed, "and where better to find that calm than in another country, where she will no longer have anything to fear . . . Where she will be surrounded by her loved ones, by Marc, her husband . . . for they are united by a link that nothing can ever destroy . . . "

"Nothing, Monsieur Vidal! But will this danger be avoided by our departure? Won't Wilhelm Storitz be able to follow us? . . . "

"No . . . and if we keep both our departure and the date of our departure a secret . . . "

"A secret," murmured Dr. Roderich.

And that word alone told me that he was asking himself, just as my brother had, whether any secret could be kept from Wilhelm Storitz . . . Whether, at that very moment, he wasn't in fact in that study, listening to what we were saying, and plotting some new machination in order to prevent us from traveling . . .

In short, we decided to go. Madame Roderich raised no objection. She longed for Myra to be taken to some other surroundings . . . far from Ragz!

As for Marc, he had no reservations at all. For that matter, I didn't speak to him about our encounter with Wilhelm Storitz and Hermann on the island. That seemed pointless. I was satisfied telling Captain Haralan all about it when he came back.

"He's in Ragz!" he howled.

As for the trip, there was no objection on his part. He approved of it and added:

"You'll accompany your brother, no doubt? . . . "

"Could I do otherwise? And isn't my presence at his side indispensable, just as yours is by the side of . . . "

"I won't go." He spoke in the tones of a man whose resolution was absolutely irrevocable.

"You won't go? . . . "

"No . . . I want to . . . I *have* to stay in Ragz . . . since he's in Ragz . . . and I have a feeling that I'm doing the right thing by staying!"

There was no point in discussing a feeling, and so I left it at that.

"So be it, Captain . . . "

"I'm counting on you, my dear Vidal, to replace me by the side of my family, a family that is already your own."

"You can count on me!"

The next day, I went to the train station, where I reserved a compartment for the 8:57 evening train, an express train that stopped only in Budapest during the night and arrived early in Vienna in the morning. From there, we would take the Orient Express, on which I reserved another compartment via telegram.

I then went to see Stepark to inform him of our plans.

"You're doing the right thing," he told me, "and it's a shame the entire city can't do the same!"

The Police Chief was visibly anxious . . . and he had reason to be after what he had heard the night before.

I went back to the Roderich home at around seven o'clock and made sure that all the travel preparations had been taken care of.

At eight o'clock, a covered landau was waiting to take Dr. and Madame Roderich, Marc and Myra, who was, alas, still in the same state of incoherence . . . As for Captain Haralan and myself, another coach was supposed to take us to the train station by another road, so as to avoid attracting attention.

When the Doctor and my brother went into Myra's room to take her to the landau, however, Myra had vanished! . . .

XVI

Myra had vanished! . . .

When this cry shot through the house, nobody seemed to understand its significance at first. Vanished? . . . That didn't make any sense . . . It was too unlikely . . .

A half hour before, Madame Roderich and Marc were still in the room with Myra, who was resting in bed, already dressed in her travel clothes, quite calm, and breathing regularly as though she were asleep. A little earlier, she had taken some food from Marc's hand . . .

The meal over, the Doctor and my brother had gone back to take her down to the landau . . . She's no longer in bed . . . the room is empty . . .[1]

"Myra!" Marc screams as he races toward the window . . .

The window is closed, the door as well.

At that moment, Madame Roderich comes running in, followed by Captain Haralan.

And then the name is called out throughout the house:

"Myra . . . Myra? . . . "

That she didn't answer was understandable, as nobody was expecting her to. But how could we explain the fact that she was no longer in her room? . . . Could she have possibly gotten out of bed . . . passed through her mother's room, and gone down the stairs without being noticed? . . .

I was in the coach, arranging the luggage, when I heard the cries and went up to the first floor.

My brother ran in and out like a maniac, repeating in a broken voice:

"Myra . . . Myra!"

"Myra?" I asked. "What are you saying . . . what do you want to do, Marc? . . . "

The Doctor barely had enough strength to answer me:

"My daughter . . . vanished!"

Madame Roderich had lost consciousness and had to be placed on her bed.

Captain Haralan, his face convulsed in anger, his eyes half crazed, came toward me and said:

"Him . . . it's still him!"

I tried to think, however. I was still posted by the door of the gallery where the landau was waiting, and, mind you, how did Myra manage to get past that door and to the garden without being seen by me? The invisible Wilhelm Storitz—so be it! . . . But her . . . her? . . .

I went down the gallery and called the servants. The garden gate opening onto Teleki Boulevard had a double lock, and I took away the key. Then the whole house, the attic, the cellars, the annexes, the tower right up to its terrace . . . I examined them all and left no corner unexplored. Then after the house, the garden . . .

Nobody, nobody!

I went back to Marc. My poor brother was weeping, tears streaming down his cheeks!

But I thought the most important thing to do at this point was to warn the Chief of Police so that he could put his men into action.

"I'm going over to the Town Hall. Come with me!" I told Captain Haralan.

We ran to the ground floor. We took our seats in the landau that was waiting for us. As soon as the gate was opened to let us out, it galloped off, and in a few minutes, we were at Liszt Square.

Stepark was still in his study. I updated him on the situation.

Although he was used to being surprised at nothing, this time he couldn't help expressing his shock.

"Mademoiselle Roderich has disappeared!" he cried out.

"Yes . . . " I replied. "It seems impossible, but it happened! She's been kidnapped by Wilhelm Storitz! . . . He entered the house invisibly, and he left invisibly . . . very well! But . . . she . . . didn't! . . . "

"And how do you know that for sure?" Stepark asked.

That reply burst from Stepark as if the reality had just flashed through his mind—wasn't it the only true and logical explanation? . . . Hadn't Wilhelm Storitz the power to make others invisible as well? . . . Hadn't we always believed in his servant Hermann's invisibility too?

"Gentlemen," Stepark offered, "will you come with me to the house? . . . "

"At once," I replied.

"I'm all yours, gentlemen . . . Just enough time to give a few orders."

He called a sergeant and told him to take a police squad to Dr. Roderich's and to keep the house under surveillance all night. Next, in lowered tones, he had a long discussion with his assistant, and then the coach took the three of us back to the Doctor's.

The most minute and detailed of searches was undertaken inside and outside the house. But it yielded nothing . . . how could it have yielded anything! . . . But Stepark did make one observation as soon as he entered Myra's bedroom.

"Monsieur Vidal," he asked me, "don't you smell a peculiar odor, one that has already reached our noses somewhere? . . . "

Indeed, there was still a vague smell in the air. It came back to me, and I shouted:

"Stepark, it's the smell of the liquid in the vial that got broken just as you were going to pick it up in Storitz's laboratory."

"That's right, Monsieur Vidal, and that liquid is the one that induces invisibility: Wilhelm Storitz made Myra Roderich invisible and carried her off as invisible as he was himself! . . . "

We were dumbstruck! Yes, that's exactly what must have happened, and I was now sure that Wilhelm Storitz had been in his laboratory during the search, and that he had broken the vial—from which the liquid had evaporated so quickly—rather than let it fall into our hands! . . . Yes! It was indeed that unusual smell, a trace of which we could detect here! . . . Yes, Wilhelm Storitz had come into this room, and had kidnapped Myra Roderich!

What a night we spent, I beside my brother, the Doctor beside Madame Roderich. One can imagine with what impatience we waited for daylight!

Daylight? . . . And what use would daylight be to us? . . . Did the daylight exist for Wilhelm Storitz? . . . Did it make him visible again? . . . Didn't he know that he was surrounded by impenetrable night? . . . [2]

Stepark stayed with us until daybreak, before he had to head off to the residence. Also, at around eight o'clock, the Governor came by to assure the Doctor that he would do everything it took to find his daughter . . .

But what could he do?

As soon as the day began, the news of the kidnapping spread throughout all the different neighborhoods of Ragz, and I can't even describe what kind of effect it produced . . .

At around ten o'clock, Lieutenant Armgard joined us at the

house and placed himself at his comrade's service. But good Lord, what for? In any case, if Captain Haralan had intended to resume his search, at least he wouldn't be all alone any longer.

And that's exactly what he had in mind, since as soon as he saw the lieutenant, he uttered only one word to him:

"Come."

As the two officers made for the door, I was suddenly seized with an irresistible desire to follow them.

I filled Marc in on it . . . Had he understood? Who knows, given the state he was in! I went outside. The two officers were already on the quay. Alarmed passersby ogled the house with a mixture of horror and shock. Wasn't that the very spot that had unleashed the tempest of fear that had engulfed the entire town?

When I caught up with the two officers, Captain Haralan looked at me without really even noticing my presence.

"You're coming with us, Monsieur Vidal?" Lieutenant Armgard asked.

"Yes, and you're going? . . . "

The question went unanswered. Where were we going? . . . Randomly, it seemed . . . and indeed, wasn't that the best course we could follow?

We walked at an uncertain pace, without exchanging a single word.

After we crossed Magyar Square and went up Prince Miloch Street, we circumnavigated St. Michael Square and walked under its splendid arcades. Occasionally, Captain Haralan would stop as though his feet had been nailed to the ground. He then resumed his indecisive steps.

When we got to the end of the square, I took a look at the Cathedral, with its doors shut, its muted bells, looking sinister in the midst of such abandonment, which still hadn't been returned to its faithful . . .

Turning left, we walked behind the cheviot, and after a short hesitation, Captain Haralan took Bihar Street.

Ragz's aristocratic neighborhood seemed cadaverous to us now, barely a few passersby rushing by, most of the homes with their windows shut as though it were a day of public mourning.

At the end of the street, Teleki Boulevard was deserted, or rather, almost deserted. Nobody went by there since the Storitz house had been burned down.

Which direction would Captain Haralan choose? Up toward the castle, or down toward Bathiany quay, toward the Danube . . .

Suddenly, he let out a cry:

"There . . . there . . . " he repeated, his eyes burned ardently, his hands pointed toward the smoke from ruins that were still smoldering . . .

Captain Haralan had stopped in his tracks, his face flushed with hatred! The ruins seemed to exert an irresistible pull on him as he threw himself toward the partially demolished gates.

A minute later, all three of us were in the middle of the courtyard.

All that was left were the remains of the walls, now blackened by flames. At their feet lay fragments of charred wood, twisted pieces of iron, heaps of ashes crowned by light clouds of smoke, furniture debris, and, at the tip of the right gable, a stem from the weathervane, on which one could discern these two letters: W.S.

Motionless, Captain Haralan stared at this pile of destruction. Ah! Why couldn't they have burned that accursed German, as they had burned the house, and with him the secret of that frightful invention! The Roderich family would have been spared such misfortune, the most horrible of all misfortunes! . . .

Lieutenant Armgard wanted to drag his comrade away from the scene, as the Captain was becoming alarmingly overexcited.

"Let's get out of here," he suggested.

"No!" declared Captain Haralan, who was no longer in any mood to listen. "No . . . I want to sift through these ruins! . . . I feel like that man is here . . . and that my sister is with him! . . . We can't see him, but he's here . . . Listen . . . there are footsteps in the garden . . . It's him! . . . him!"

Captain Haralan extended his ear . . . motioning to us not to move . . .

And perhaps it was just a hallucination, but I too thought I heard a rustling on the sand . . .

Then, pushing away the Lieutenant, who was encouraging him to leave, Captain Haralan leapt through the ruins, his feet immersed in rubble and cinders, and stopped at the spot where the ground-floor laboratory had been, on the side of the courtyard . . . And he shouted:

"Myra . . . Myra . . . "

And it seemed as though an echo repeated the name . . .

I glanced at Lieutenant Armgard, who was looking at me, on the verge of asking me a question . . .

At that moment, Captain Haralan went all the way to the garden, across the ruins. He went down the steps in one leap, and fell back among the weeds that straggled along the grass.

We were about to join him, when he made certain movements as if he had knocked against some sort of physical obstacle . . . He advanced, he retreated, he extended his arms then drew them together, he bent over, he stood up like a wrestler who had just locked his opponent in a hold.

"I've got him!" he yelled.

Lieutenant Armgard and I raced over toward him. I could suddenly hear compressed breathing puffing from his chest . . .

"I've got him, the bastard . . . I've got him . . . " he repeated. "Help me, Vidal . . . help me, Armgard!"

All of a sudden, I feel myself hurled backward by an arm I can't see, while noisy breath lands right in my face!

No . . . Yes! . . . It's real hand-to-hand combat! He's there, that invisible being. Wilhelm Storitz or someone else! . . . Whoever it is, we've got him . . . we'll never let him go . . . We'll know how to make him tell us where Myra is!

As I expected, even if he has the power to destroy his visibility, at least his physical self subsists! It's not a ghost; it's a body that we're trying to paralyze, at the expense of our herculean efforts! . . . And Wilhelm Storitz is by himself, since if other invisible ones had been in the garden at the time when he was caught, they would have been all over us by now! Yes . . . he's alone . . . but why didn't he flee when he saw us coming? . . . Had he been abruptly surprised and grabbed by Captain Haralan? . . . That's got to be the reason! . . .

At present, our invisible adversary's movements have been impaired. I'm holding on to him by one arm, Lieutenant Armgard by the other.

"Where's Myra . . . where's Myra? . . . " Captain Haralan screams at him.

Instead of answering, he tries to free himself, and I feel as though we're dealing with a very vigorous man who is violently struggling to break loose from us, and if he succeeds, he'll thrust himself across the garden, across the ruins, he'll reach the boulevard, and we'll have to give up all hope of ever capturing him again!

"Will you tell us where Myra is? . . . " Captain Haralan repeats.

At last we hear these words:

"Never! . . . Never!"

It is indeed Wilhelm Storitz. His very voice! . . .

This battle can't go on any longer . . . Even though we're three against one, we're starting to weaken. At that moment, Lieutenant Armgard is viciously thrown on to the grass, and that arm I was holding on to slips away. And before the Lieutenant can get back up, his saber is suddenly pulled out of its sheath, and the hand that is now brandishing it is Wilhelm Storitz's . . . Indeed . . . his wrath has gotten the better of him. He is no longer trying to escape . . . He wants to kill Captain Haralan, who brandished his own saber. There they were, now face to face, as though they were locked in a duel: one opponent whom we could see, the other whom nobody could see! . . .

We were unable to intervene in this strange combat, during which Captain Haralan was at a complete disadvantage. While he successfully defended himself against his attacker's blows, it was difficult for him to return them. Moreover, he was only interested in attacking . . . in attacking his opponent without trying to defend himself. The two swords were clashing together, one held by a visible hand, the other by an invisible one.

It was clear that Wilhelm Storitz knew how to handle a sword, and during a swiftly parried cut to the arm, Captain Haralan took a hit in the shoulder . . . But his saber flashed forward . . . a cry of pain rang out . . . The grass on the lawn was flattened.

Wilhelm Storitz had probably been pierced through the chest . . . A jet of blood began to spurt from it, and as life was leaving it, the invisible body gradually took on its material form . . . It was there before our very eyes, reappearing during the supreme convulsions of death.

Captain Haralan threw himself on Wilhelm Storitz once more and cried out:

"Myra . . . my sister, where's Myra? . . . "

There was nothing but a corpse, its face contorted, its eyes wide open, its gaze still menacing—the visible body of that strange person who had once been Wilhelm Storitz![3]

XVII

Such was the tragic end of Wilhelm Storitz. Yet even though the Roderich family had no longer anything to fear from him, hadn't the situation gotten worse as a result of his death? . . .

The most urgent task was to alert the Chief of Police, so that he could enact the necessary measures, and this is what was decided:

Captain Haralan,—who was only lightly wounded—would go to the Roderich residence and warn his father.

I would rush over to the Town Hall in order to update Stepark on what had just happened.

Lieutenant Armgard would stay in the garden next to the corpse.

We went our separate ways. As Captain Haralan went down Teleki Boulevard, I took Bihar Street and, at a fast clip, walked toward Town Hall.

Stepark saw me immediately, and as soon as I had told him about the unbelievable duel, he said to me, with as much surprise as doubt in his voice:

"So is Wilhelm Storitz really dead? . . ."

"Absolutely . . . from a saber wound that Captain Haralan inflicted on him right in the chest."

"Dead? . . . What we refer to as dead? . . . "

"Come with me, Mr. Stepark, and you'll see it with your own eyes . . . "

"I'll see? . . . "

Surely, Stepark must have been wondering if I was in full command of my faculties. I then added:

"The invisibility did not last past death, and as the blood flowed from his wound, Wilhelm Storitz regained his human form . . . "

"You saw it? . . . "

"Just as I'm seeing you, and as you'll see for yourself! . . . "

"Let's get going," the Chief of Police announced, after having given the order to the sergeant to follow him with about a dozen men.

As I have already mentioned, nobody walked along Teleki Boulevard after the Storitz house fire. Not a soul had gone by it since I left. But the latest news hadn't yet spread, and Ragz didn't know that it had been saved from this nefarious individual.

As soon as Stepark, his men, and I went through the gate and crossed the ruins, Lieutenant Armgard came forward.

The body was stretched out on the grass and still rigid with death, a bit turned over on its left side, his clothes soaked in blood, with a few drops oozing from his chest, his face discolored, his right hand still grasping the Lieutenant's saber, his left arm bent under him. An already chilled cadaver that was ripe for the grave.

Stepark, after staring at it for a while, announced:

"It's him!"

With some trepidation, his men had come closer and recognized him as well. To match the visual certainty with a tactile one, Stepark touched the body from head to foot.

"Dead . . . stone cold dead!" he said.

He then turned to Lieutenant Armgard:

"No one came? . . . "

"No one, Monsieur Stepark."

"And you heard nothing in the garden . . . any footsteps? . . . "

"None!"

There was then good reason to believe that Wilhelm Storitz had been alone in the midst of the ruins of his house when we surprised him.

"And what now, Mr. Stepark?" asked the Lieutenant.

"I'll have the body taken to the Town Hall . . . "

"Publicly? . . . " I asked.

"Publicly," the Chief of Police replied. "Ragz must know that Wilhelm Storitz is dead, and the only way they'll believe it is once they see his body pass by! . . . "

"And once he's buried! . . . " Lieutenant Armgard added.

"If we bury him! . . . " Stepark replied.

"If we bury him? . . . " I repeated.

"First of all, Monsieur Vidal, we ought to do an autopsy . . . Who knows? . . . By examining his organs, after analyzing the deceased's blood, perhaps we might discover what we still don't know . . . the nature of the substance that produces invisibility."

"A secret that must be destroyed!" I shouted.

"Then," the Chief of Police explained, "to my mind, it would be best if we burned the corpse and scattered its ashes to the wind, as they used to do with sorcerers in the Middle Ages."

Stepark sent for a stretcher, and we left him, Lieutenant Armgard and I, on our way back to the Roderichs' house.

Captain Haralan was by his father's side, having told him everything. In Madame Roderich's state, he thought it wisest not to tell her what had happened. For that matter, Wilhelm Storitz's death would do nothing to bring back his daughter!

As for my brother, he knew nothing of all this yet, and that's why we had word sent to him that we were waiting for him in the Doctor's study.

He didn't receive the news with a feeling of satisfied vengeance, however! He burst into sobs, while desperate words managed to barely escape from his lips:

"He's dead! . . . You killed him! . . . He's dead, without telling us where Myra is! . . . Alive . . . Myra . . . my poor Myra . . . I'll never see her again!"

And what could we tell him after such an outburst of grief? . . .

I tried anyway, just as we would with Madame Roderich. No, we mustn't give up all hope . . . We didn't know where Myra was . . . if she had been kept in some hideout in town, or if she had left it . . . But one man knew . . . He had to know . . . Wilhelm Storitz's servant Hermann . . . We were going to look for him . . . Even if it meant going to the deepest parts of Germany, we would find him! . . . Unlike his master, there would be no reason for him to keep quiet! . . . He'd speak . . . We'd force him to speak . . . even if we had to give him an entire fortune! . . . Myra would be returned to her family . . . to her fiancé . . . to her husband . . . and sanity would come back to her as a result of loving care, of tenderness and love! . . .

Marc heard none of this . . . he didn't want to hear any of it . . . As far as he was concerned, the only one person who could have told him anything was dead . . . We shouldn't have killed him . . . We should have wrenched his secret from him first! . . .

I wondered how on earth I was going to calm my brother down, when our conversation was suddenly interrupted by a raucous din outside.

Captain Haralan and Lieutenant Armgard rushed to the window, which opened onto a corner of the boulevard and Bathiany quay.

What could possibly be going on now? . . . And in our present state of mind, I suppose nothing could have surprised us, not even Wilhelm Storitz's resurrection! . . .

It was the funeral procession. The corpse, lying on a stretcher with not even a sheet to cover it, was being carried by two policemen, followed by the rest of the squad . . . So all of Ragz would soon know that Wilhelm Storitz was dead and the reign of terror finally over!

After taking Bathiany quay all the way to Stephen II Street, the procession was supposed to go through the Coloman Square marketplace, and then the city's busiest neighborhoods, before getting to Town Hall.

In my opinion, it would have been better if it hadn't passed by the Roderich house.

My brother had joined us by the window, and from there, he let out a cry of despair upon seeing the bloodied corpse. He would have gladly restored it to life, were it at the price of his own! . . .

The crowd gave itself up to the most violent demonstrations, men, women, children, the middle class, peasants from the Puszta! . . . Alive, Wilhelm Storitz would have been torn to pieces by them! Dead, his body was spared. But as Stepark had suggested, they certainly didn't want him to be buried in holy soil. Rather, they insisted that he be burned in the public square or thrown into the Danube, whose waters would carry him off to the far-distant depths of the Black Sea.

For a half an hour, the screams rang out in front of the house, then silence.

Captain Haralan then told us that he wanted to go back to the Town Hall. He wanted to talk to the Governor about finding Hermann. Berlin had to be contacted, the Austrian embassy; the German police had to be mobilized, as they would no doubt hasten to come to our aid . . . the press would help out . . . Rewards would be offered to anyone with any information leading to Hermann's whereabouts, this single repository of Wilhelm Storitz's secrets, and no doubt the guardian of his victim.

After he had gone up to his mother's room, Captain Haralan left the house, accompanied by Lieutenant Armgard.

I stayed with my brother. One can imagine how painful the hours were spent by his side! I had no way of calming him down, and his increasingly overexcited mind sent shivers down my spine! I was losing him, I felt it quite clearly, and I dreaded some sort of attack from which he might never recover! . . . He was delirious! . . . He wanted to leave, to leave that very night for Spremberg . . . Hermann must have been known there . . . Why wouldn't he be in Spremberg . . . and Myra along with him? . . .

It was entirely plausible to assume that Hermann was in Spremberg. But not Myra, that was out of the question. She had disappeared the night before, and this morning, Wilhelm Storitz was still in Ragz . . . I was more inclined to believe that she had been led to some surrounding area of town . . . to a house where Hermann kept an eye on this poor soul deprived of her senses, to whom he had probably not returned her visible form! . . . And, under those conditions, could one hang on to any hope of finding her? . . .

Well, my brother refused to listen to me . . . He wouldn't even discuss it . . . He had just one idea . . . an idée fixe . . . to set off for Spremberg! . . .

"And you'll come with me, Henry," he said.

"Yes . . . my poor friend," I answered. I wasn't sure I was going to be able to dissuade Marc from this useless trip!

All that I could get him to do was push back our departure to the next day . . . I had to see Stepark, ask him for letters of recommendation for the Spremberg Police, and then warn Captain Haralan, who would no doubt insist on accompanying us.

At around seven o'clock, he and Lieutenant Armgard came back to the house. The Governor had given them his assurance that the promptest of searches was going to be organized in the area surrounding Ragz, where he thought (and I also thought) that Myra must be held by Hermann.

Dr. Roderich was still at his wife's side. There were only the two officers in the drawing room, as well as my brother and me.

The blinds drawn, the servant brought a lamp that was placed on one of the console tables. We were to go to the dining room only when the Doctor had come down.

Seven-thirty had just rung. As I was sitting next to Captain Haralan, I was about to talk to him about our Spremberg trip when the gallery door suddenly opened rather vigorously.

No doubt, a gust of air coming in from the garden must have thrust open the door, as nobody else was around. But what was even more extraordinary was that the door had shut all by itself . . .

And then—no! I'll never forget that scene!

We heard a voice . . . not like that coarse voice that had insulted us with its rendition of "Song of Hatred" on the evening of the engagement party—but a fresh, joyful voice, a voice that we all loved, the voice of our dear Myra! . . .

"Marc . . . my dear Marc," she said. "And you, Monsieur Henry . . . and you, my brother? . . . Well then, it's time for dinner! . . . Has anyone told my mother and father? . . . Haralan . . . go get them and we can all sit down to dinner . . . I'm dying of hunger! . . . Are you joining us, Monsieur Armgard? . . . "

It was Myra . . . Myra herself . . . Myra who had regained her reason, Myra cured! . . . It was as if she had come down from her room as usual. It was Myra who could see us but whom we could not see! . . . It was an invisible Myra! . . .

Open-mouthed, nailed to our seats, we dared neither move, nor speak, nor go toward the place where the voice was coming from . . . And yet Myra was there, alive, and, we were sure of it, tangible in her invisibility! . . .

Where had she come from? . . . From the house where her kidnapper had taken her after absconding with her from the Roderichs' home? . . . Had she then been able to escape, to get past

Hermann's watchful eye, cross town, come home without anyone noticing her? . . . And yet, the doors of the house had been shut, and nobody could have opened them! . . .

No, the explanation for her presence was going to be given to us soon . . . Myra had come down from her room, where Wilhelm Storitz had made her and left her invisible . . . While we thought she had been taken out of the house, she had never left her bed . . . She had stayed there, stretched out, unable to move, still silent and unconscious, for those twenty-four hours! . . . It had never entered anybody's mind that she might be there, and indeed, why should anyone have thought of it?

And if Wilhelm Storitz had not taken her off right then and there, it must have been because something prevented him from doing so, no doubt; but he would have surely come back to finish off his crime, if, that very morning, he had not been killed by Captain Haralan! . . .

And here was Myra, in full command of her faculties, perhaps under the influence of that liquid that had put her in this state of invisibility . . . Myra, who had been oblivious to what had been going on all week. Myra was in this very drawing room, speaking to us, seeing us, unable as she came down from her room in the darkness to realize that she couldn't even see herself! . . .

Marc had gotten up, his arms extended as if to hug her . . .

And she continued:

"But what's the matter with you, my friends? . . . I'm talking to you, and you're not answering? . . . You all seem so surprised to see me? . . . What's happened? . . . And why isn't my mother here? . . . Is she ill by any chance? . . . "

She wasn't able to finish her sentence, as the door opened once again when Dr. Roderich came in.

Myra immediately ran toward him—at least that's what we thought—as she cried out:

"Oh, Father! . . . What's wrong? . . . And my mother's not coming down? . . . Is she sick? . . . I'm going to go up to her room . . .

The Doctor, frozen on the threshold, understood.

Yet Myra was next to him; she kissed him and repeated:

"My mother . . . my mother! . . . "

"She's not sick! . . . " he stammered. "She'll come down . . . Stay here, my child, stay right here!"

At that very moment, Marc found Myra's hand, and he led her gently, as he would a blind person . . . Which, of course, she wasn't. We who could not see her were the blind ones!

My brother then sat her down beside him . . .

Frightened by the effect her presence had produced, she did not speak, and Marc, in a trembling voice, murmured words that she no doubt could not understand.

"Myra . . . my dear Myra! . . . Yes! . . . It's really you . . . I feel you here . . . by my side! . . . Oh, I beg of you . . . my beloved . . . don't leave me . . . "

"My dear Marc . . . This bewildered attitude . . . All of you . . . you're frightening me . . . Father . . . answer me! . . . Has some sort of tragedy taken place? . . . Mother . . . Mother! . . . "

Marc felt her getting up, and he drew her down again . . . gently . . .

"Myra . . . my dear Myra . . . speak . . . speak to me some more! . . . Just so I can hear your voice . . . you . . . you . . . my wife! . . . My beloved Myra! . . . "

And we remained there, horrified by the thought that the only one who could restore Myra to her visible form was dead and had taken his secret with him!

XVIII

Would this situation, over which we no longer had any control, have a happy ending? . . . Who could have maintained that hope? . . . And how could one not start to despair, to tell oneself that Myra might be forever erased from the visible world? . . . Moreover, mixed with our intense delight at having found her, there was also an intense distress that she had not been visibly restored in all her grace and beauty!

It could well be imagined what kind of life the Roderich family could look forward to under these conditions!

First of all, in that drawing room, right in front of all of us, Myra let out an anguished scream . . . As she went past the mirror on the mantelpiece, she wasn't able to see her own reflection . . . and when she went by the lamp that had been placed on the console, she couldn't see her shadow behind her! . . .

We had to tell her everything that had happened. That's when we heard the sobs bursting from her breast while Marc, kneeling beside her chair, tried in vain to calm her down. He loved her visible, he would love her invisible. It was enough to break our hearts.

Later in the evening, the Doctor insisted that Myra go up to her mother's room. Madame Roderich was better off knowing that her daughter was by her side, and hearing her speak . . .

A few days went by! Well then, Myra had resigned herself to her condition. Thanks to her spiritual strength, it seemed as though our everyday lives could at last go back to normal. Myra would show us that she was there by speaking to one of us, and by asking us questions. I can still hear her saying:

"I'm still here, my friends . . . Do you need anything? I'll get it for you! . . . My dear Henry, what are you looking for? . . . That book that you placed on the table, here it is! . . . Your newspaper? It fell right next to you! . . . My father . . . this is the time when I usually give you a kiss! . . . And you, dear brother, why do you look at me with such sad eyes? . . . I can assure you I'm all smiles! . . . Why worry yourself over nothing! . . . And you . . . you, my dear Marc, here are my two hands . . . take them . . . Do you want to come out into the garden? . . . We can walk around it together . . . Give me your arm, Henry, and we'll talk about thousands and thousands of different things!"

That dear, adorable creature, so filled with goodness, did not want any change to be made in the life of the family. She and Marc spent long hours together, and she never stopped murmuring encouraging words in his ear as he held her hand . . . She tried to console him, declaring that she was full of confidence in the future, that one day her invisibility would end . . . But did she really have faith in that?

One change, and one alone, however, was made to our daily life. Myra, realizing that under such conditions her presence among us would have been painful, never came to take her place with us at table. But when the meal was over, she would come down to the drawing room. We could hear her opening and closing the door, saying:

"Here I am, my friends, I'm here!"

And she didn't leave us until it was time to go back to her room, after having wished us all goodnight.

I need hardly mention that as Myra Roderich's disappearance had made such a stir in town, her reappearance—if that's the word I should be using!—produced an even greater one. Expressions of sympathy came in from everywhere, and visitors flocked to her home. Myra had given up on her walks through the streets of Ragz, and went out only by coach, accompanied by her father and mother, Marc and Captain Haralan, and occasionally, she could hear affectionate words that went straight to her heart. But above all, she preferred to sit in the garden, to be with everyone she loved, and to whom, morally at any rate, she had been completely restored!

We hadn't forgotten that after Wilhelm Storitz's death, the Governor of Ragz had undertaken a massive investigation in search of Hermann. They had planned on finding out where Myra was hidden, since we supposed, reasonably, that she must have been held prisoner by Wilhelm Storitz's servant.

The investigation would continue, however, as everything pointed to the fact that Hermann must have been his master's confidant, that he must have shared some of his secrets, and we had no doubt that he would be able to return Myra's lost visibility.

Indeed, Wilhelm Storitz certainly had the capacity to make himself either visible or invisible whenever he wanted, and whatever he could do, Hermann could do. Once he had been captured, we would know how to extract the secret from him, either by promising him large sums of money or by threatening to make him responsible for the crimes of his master, as hadn't he committed one of the most despicable crimes imaginable?

The subject was approached with the utmost diligence. Nonetheless, the situation had huge repercussions. The press had written about it in great detail, and unrelentingly kept the entire world abreast of each development. People were passionate about Myra Roderich! The German chemist's discovery was debated everywhere, especially in regards to its terrifying consequences in terms of public safety. It was crucial that the secret never be divulged by the only man, in all likelihood, who possessed the formula.

I say in all likelihood because if others like him had known it, they would not have been able to resist the myriad of rewards that had been offered, not only by the Roderich family, but by the police departments of both the Old and the New Worlds.

Still, not a single revelation had been produced, and it was understood that Wilhelm Storitz's servant must have been the only one who shared his secret.

Furthermore, the investigations that had been launched in Spremberg yielded no information whatsoever. The authorities had lent their full support, which was considerable, as the Prussian police force is known to be one of the best in Europe. It was just impossible to find out where Hermann had taken refuge, whether in Spremberg or elsewhere.

Alas, it soon became apparent that these searches would never come to fruition.

The government of Ragz had decided that, in order to obliterate any memory of this sorrowful affair forever, the ruins of the Storitz house should disappear. The rubble would be taken away, the last vestiges of the walls knocked down, so that of this abode, isolated along a side lane of Teleki Boulevard, not a trace would remain.

Yet on the 2nd of June, in the morning, as the workers reached the Storitz house in order to proceed with the cleanup, they discovered a corpse lying at the end of the garden. It was Hermann's. His body was immediately recognized. If the old servant had come there invisibly, death, as it had for his master, had returned his visibility to him. Incidentally, we learned that he had died of heart failure.

Our last hope died with him, however, as Wilhelm Storitz's secret had passed away as well.

Indeed, after a painstaking analysis of the papers that had been deposited at Town Hall, nothing was found but vague formulas with Chemistry- and Physics-related annotations. It was possible to decipher the double intervention of Roentgen rays and electricity but impossible to deduce anything that might lead to a reconstitution of the substance that could make someone instantaneously visible or invisible! . . .

Would the unfortunate Myra be doomed to visibly reappear only at that moment when life would leave her, when she'd be stretched out on her deathbed? . . .

My brother came by to fetch me on the 5th of June, in the morning. He seemed relatively calm to me when he said:

"My dear Henry, I want to discuss a decision I've arrived at. I think you'll approve of it and that everyone else will approve of it as well."

I had to admit, and why not admit it, that I sensed where Marc was going with all this.

"My friend," I told him, "speak freely! . . . I know that you would only listen to the voice of reason . . . "

"Of reason and of love, Henry! Myra is my wife in the eyes of the law . . . Our wedding still lacks its religious consecration, and I want to ask for that consecration . . . I want to obtain it . . . "

I took my brother in my arms, and told him:

"I understand you, Marc, and I can't see what would stand in the way of your wedding . . . "

"An obstacle could only come from Myra," Marc replied, "and Myra is ready to kneel beside me at the altar! If the priest can't see her, at least he'll hear her declare that she takes me for her husband just as I take her for my wife! . . . I can't imagine that the ecclesiastical authorities would raise any difficulties, and, besides, if I had to go . . . "

"No, my dear Marc, no, and I'll take care of all the arrangements . . . "

It was at first the priest at the Cathedral to whom I turned, then to the Arch-Priest who had officiated at that nuptial mass that had been interrupted by the unprecedented profanation. The venerable old man assured me that the case had already been looked into, and that the Archbishop of Ragz had given a favorable decision. Invisible though she might be, there was no doubt that the bride was alive, and that she was therefore open to receive the sacrament of marriage.

In short, the date of the ceremony was set for June 12th.

The night before, Myra told me, as she had said to me once before:

"Don't forget, Henry! . . . It's tomorrow."

The wedding would take place in St. Michael's Cathedral, now reconciled according to liturgical rules, under the same conditions, with the same witnesses, the same friends and guests invited by the Roderich family, the same influx of people.

Granted, there was an unusually high dose of curiosity at the wedding, a curiosity that could certainly be understood and forgiven! No doubt, there were among those present certain misgivings that time alone could overcome! Yes, Wilhelm Storitz was dead; yes, his servant Hermann had been found dead in the garden of that cursed house . . . And yet more than one guest was asking himself if this second wedding mass would not be interrupted like the first one . . . or whether some new phenomena might disturb the nuptial ceremony . . .

Here is the engaged couple in the choir of the cathedral. Myra's chair seems empty. And yet she's right there in her wedding gown, all white and as invisible as she is . . .

Marc is standing up and turns toward her. He cannot see her, but he knows that she is by his side; he takes her hand, as though to demonstrate her presence before the altar.

Behind them the witnesses, Judge Newmann, Captain Haralan,

Lieutenant Armgard, and myself; then Dr. and Madame Roderich, the poor mother on her knees, imploring the Almighty to work a miracle on her daughter's behalf! . . . Hoping perhaps that it might occur in God's sanctuary. Friends are jammed in every corner, the notables of the town fill the great nave, and the aisles swarm with people.

The bells ring with abandon, the organs blast with joy.

The Arch-Priest and his acolytes arrive. The mass begins, its ceremonies proceeding to the chanting of the choir. At the offertory, Marc can be seen leading Myra to the first step of the altar . . . and then bringing her back, after her offering has fallen into the deacon's alms-purse.

Finally, after the elevation, after the three tinkles of the bell, the wafer is finally raised heavenward, and this time, the consecration is completed before the deeply silent faithful! . . .

The mass over, the old priest turned toward the congregation. Marc and Myra came forward, and he said:

"Myra Roderich, are you there? . . . "

"I'm here," Myra replied.

Then he turned to Marc:

"Marc Vidal, do you agree to take Myra Roderich, present here, as your wife in accordance with the rites of our Holy Church?"

"I do," Marc replied.

"Myra Roderich, do you agree to take Marc Vidal, present here, as your husband in accordance with the rites of our Holy Church?"

"I do," Myra answered in a voice everyone could hear.

"Marc Vidal," the Arch-Priest continued, "do you promise to remain true in all things, as a loyal husband owes to a wife, according to God's commandments?"

"Yes . . . I promise."

"Myra Roderich, do you promise to remain true in all things, as a loyal wife owes to a husband, according to God's commandments?"

"Yes . . . I promise."

Marc and Myra were then united by the sacrament of marriage.

After the ceremony, the married couple, their witnesses, their friends, gathered at the sacristy in the middle of a crowd so thick that they could barely navigate away from it.

There, on the registers in the vestry, to the signature of Marc Vidal another name was added, traced by a hand that nobody could see . . . Myra Roderich![1]

XIX

And this is how the story ends as we await a happier ending?

It goes without saying that the newlyweds gave up on their earlier plans. There could be no trip to France. I could even predict that my brother would only make rare appearances in Paris, and that he would settle permanently in Ragz. This was a great loss for me, but I had to resign myself to it.

The best thing would be for him and his wife to live in the old mansion, near Dr. and Mrs. Roderich.[1] Time would settle it, and Marc would get used to that life, and as for Myra, it seemed as though we could see how gracious and smiling she was . . . She revealed her presence by her words, by the warmth of her hand! We always knew where she was and what she was doing. She was the soul of the house,—invisible like a soul!

And then there was that remarkable painting of her that Marc had made. Myra liked to sit near the canvas, and with that soothing voice of hers, she would say:

"As you can see . . . it's me . . . There I am . . . I've become visible again . . . and you see me as I see myself!"

Once I obtained an extension to my leave of absence, I stayed a few weeks longer in Ragz, at the Roderichs' home, in the most complete intimacy of that much-tried family. I couldn't think without regret about the day when I would have to leave them! . . .

And I sometimes ask myself whether I have to permanently give up any hope of ever seeing that young woman in her physical form again, whether some sort of physiological phenomenon might possibly occur, or even whether the simple passage of time might bring back her lost visibility, whether, one day, Myra might finally reappear before our eyes, radiating with her youth, grace and beauty? . . .

The future might well decide in the end, but for the sake of Heaven, I pray that the secret of invisibility may never ever resurface again, and that it remain forever buried deep down in Otto and Wilhelm Storitz's grave!

Afterword

Jules Verne's Invisible Man and Other Discoveries

"Death doesn't destroy," Sandorf tells us in Jules Verne's *Mathias Sandorf* (1885); "it just makes one invisible."[1] In one of Verne's very last novels, however, *The Secret of Wilhelm Storitz*, it's not death that makes one invisible, but rather, the unrequited love the diabolical protagonist of the novel's title feels for the lovely Myra, whose name also suggests, in Spanish, *mira*, or *see*. Indeed, the famous line from *Michel Strogoff*, "Look, with all your eyes, look!" could also apply to this enigmatic novel. Storitz succeeds in rendering invisible not only himself but also the target of his affections. As opposed to other Vernian bachelors, such as Phileas Fogg and Michel Ardan, who race across the globe (or around it in outer space) with great alacrity, or even Robur, who dreams of great flying inventions, Storitz is enveloped in a type of hatred that limits him spatially and emotionally despite the great freedom of movement allowed by his invisibility. This hatred pushes him toward a horrifying solitude that often echoes the pessimism found in many other of Verne's later novels, as well as in his very first novel, the ill-fated *Paris in the Twentieth Century*, which was so grim that his publisher wouldn't publish it during his lifetime (it was finally published posthumously in 1994). How does this sinister bachelor construct his narrative space? How does Verne frame notions of visibility and invisibility at the dawn of the twentieth century, just as his own life was coming to an end? From Storitz's bedroom to the Hungarian city of Ragz that Storitz petrifies, Verne seems to give equal importance both to a typically "fantastic" narrative space and to a nineteenth-century bachelor's one as well.

Writing about H. G. Wells's *Invisible Man*, Nathalie Prince remarks that Griffin "lives like a bachelor and asserts his bachelordom. . . . His entire character lends itself to a comparison with the figure of the bachelor. Isn't the bachelor a secretive creature who hides or cloaks himself in some way, who flees others, their stares, who has no relations, no friends to speak of? Isn't he always shrinking away from others, and cultivating his own private garden?"[2] Indeed, a detailed comparison of these two invisible men—Wells's and Verne's—would yield interesting similarities and patterns. Yet all one has to do is deconstruct Prince's description in order to trace a true "invisible bachelor paradigm," through which Storitz shrouds himself in mystery, as Griffin does, or even a type of obsessive madness that isolates him both spatially and socially from the rest of the world.

"Invisibility, like bachelordom, depends on a gaze," Prince continues. Indeed, in Ragz, Storitz finds a place that is particularly propitious to his efforts at spreading terror among the villagers and a fertile ground for his theatrical manipulations. According to Verne's narrator, Henry Vidal, the brother of Myra's fiancé, any kind of seemingly supernatural act can cause the superstitious Ragzians to panic:

Would [they] accept a natural explanation of these events? This was not France, where no doubt these wonders would have been made into jokes by the press and ridiculed in song in all the taverns of Montmartre! Things were different in this country. As I have already pointed out, the Magyars have a natural tendency toward the marvelous, and superstition, among the uneducated classes, is ineradicable.

Verne underlines the fact that the Ragzians, by refusing any kind of scientific explanation for the extraordinary events caused by Storitz, allow themselves to be completely manipulated by his macabre spectacle. As such, Storitz's malevolent powers can grow in relation to his actions, which, despite his physical invisibility, remain extremely visible, if not ostentatious: "For the most sophisticated, these strange goings-on could only be the result of some discovery in Physics or Chemistry. But when it comes to unenlightened minds, everything is explained by the intervention of the devil, and Wilhelm Storitz would pass for the devil incarnate." Storitz succeeds in projecting such a horrible image of himself onto Ragz because he knows how to exploit the fact that he is not only strange, but a stranger as well, and a foreigner in particular. On the one hand, as a German he represents the Magyars' fearsome enemy; on the other, as a *strange* foreigner he represents the danger associated with the figure of the intruder who can not only invade the country with troops and canons but also—within the realm of the fantastic, where *anything* is possible (especially when it comes to evil)—gain access to the private spaces of the villagers, at any hour or moment of the day: "Yet if a man had the power to make himself invisible [. . .] then public order would be completely compromised! No more personal security."

As he describes the panic provoked by Storitz's invisibility, Verne underlines the type of collective trance that hypnotizes the Ragzian people, just as it destabilizes the internal politics of the village: "The situation was still rather worrisome," Verne writes, "and public safety had been completely compromised. We were living as though we were in a trance. We felt safe in neither houses nor streets, neither at night nor in the day." The comforting aspects of home and hearth, so dear to the bourgeois psyche of nineteenth-century France, are suddenly assaulted by that antithesis of the nuclear family, the monstrous bachelor whose only goal is to destroy the "holy" union between Marc Vidal and Myra Roderich and then, accordingly, all the harmony associated with the marital bliss of all the other families in Ragz. As Jean Borie explains it, this is in keeping with the nineteenth-century bachelor's negative image: "Because he is placed outside of marriage, the bachelor is dangerously close to that badly guarded box in which all the most deviant monsters of savage sexuality are parked: his own territory is a cramped one, stuck between the conjugal home and purveyors of crime and placed somewhere among prisons and asylums, and therefore, attached to all that is criminal, perverted, mad, and sick."[3] Moreover, Borie quotes from a pamphlet written in 1871 proposing a special tax on bachelors, who are responsible (according to the author of the pamphlet) for whatever disorder threatens the family unit or even the nation as a whole: "Yet the bachelor is not just a sterile being, he is a bad example, and moreover an agent of corruption. [. . .] In society, he provokes disorder incessantly, as well as misery and depravity. As much as the family consolidates the social edifice, the bachelor is the utmost agent of destruction."

Although Storitz *wants* to marry the lovely Myra, he is already marginalized in relation to society: the fact that he is categorically rejected by the Roderich family pushes him toward his phantom-like and diabolical incarnation, which turns him into an "anti-man" rather than a virile man, since he remains fundamentally unnatural. Phileas Fogg may well begin *Around the World in Eighty Days* as a bachelor, but by the end of the novel he is married to Aouda, as the qualities associated with his "fogginess" allowed him to circumnavigate the world as though he were some sort of vaporous fog, only to complete his great voyage and reach London more complete than when he began. Storitz, on the other hand, is incapable of "completing" himself spiritually through marriage and therefore must dissipate, morally and physically, by transforming himself literally into a type of metaphysical fog. In this way he succeeds, just like Ulysses before him, in being everywhere and nowhere at the same time. As the French philosopher Paul Virilio explains, linking Ulysses to his pseudonym "Nemo," "Since he does not occupy one single spot, he wishes to be unidentifiable, but above all, wishes to be identified with nothing. He is no one because he wants to be nobody, and to be nobody, one has to be simultaneously everywhere and nowhere."[4] Just as Captain Nemo, disgusted with society on land, decides to retreat beneath the seas and become invisible—or no one—in relation to the life he may have known before, and becomes visible only in order to sink warships with his *Nautilus* in *Twenty Thousand Leagues under the Sea*, Storitz also chooses to be nobody. Storitz is able to terrorize so effectively not only through his nefarious apparitions (such as when he steals Myra's bridal wreath) but through his constant presence, which becomes unpredictable and omnipresent. If, as Borie affirms, "the bachelor against whom there is no legal evidence, and [who] thinks of himself within the bounds of legality, remains nonetheless fundamentally *suspicious*," Storitz, via his metamorphoses, creates a collective hysteria during which "*everything* seemed suspicious." He can penetrate without penetrating, and he can underline his presence by his absence:

During the comings and goings of domestic life, at table during meals, in the evenings during get-togethers, at night during sleep—supposing that sleep were possible—we never knew whether some intruder were violating, by his presence, the inviolability of hearth and home! Whether this Wilhelm Storitz, or someone else for that matter, might not be there, spying on our actions, listening to our words, at last penetrating the most intimate of family secrets.

Indeed, if Nemo becomes a type of aquatic phantom who torpedoes instruments of war, Storitz is also a torpedoer, as well as a violator of that which is the most private and intimate: the family.

Repeatedly, the characters who seek Storitz out try to catch him physically, but can only sigh sadly in defeat. Captain Haralan, after a search of Storitz's house, cries out, "Nobody! Nobody!" Similarly, after "the light had disappeared," Stepark waits for Storitz in the darkness, as though he were waiting for a vampire, but found "no one." And when an angry mob cries out for Storitz's head, those who try to find him are again faced with the same result: "And thus: nobody! . . . Or the individual,—let's say Wilhelm Storitz,—had had enough time to escape, or else he was hiding in a corner of the belfry, invisible and intangible." Later the frenzied crowd, gathered in front of the Storitz house that they have just burned to the ground, yells out in frustration: "Nobody! Nobody!" And literally, there is no "body" for them to hold on to. After hearing the horrible bell knolls Storitz rings out, they are once again confronted with the "storitzian" void: "When the policemen entered the chamber where the muted bells had just stopped swinging, the invisible bell ringers had already disappeared."

Storitz, in fact, exploits an "aesthetic of disappearance" that allows him to transform himself into a superhuman (an archangel, though not the head of a family, as he would have no doubt aspired to if he had been able to marry Myra). His invisibility allows him to cultivate his other talent, however, linked to his power—that of terrifying others. As such, he can attempt to substitute an impression of power for the impotence he feels regarding his exclusion from the Roderich family world. Yet despite his actions, and while Marc's love for Myra becomes increasingly consolidated, Storitz can only act within an aesthetic Akbar Abbas calls the *déjà disparu* (the already disappeared)—that is to say, a space "where the visual is both ineluctable and elusive at the same time. [. . .] It is [. . .] the (negative) experience of an invisible order of things, always teetering just on the brink of consciousness."[5] For Abbas the notion of the *déjà disparu* is also a consequence or a symptom of unresolved desire, which helps to construct a ghostly space. In Storitz's case Storitz becomes his own ghost, or at least the specter of what he has become, by remaining Myra's permanently unrequited lover. Abbas explains: "The ghost story becomes a study of affectivity and the way it unfolds in a space of disappearance.

It goes without saying that when Stepark, Haralan, Henry Vidal, and the policemen ransack Storitz's house in order to grab this "unattainable being," the space that surrounds the house is barren and covered with fog: "At most, two or three passersby had stopped to see what was going on. Few were on the streets that foggy morning on Teleki Boulevard." Storitz concurrently changes into a type of fog himself, reconstructing himself in vaporific matter. If the novel begins with a commemoration at a cemetery in honor of Storitz's father, Otto, a famous scientist in Spremberg, Germany, Ragz becomes, for his son, a giant cemetery for his love of Myra and the wasteland for his desire. The name of the father, so rich in brilliant scientific discoveries, is reduced to the "unnameable" in the case of Wilhelm, in whom the villagers of Ragz can see only a destructive ghost who haunts the town malevolently. Storitz is far from resembling the romantic German cliché of Goethe's lovelorn young Werther: "In every house, among every family, the name of Wilhelm Storitz could no longer be uttered without arousing the memory, or rather, the ghost, of this strange character whose existence was spent between the silent walls and behind the closed windows of the house on Teleki Boulevard."

For Jacques Nassif, Storitz's appearances/disappearances are essentially linked to the act of writing itself, in which he sees a Freudian link between the word *secret* and the French verb meaning *to create—secret/se créer*. Nassif reads *The Secret of Wilhelm Storitz* as a metaphor for Jules Verne the writer: "Under cover of test tubes and notions of invisibility, it is surely the powers of writing that Jules Verne is dealing with here: and it has as much to do with the demon of Asmodeus as it does with the ring of Gyges, which he would no doubt enjoy finding and putting into action."[6] Indeed, whether or not Storitz's secret is related to one of Verne's, it is clear that creation is inexorably linked to Storitz's mission for no other reason than Storitz re-creates himself by annihilating his physical form. He in fact creates an invisible man who torments the citizens of Ragz and is monomaniacally bent on abolishing Marc and Myra's wedding. His spectral presence is invented just to destroy it. In fact, when he succeeds in haunting the village, all the characters in the book become victims of his powers of attraction/repulsion. As he leaves Storitz's empty house, for example, Henry Vidal admits that he has been overcome by the idée fixe that Storitz has become for everyone: "And yet,—as a testament to the power obsession can have over someone—despite everything I was telling Marc and Captain Haralan, and despite what I was telling myself, if I had seen a wisp of smoke rising from the laboratory chimney, or a face appearing behind the windows of the belvedere, I would not have been at all surprised."

If the boundaries between reality and the fantastic are constantly being blurred for the characters in the novel, thanks to the master of horror Storitz embodies for them, Henry Vidal can only picture him in terms of personal trauma: "The truth of the matter was that, while the people of Ragz were recovering from their initial fright and no longer mentioned those strange happenings," Henry remarks, "it was really Dr. Roderich, it was really my brother, it was really Captain Haralan, it was really myself—we were the ones haunted by Wilhelm Storitz's ghost." They might stop him from marrying Myra, Storitz seems to be saying, but nothing will stop him from profaning the most sacred places in Ragz, such as the churches and the main cathedral. Even when he does nothing, he succeeds in cloning himself ad infinitum within the imaginations of others:

And yet, even though no other incident had taken place since Wilhelm Storitz had, for all intents and purposes, screamed from the top of the belfry, "Here I am . . . still here!" the horror had taken over the entire city. There was not one single house that hadn't thought it was haunted by the invisible one! And he wasn't alone! . . . He had his gang at his command! . . . The churches couldn't even be used as safe havens anymore after what had happened in the Cathedral! . . . The papers tried very hard to intervene, but without success, and what could they do against the terror in any case? . . .

Unable to procreate, Storitz never ceases to reinvent himself by creating a "new Storitz," the abominable "author," so to speak, of obsessive crimes of passion against happiness itself, against love, and against marriage. As Henry Vidal asserts, Storitz is above all the author of texts that might never end. The enigma becomes his only truly creative act: "Put a stop to this? . . . What did he mean by that? . . . What did he have in mind? . . . That Wilhelm Storitz had returned to Ragz, and that he was responsible for this profanation, there was no doubt whatsoever! . . . But where could we find him, and how could we hold on to this unattainable creature? . . . " Even though the aesthetic of disappearance dominates Storitz's willing space and condemns him to being universally hated, in keeping with his favorite song, "Song of Hatred" (which he sings when he haunts the Roderich house for the first time and disturbs Marc and Myra's engagement party), the end of the novel may also prove that not *all* disappearances are made of self-destruction or spite, for if Myra must remain invisible for the rest of her life, she will never lose her incredible external beauty or her internal/spiritual loveliness. Of course, Marc has made her into a magnificent art object by painting her and immortalizing her in that way . . . but it is her soul, the purest element of her person, that lights up the entire home: "It seemed as though we could see how gracious and smiling she was. [. . .] She was the soul of the house,—invisible like a soul!" Marc, as opposed to Storitz, ceases to be a bachelor and affirms his devotion to Myra, despite the fact that she is invisible: "He loved her visible, he would love her invisible." He thus overdetermines the fact that the "Song of Hatred" proclaimed by Storitz is quite weak compared to the power to love. Indeed, *amor vincit omnia*: if Henry Vidal can ask, at the beginning of the novel, "Does this Mademoiselle Myra really exist?" the Spanish version of her name, *mira*, proves that while the deepest love, and the most intense beauty, might still be just as literally invisible as Wilhelm Storitz—their troubled and ghostly antithesis—they remain nonetheless much more solid and glowing.

Notes

Introduction

1. Verne here refers to Hetzel's *Magasin d'Education et de Récréation*, which published Verne's very first published novel, *Cinq semaines en ballon* (1863, *Five Weeks in a Balloon*) and his subsequent novels as well.

2. Letter A512, Jules Verne to Louis-Jules Hetzel, Amiens, Sunday, Mar. 5, 1905 (my translation), in *Correspondance Verne-L.J. Hetzel II 1897–1914*, ed. Olivier Dumas, Volker Dehs, and Piero Gondolo della Riva (Geneva: Editions Slatkine, 2006), 147.

3. See Arthur B. Evans's excellent biography of Jules Verne, on which the following paragraph is based: "Jules Gabriel Verne: A Biography," in *The Begum's Millions* (Middletown CT: Wesleyan University Press, 2005), 253–61.

4. Jules Verne to Pierre Verne, July 28, 1870, in *Bulletin de la Société Jules Verne* 144 (2002): 10.

5. Jules Verne to German reader, May 9, 1890, *Bulletin de la Société Jules Verne* 144 (2002): 17.

6. H. G. Wells, *The Invisible Man* (New York: Signet Classics, 2002), 153.

Chapter I

1. Wilhelm Hoffmann, otherwise known as E. T. A. Hoffmann (1776–1822), was known for his supernatural, romantic tales that were fictionalized by Offenbach in his popular late-nineteenth-century operetta *The Tales of Hoffmann*. Verne sets up the uncanny aspects of his story with a wink at Hoffmann by calling his own supernatural protagonist "Wilhelm."

2. Verne had a deep appreciation of Edgar Allan Poe and even wrote a sequel to *The Narrative of Arthur Gordon Pym* called *Le sphinx des glaces* (*An Antarctic Mystery*) in 1897. Poe was in fact one of Verne's favorite authors. He had even written his only literary study on him, the article "Edgard [*sic*] Poe et ses oeuvres," in 1864.

3. Léon Bonnat was a French academic painter (1833–1922) known for his portraits and for being a teacher of many well-known artists, such as Thomas Eakins, Gustave Caillotte, and Henri de Toulouse-Lautrec. His subjects included many prominent figures, such as Victor Hugo, Louis Pasteur, J. A. D.-Ingres, and other contemporaries of Verne's.

4. Ragz is a fictitious Hungarian town invented by Verne that he also used in *Le beau Danube jaune* (The beautiful yellow Danube), a posthumous novel that had been reworked by his son Michel as *The Danube Pilot* in 1908. Verne originally intended to set it in a Hungarian town called "Wieg-Varda," according to a letter he wrote to Louis-Jules Hetzel (A512, Mar. 5, 1905, Verne, *Correspondence*, 147). According to the editors of this volume of Verne's correspondence, Verne may have intended to write Vieg-Yaszsa (see Verne, *Correspondance*, 147 n. 4).

5. Ocular imagery is very important in many novels, such the famous line in *Michael Strogoff*: "Look, with all your eyes, look!" In *The Secret of Wilhelm Storitz* seeing is equally important, in terms of both visible, external beauty and inner, invisible beauty.

6. The "Diet" is the Hungarian legislature.

7. *Dampfschiff* is the German word for "steamship."

Chapter II

1. Verne here begins a leisurely, descriptive "travelogue" of Henry's trip down the Danube. Such travelogues are inserted into many of his books, even though they might not have anything to do with the actual plot or narratives. According to Verne scholar Terry Harpold, they act like musical interludes in a Bollywood film.

2. The Alsace-Lorraine region has been an unfortunate "football," changing hands three times during the Franco-Prussian war Verne alludes to here, when France lost the region to the Germans in 1871. France regained the region after World War I, with the Treaty of Versailles in 1919; lost it again during the German Occupation of World War II (1940–45); and finally reclaimed it, holding control to this day.

3. Ulm was where Napoleon surrounded a large Austrian army in 1805, forcing it to surrender. It was a staging point for the campaign that led to his victory at Austerlitz.

4. Victor Duruy (1811–90) was a French historian and politician. His "Récit de voyage de 1860 entre Paris et Bucharest" is mentioned in *Storitz.* His remarks about his trip to Ulm (Germany) are quoted in *The Golden Volcano.*

5. Verne wrote luxurious and beautiful descriptions of the Amazon in *La Jangada* (1881), which takes place there.

6. Wagram was one of the first Napoleonic victories that didn't cost Napoleon excessive casualties. No doubt Verne was sentimental about this victory against the Austrians, as he had been so disillusioned and bitter after France's defeat at the hands of the Germans in the Franco-Prussian war.

7. Verne's claim that there were bloody battles between the French and the Turks in the sixteenth century is puzzling, as no major wars between the two countries seem to have been fought then. He may be referring to the imperial *autrichiennes* troops from Artois, Flanders, or Charolais, or the famous Walloon troops

from Hainaut, Luxemburg, the Ecclesiastic principality of Liege, the Count of Namour, or the imperial Burgundy troops, all of which were francophone but not actually French. Similarly, the troops loyal to the Dukes of Lorraine and Savoie were also francophone and strongly implicated in the fight against the Turks, although not technically French. During the reign of Louis XIV the French supported Imn Thokly with troops to aid him in his fight against the Habsburgs and helped liberate Upper Hungary (now Slovakia) in 1664.

8. The Battle of Austerlitz (also known as the Battle of the Three Emperors) was one of Napoleon's biggest victories against the Third Coalition and against the French Empire. The ensuing Treaty of Presburg decisively took Austria out of the war and sent Tsar Nicolas's army back to Russia in defeat.

9. The Habsburg Austrian Empire faced many revolts from March 1848 through July 1849, from Austrian Germans, Hungarians, Slovenes, Poles, Czechs, Slovaks, Ruthenians, Romanians, Serbs, Italians, and Croats, who all sought independence. After a failed but valiant uprising in 1848, Hungary tried again in March 1849 to resist Habsburg domination, but the insurgency was crushed when the Empire called on Russian intervention, which successfully defeated Hungarian insurgents in late August 1849.

10. The tomb is an important place for Muslim pilgrims. The Turkish armies took possession of Buda in 1541. Gull Baba, who arrived in Buda with the armies, died in the Nagyboldogasszony temple during the victory celebrations. The tomb was renovated in 1885 and 1962 by the Turkish government.

11. Mary-Theresa of Austria (1717–80) was the reigning Archduchess of Austria and Queen of Hungary and Bohemia and a Holy Roman Empress. Opposition to her rule led to the War of Austrian Succession in 1740 and later to the Seven Years' War with the King of Prussia. She brought unity to the Habsburg Monarchy

and was well respected as a leader and skillful administrator. She was also the mother of Marie-Antoinette. At the time the Turks were considered "infidels" and natural enemies of the Hungarians.

Chapter III

1. Galatea was the beautiful ivory statue that Pygmalion brought to life in Grecian mythology. There are many references to the Pygmalion myth and notions of ideal artistic beauty throughout the novel.

2. In 1849 Jules Verne wrote the following poem:

Le passé n'est pas, mais peut se peindre
[. . .]
L'avenir n'est pas, mais il peut se peindre
[. . .]
Le présent seul est, [. . .]

The past is not, but it can be painted,
[. . .]
The future is not, but it can be feigned,
[. . .]
There is only the present [. . .]

See "La vie" (Life), *Bulletin de la Société Jules Verne*, no. 87 (1987): 27 (note from the 1996 L'Archipel edition).

3. Verne sets up a type of Platonic love triangle here that will continue throughout the novel, as both brothers are infatuated with Myra. Henry always describes her in a quasi-romantic manner.

Chapter IV

1. Verne is describing his own house here on 2, rue Charles-Dubois, in Amiens. For more on the parallels between the Roderich house and Verne's, see Cécile Compère's wonderful article "Amiens

sur le Danube?" in *Visions nouvelles sur Jules Verne* (Amiens: Centre de Documentation Jules Verne, 1978), 84–94.

2. Verne never finished his list of plants (note from the 1996 L'Archipel edition).

3. Frans Van Mieris, the elder, was a Dutch Baroque painter from Leiden (1635–81) known for his paintings of the leisure class, with many scenes of piano lessons and duets.

4. Élisée Reclus was a nineteenth-century French geographer (1830–1905), a great traveler and anarchist. Verne often alluded to him in such texts as *The Carpathian Castle*, in which he is quoted: "Vulkan, as the great geographer Élisée Reclus puts it, is 'the last outpost of civilization in the valley of the Wallachian Syl,' and it is not astonishing that Werst is one of the most backward villages of the country of Kolosvar" (trans. I. O. Evans [London: Arco Publications, 1963], 31).

5. Sandor Petröfi was known for his poetry and for writing the lyrics of national Hungarian songs during the Hungarian revolt in the mid-nineteenth century.

6. The theme of real and illusionary love objects can also be seen in other Verne works, notably *The Carpathian Castle*, in which Baron Rudolph of Gortz creates a hologram of his beloved, the opera singer La Stilla.

7. He repeats this word three times, as though it were a magic spell or incantation, a touch that contributes to the supernatural and mysterious atmosphere of the novel.

Chapter V

1. "Little Russians" refers to Ukrainians (note from the 1996 L'Archipel edition).

2. The "Four Circles Committees" is a reference to the Hungarian Estates General Assembly, where until 1848 important decisions were made in committees and sessions the county deputies

held according to the four traditional parts (districts or circles) of Hungary.

3. Verne often referred to American cities as made up of "right angles and squares" in such texts as *Les cinq cents millions de la Begum* (1879, *The Begum's Millions*) and *Le tour du monde en quatre-vingts jours* (1873, *Around the World in Eighty Days*).

4. Café concerts, like music halls and cabarets, were very popular at the end of the nineteenth century, especially in Paris, where artists and writers such as Aristide Bruant performed songs as people ate and drank, often about the lower classes.

5. Much has been written about Verne's possible anti-Semitism, especially in such novels as *Hector Servadac* (1877) and *Le château des Carpathes* (1892, *The Carpathian Castle*), which begins with a description of a Jew as an unscrupulous peddler: "Was this one an Italian, a Saxon, or a Wallachian? No one could say, but he was a Jew—a Polish Jew, tall, thin, hook-nosed, with a pointed beard, a prominent forehead, and lively eyes. [. . .] These vendors of thermometers, barometers, and cheap jewelry always seem to be a people apart, with something Hoffmanesque in their appearance. This comes from their trade. They sell time and weather in all forms" (trans. I. O. Evans, 13).

6. Verne's comments on superstitious villagers are echoed in *The Carpathian Castle*: "The reader must put himself in the place of the people of Werst and then he will not be astonished at what follows. He is not asked to believe in the supernatural, but to remember that this ignorant people believed in it without reservation" (trans. I. O. Evans, 38–39).

Chapter VI

1. In the original manuscript Verne wrote "Téléki," as in the Baron Telek, the protagonist of *The Carpathian Castle*. Christian Chelebourg explains: "Jules Verne hesitates in the spelling (retained)

of 'Téléki' and 'Tékéli': 'Téléki' in honor of the Count Teleki, a famous Hungarian patriot, and 'Tekeli-li,' the obsessive cry that defines the rhythm of the ending to [Poe's] *The Adventures of Arthur Gordon Pym*" ("Le blanc et le noir," *Bulletin de la Société Jules Verne* no. 77 [1986]; my translation) (note from the 1996 L'Archipel edition).

2. Verne planned on adding a hand-drawn representation of this signature (note from the 1996 L'Archipel edition).

Chapter VII

1. It is interesting to note that I. O. Evans's version attributes "Song of Hatred" to Frederick Margrave (Frederick II), rather than to the German revolutionary poet and friend of Bakhunin Georg Herwegh (1817–75), to whom Verne is actually referring. Was Evans thinking of Ernst Lissauer's "Hymn of Hate" ("Gott strafe England"), the German fight song so popular among German soldiers during World War I? Ironically, Storitz is singing a Marxist revolutionary song, as Herwegh had been exiled from Prussia and was living in Paris. Moreover, he was a harsh critic of German nationalism and the Franco-Prussian war. An English translation of "Song of Hatred" appeared in Longfellow's *The Poets and Poetry of Europe* (Boston: James Osgood and Co., 1871):

Brave soldier, kiss the trusty wife,
And draw the trusty blade!
Then turn ye to the reddening east,
In freedom's cause arrayed
Till death shall part the blade and hand,
They may not separate:
We've practiced loving long enough,
And come at length to hate!

To right us and to rescue us

Hath Love essayed in vain,
O Hate! Proclaim thy judgment day,
And break our bonds in twain.
As long as ever tyrants last,
Our task shall not abate:
We've practiced loving long enough,
And come at length to hate!
Henceforth let every heart that beats
With hate alone be beating;—
Look around! What piles of rotten sticks
Will keep the flame a-heating!
As many as are free and dare,
From street to street go say't:
We've practiced loving long enough,
And come at length to hate!

Fight tyranny while tyranny
The trampled earth above is;
And holier will our hatred be,
Far holier than our love is.
Till death shall part the blade and hand,
They may not separate:
We've practiced loving long enough,
Let's come at last to hate! (369)

Chapter VIII

1. Storitz's name in fact can be read as an allusion to the German word for "disturb," *storen*.

2. Jules Verne, who had also written poetry as a young man, greatly appreciated Victor Hugo's work, in which shadows often play a major role. In this instance Verne might be alluding to Hugo's great poem "Ce que dit la bouche d'ombre" ("What Says the Shadow's Mouth"), in *Les contemplations*, or to a line in "Le

bien germe parfois" ("Good can sometimes sprout . . ."), in the collection *Toute la lyre*:

Good can sometimes sprout from the bramble of evil [. . .]
I can see blooming, deep within a nameless glow,
Monstrous flowers and terrifying roses:
I think it is out of a sense of duty that I write all these things
That seem, from the wild and trembling parchment, to
Spring sinisterly from the shadow of my hand.
Is it by chance, great, mad breath of the Prophets,
That you disturb my thoughts?
Where am I being taken in this nocturnal azure?
Is it sky I see? Is it the obscure dream
With the wide-open door I see before me?
Do I obey? Do I lead?
Darkness, am I in flight? Am I the one who chases?
Everything is collapsing; at times, I don't know if I'm
The formidable horseman or the untamed horse;
I hold the scepter in my hand and the bit in my mouth;
Open up so I can come through, you abysses, blue pit,
Black pit! (my translation)

Chapter IX

1. Daniel, Denner, and the Sandman are all characters in Hoffmann's fantastic tales but were not included in Offenbach's famous nineteenth-century operetta *Tales of Hoffmann* (Coppelius does appear in Offenbach's version). Verne is establishing both a literary and a fictionalized framework to add weight to the mysterious goings-on created by Storitz.

2. The Ruhmkorff induction coil was invented by E. Ducretet et LeJeune of Paris. The coil is almost thirty-six centimeters long, and the circular glass ends are two centimeters thick. This sort of

coil is often called a Ruhmkorff coil, after the Parisian apparatus manufacturer Heinrich Daniel Ruhmkorff (1803–77). Although Ruhmkorff did not invent the induction coil, his name is often associated with it (particularly in Europe) because he successfully put together all of its elements. Verne makes frequent use of it in such novels as *Twenty Thousand Leagues under the Sea* (1869), *Journey to the Center of the Earth* (1864), and *The Black Indies* (1877, *Les Indes noires*), as his characters often explore underwater or underground.

3. Henri Moissan was a late-nineteenth-century chemistry professor at the University of Paris who won the Nobel Prize in 1906. He invented an electric furnace that was able to produce microscopic diamonds, reproducing how they are formed in nature by suddenly cooling, from a very high temperature, a molten pig of iron containing carbon. Verne often included precise scientific information in his novels to make them educational, as well as to add credence to his stories.

4. "Roentgen rays" is a term coined around 1890 that preceded the term "X-ray" and is now synonymous with it. It refers to Wilhelm Roentgen, a German professor of physics who wanted to prove his hypothesis that cathode rays could penetrate substances besides air. When he saw that he could film his thumb and forefinger and their bones on a screen, the story goes, he replaced the screen with a photographic plate and X-rayed his wife's hand. Roentgen's report of his findings, "On a New Kind of Rays," was published by the Physical-Medical Society of Würzburg in December 1895 (see http://www.medecine.net). The German connection between Otto Storitz's experiments and Roentgen's reinforces both Verne's attempts to make his novel more realistic, on the one hand, and his constant desire to incorporate the latest scientific discoveries into his works. Verne would claim that this is what separated him from H. G. Wells, for example, whom he considered purely

a fantasy fiction writer who did not conduct the type of research Verne undertook each time he wrote.

5. This description of Storitz's room resembles that of Count Dracula's, when Von Helsing and Jonathan Harker storm his London flat and see "a sort of orderly disorder on the great dining room table. There were title deeds of the Piccadilly House in a great bundle, note paper, envelopes, and also a clothes brush, a brush and comb, and a jug and basin, the latter containing dirty water which was reddened as if by blood" (Bram Stoker, *Dracula* [New York: Bantam Press, 2004], 288).

Chapter X

1. "Immutable": this was a rare word in French at the time Jules Verne penned it. He also used it in *Autour de la lune* (1870, *Around the Moon*) and *Le pays des fourrures* (1873, *The Fur Country*) (note from the 1996 L'Archipel edition).

Chapter XIII

1. In a recent *New York Times* article in "Science Times" (June 12, 2007), titled "Light Fantastic," Kenneth Chang writes that physicists are now "flirting with invisibility by constructing materials that bend light the 'wrong' way, an optical trick that could [. . .] even make objects disappear." "New materials," Chang asserts, "can bend some wavelengths of light around an object [. . .] to make it vanish." Perhaps Verne was indeed as prescient about the possibilities of invisibility as he was about submarines and space travel.

2. Montmartre, a northern neighborhood in Paris, was home to many artists and influential cafés and café concerts, in which satirical skits lampooning daily events were presented in cabaret form. The opening of *Twenty-Thousand Leagues under the Sea* describes how the *Nautilus*, considered a sea creature, was celebrated: "In

all the great centers the monster became fashionable. They sang of it in the cafés, ridiculed it in the papers, and staged it in the theater" (intro. and notes Emanuel J. Mickel [Bloomington: Indiana University Press, 1991], 94).

3. Here is one of the many parallels with *The Carpathian Castle*, in which Verne also decries the Transylvanians' deep-seated superstition: "A castle deserted, haunted, and mysterious. A vivid and ardent imagination soon peopled it with phantoms; ghosts appeared in it, and spirits returned to it at all hours of the night. Such opinions are still common in some of the superstitious countries of Europe, and Transylvania is one of the most superstitious." (trans. I. O. Evans, 25).

4. According to legend, Gyges, a favorite and successor of King Candaule, would have possessed a ring enabling him to become invisible (note from the 1996 L'Archipel edition).

Chapter XIV

1. Verne was severely marked by the Franco-Prussian war and by Germany's occupation and invasion of France. He wrote to his father at the start of the war: "What a debacle of public funds and stocks! [. . .] What a great year 1870 turned out to be, the plague, the war, and famine. God protect France" (Jules Verne to Pierre Verne, July 28, 1870, *Bulletin de la Société Jules Verne* 144 [2002]: 10).

2. With the constant, obsessive repetition of the words "nothing, nothing," "nobody, nobody," and "no one, no one," Verne underlines this notion of intangibility, the feeling of frustration attached to constantly grasping at different goals (for Storitz it is Myra; for Henry Vidal it is Captain Haralan; for Stepark it is Storitz; for the villagers it is Storitz's body; and for Marc Vidal it is marriage to his fiancée).

3. The rhythm and destructive force of the mob are reminiscent of similar scenes in great nineteenth-century works such as Victor

Hugo's *Les Miserables* and *Notre-Dame de Paris* and Charles Dickens's *A Tale of Two Cities*, in which the crowd takes on an unbridled energy of its own, as though it were performing a cathartic act of unleashing its pent-up frustrations. Similarly, mob violence also occurs in other works by Verne, including *Le superbe Orénoque* (1898, *The Mighty Orinoco*), *La chasse au météore* (1908, *The Meteor Hunt*), and *Around the World in Eighty Days*.

Chapter XV

1. Verne's encomium to Eastern European freedom fighters is in keeping with his original vision of Captain Nemo as a Polish revolutionary who, at the end of *L'ile mystérieuse* (1874–75, *The Mysterious Island*) yells out, "Freedom! Freedom!" on his deathbed, rather than "God and my Fatherland!" which his editor, P. J. Hetzel, insisted on.

Chapter XVI

1. Verne uses the present tense here as a stylistic device to underline both the immediacy of the situation and Marc's panicked state. The memory is so intense and traumatic for him that he has to revert to the scene of the trauma in his mind. The detective fiction of Georges Simenon is similar in its intermittent use of the present tense to denote an indescribable and sudden trauma set in the past.

2. Once again Verne shrouds Storitz with supernatural characteristics similar to Bram Stoker's descriptions of Dracula.

3. Storitz's macabre "last appearance" is similar to other powerful images Verne creates to mark the end of a particularly frightening villain. Toward the end of *The Begum's Millions*, for example, Schultze, the maniacal German tyrant who threatens the world with a secret, proto-nuclear weapon, is found eerily frozen in his secret laboratory: "In the middle of the room and bathed in this

radiance, an enormous human form, enhanced by the refraction from the lens and appearing as large as one of the sphinxes from the Libyan desert, was seated in an immobility of marble. [. . .] It was Herr Schultze! He was recognizable by the horrible smile on his face and by his gleaming teeth" (trans. Stanford L. Luce, ed. Arthur B. Evans, intro. and notes by Peter Schulman [Middletown CT: Wesleyan University Press, 2005], 184).

Chapter XVIII

1. Verne uses the word *fabrique* here for "vestry." This is an esoteric word Verne uses instead of "parish" (note from the 1996 L'Archipel edition).

Chapter XIX

1. Verne uses the word *hôtel* here, which is more like a townhouse, in the sense of *hôtel particulier*.

Afterword

1. Jules Verne, *Mathias Sandorf* (ROH Press, 2007), 1.

2. Nathalie Prince, *Les célibataires fantastique: Essai sur le personnage célibataire dans la littérature fantastique de la fin du XIXème siècle* (Paris: L'Harmattan, 2002), 127. (Unless otherwise noted, all translations here are my own.)

3. Jean Borie, *Le célibataire français* (Paris: Livre de Poche, 2002), 63.

4. Paul Virilio, *Esthétique de la disparition* (Paris: Galilée, 1989), 36.

5. Akbar Abbas, *Hong Kong: Culture and the Politics of Disappearance* (Minneapolis: University of Minnesota Press, 1997), 42–48.

6. Jacques Nassif, "Freud aurait-il retrouvé le secret perdu de Wilhelm Storitz?" *La Revue des Lettres Modernes* 1193–1200 (1994): 117–47.

IN THE BISON FRONTIERS OF IMAGINATION SERIES

Gullivar of Mars
By Edwin L. Arnold
Introduced by Richard A. Lupoff
Afterword by Gary Hoppenstand

A Journey in Other Worlds: A Romance of the Future
By John Jacob Astor
Introduced by S. M. Stirling

Queen of Atlantis
By Pierre Benoit
Afterword by Hugo Frey

The Wonder
By J. D. Beresford
Introduced by Jack L. Chalker

Voices of Vision: Creators of Science Fiction and Fantasy Speak
By Jayme Lynn Blaschke

The Man with the Strange Head and Other Early Science Fiction Stories
By Miles J. Breuer
Edited and introduced by Michael R. Page

At the Earth's Core
By Edgar Rice Burroughs
Introduced by Gregory A. Benford
Afterword by Phillip R. Burger

Back to the Stone Age
By Edgar Rice Burroughs
Introduced by Gary Dunham

Beyond Thirty
By Edgar Rice Burroughs
Introduced by David Brin
Essays by Phillip R. Burger and Richard A. Lupoff

The Eternal Savage: Nu of the Niocene
By Edgar Rice Burroughs
Introduced by Tom Deitz

Land of Terror
By Edgar Rice Burroughs
Introduced by Anne Harris

The Land That Time Forgot
By Edgar Rice Burroughs
Introduced by Mike Resnick

Lost on Venus
By Edgar Rice Burroughs
Introduced by Kevin J. Anderson

The Moon Maid: Complete and Restored
By Edgar Rice Burroughs
Introduced by Terry Bisson

Pellucidar
By Edgar Rice Burroughs
Introduced by Jack McDevitt
Afterword by Phillip R. Burger

Pirates of Venus
By Edgar Rice Burroughs
Introduced by F. Paul Wilson
Afterword by Phillip R. Burger

Savage Pellucidar
By Edgar Rice Burroughs
Introduced by Harry Turtledove

Tanar of Pellucidar
By Edgar Rice Burroughs
Introduced by Paul Cook

Tarzan at the Earth's Core
By Edgar Rice Burroughs
Introduced by Sean McMullen

Under the Moons of Mars
By Edgar Rice Burroughs
Introduced by James P. Hogan

The Absolute at Large
By Karel Čapek
Introduced by Stephen Baxter

The Girl in the Golden Atom
By Ray Cummings
Introduced by Jack Williamson

The Poison Belt: Being an Account of Another Amazing Adventure of Professor Challenger
By Sir Arthur Conan Doyle
Introduced by Katya Reimann

Tarzan Alive
By Philip José Farmer
New foreword by Win Scott Eckert
Introduced by Mike Resnick

The Circus of Dr. Lao
By Charles G. Finney
Introduced by John Marco

Omega: The Last Days of the World
By Camille Flammarion
Introduced by Robert Silverberg

Ralph 124C 41+
By Hugo Gernsback
Introduced by Jack Williamson

Perfect Murders
By Horace L. Gold
Introduced by E. J. Gold

The Journey of Niels Klim to the World Underground
By Ludvig Holberg
Introduced and edited
by James I. McNelis Jr.
Preface by Peter Fitting

The Lost Continent: The Story of Atlantis
By C. J. Cutcliffe Hyne
Introduced by Harry Turtledove
Afterword by Gary Hoppenstand

The Great Romance: A Rediscovered Utopian Adventure
By The Inhabitant
Edited by Dominic Alessio

Mizora: A World of Women
By Mary E. Bradley Lane
Introduced by Joan Saberhagen

A Voyage to Arcturus
By David Lindsay
Introduced by John Clute

Before Adam
By Jack London
Introduced by Dennis L. McKiernan

Fantastic Tales
By Jack London
Edited by Dale L. Walker

Master of Adventure: The Worlds of Edgar Rice Burroughs
By Richard A. Lupoff
With an introduction to the
Bison Books edition by the author
Foreword by Michael Moorcock
Preface by Henry Hardy Heins
With an essay by Phillip R. Burger

The Year 3000: A Dream
By Paolo Mantegazza
Edited and with an introduction
by Nicoletta Pireddu
Translated by David Jacobson

The Moon Pool
By A. Merritt
Introduced by Robert Silverberg

The Purple Cloud
By M. P. Shiel
Introduced by John Clute

Shadrach in the Furnace
By Robert Silverberg

Lost Worlds
By Clark Ashton Smith
Introduced by Jeff VanderMeer

Out of Space and Time
By Clark Ashton Smith
Introduced by Jeff VanderMeer

The Skylark of Space
By E. E. "Doc" Smith
Introduced by Vernor Vinge

Skylark Three
By E. E. "Doc" Smith
Introduced by Jack Williamson

The Nightmare and Other Tales of Dark Fantasy
By Francis Stevens
Edited and introduced by Gary Hoppenstand

Tales of Wonder
By Mark Twain
Edited, introduced, and with notes by David Ketterer

The Chase of the Golden Meteor
By Jules Verne
Introduced by Gregory A. Benford

The Golden Volcano: The First English Translation of Verne's Original Manuscript
By Jules Verne
Translated and edited by Edward Baxter

Lighthouse at the End of the World: The First English Translation of Verne's Original Manuscript
By Jules Verne
Translated and edited by William Butcher

The Meteor Hunt: The First English Translation of Verne's Original Manuscript
By Jules Verne
Translated and edited by Frederick Paul Walter and Walter James Miller

The Secret of Wilhelm Storitz: The First English Translation of Verne's Original Manuscript
By Jules Verne
Translated and edited by Peter Schulman

The Croquet Player
By H. G. Wells
Afterword by John Huntington

In the Days of the Comet
By H. G. Wells
Introduced by Ben Bova

The Last War: A World Set Free
By H. G. Wells
Introduced by Greg Bear

The Sleeper Awakes
By H. G. Wells
Introduced by J. Gregory Keyes
Afterword by Gareth Davies-Morris

The War in the Air
By H. G. Wells
Introduced by Dave Duncan

The Disappearance
By Philip Wylie
Introduced by Robert Silverberg

Gladiator
By Philip Wylie
Introduced by Janny Wurts

When Worlds Collide
By Philip Wylie and Edwin Balmer
Introduced by John Varley

To order or obtain more information on these or other University of Nebraska Press titles, visit www.nebraskapress.unl.edu.